Mixed Messages

LaTonya Y. Williams

United Brothers
www.urbanbooks.net

United Brothers
P.O. Box 3045
Farmingdale, NY 11735

© Copyright 2004 LaTonya Y. Williams

ISBN09712370-4-2

First printing December 2004

10 9 8 7 6 5 4 3 2 1

United Brothers is an imprint of Urban Books LLC

Printed in Canada

*This book is dedicated
to my grandmother, Lula Mae Peoples,
who first taught me to love Jesus Christ
and be kind to others.*

Acknowledgements

It's been a long journey. These are the people who have been instrumental throughout this process. I can't thank you enough.

God: my father, for without you I am nothing. All the glory goes to you.

Shawn: my husband, my best friend, thanks for putting up with my craziness all these years. I love you.

Lil' Shawn: my son, the love of my life, you make me so proud to be your Mama.

Christopher: my newborn son, I've prayed, dreamed, and waited so long for you, I'm truly blessed.

Avis: my mother, you're so wonderful for providing structure in my life, always encouraging me to reach higher, even when I was rebellious and didn't want to.

My sisters T'Ronda, Cabrina, Natalie, my aunt Caroline, Susan Malone, and Tabitha Griffin: thanks for reading my manuscript from cover to cover. Your advice, critiques, and encouragement helped me complete this project.

My Family: ya'll have been so supportive with your love to help me get through the difficult times. I need you now more than ever.

Carl Weber (Big Daddy): my publisher, I will be forever grateful to you for believing in my work.

Carla Dean: my editor, thanks for working on my book. Your support was more than I could have asked for.

Ruthie Sanchez: my publicist, all of your promotional work will finally pay off.

Urban Books Family : Robilyn (Momilyn), you are the backbone, thanks for working on my behalf long before I even knew you. Trista Russell (stepchild, lol), your book, *Going Broke*, is going to blow up. Thanks for the friendship. To all the Urban authors, thanks for paving the way for me. We are family!

Tina Brooks McKinney: author of *All That Drama*, if it weren't for you, my sista, I wouldn't be where I am today. Thanks for the wonderful review!

My girlfriends: Nicole, Tabitha, Shauna, LaNisa, Tracey, Kenyetta, Ericka, and my sister Lisa, forgive me for the unanswered and unreturned phone calls, but a sistah had to write. Thanks for listening to my problems and helping me remain sane. Your friendship means the world to me.

To all reviewers, book clubs, book store owners, and readers who support African American writers.

Because of you, I am able to do what I love and make a living doing it.

God bless you all!

MIXED MESSAGES

+++++++

Chapter 1
Good Friends?

A revealed secret can have a devastating effect on a person. Especially if the girl thought she was the shit, and everything in her life was so damn perfect. And why wouldn't she think that? If you had a new gold-toned Lexus ES 300, credit cards with six-digit limits, a nice loft-style apartment, clothes and shoes that could fill three closets, and never had to work a day in your life, you would, too.

It's too bad the strong desire proved to be far more difficult to quench. Existing internally ever since she was seven years of age, Kailah believed this strong and very overpowering desire to be genetic. Even though very young, she knew better than to share her secret with anyone. No one could ever know. What would they think of her? No, she wouldn't think of it. She worked way too hard to maintain an unblemished reputation to allow someone to simply step in and fuck it all up.

What went wrong? While still trying to figure out how she allowed herself to get in the most complicated situation, she'd successfully suppressed it. But after ten years, Kailah found herself losing control. Underestimating the overwhelming power of a man, she lost the battle, and now the record was 0-31. She had crossed the line, past the point of no return. Seductively presented as a challenge, Kailah never intended to see this thing through to the end. It just got out of hand, and before she knew it, she was knee-deep in it.

Damn. Who was she fooling? It's not like she hadn't done this kind of thing before. But never so close to home. Kailah used to have her limits, such as never with a married man, with another woman, with more than one man at a time, or taking it

1

in the ass. As she experienced each one that she once considered taboo, she began to take it to new heights and levels never once thought of or even imagined. The risks had grave consequences, but to her dismay, it only made the actual experience sweeter like the taste of warm honey.

Kailah looked at her watch for the umpteenth time. Hour after hour had passed, and still, no customers. Sundays were always slow. A mad rush of people would come in around noon until three, and then no one until the last hour. One more mad rush and that would be it. The workday would then be over.

So tired, Kailah could barely keep her eyes open while she stood at the counter. The latest single from Britney Spears blasted from the store speakers…anything to entice the young white teenagers inside long enough to spend all their parents' money. Every single item in the store was ridiculously overpriced.

Being assistant manager had its drawbacks for Kailah; long hours standing on her feet, working weekends when she could be out partying, and working evenings when she really needed to be at home studying for exams. However, money was tight. At least until the end of the semester, at which time Kailah planned to move as far away from Florida as fast as possible. Well, as soon as she could get a good job from a respectable company. Actually, any job offer would do at this point. With only three weeks until graduation, she'd signed up at the career-resource center and interviewed with several large companies. Not one single call back. No second interview. She was doing her best to remain optimistic, but at the same time, a little fear crept in.

How easy life was for her best friend and roommate, Mona! Five major law firms were bidding to hire her. A hot commodity in the legal world, it looked as if Mona was going to finally go with Thomas & Clarke in Miami. Why wouldn't she?

MIXED MESSAGES

She had the job in her back pocket. And why not? Especially since her family and the firm's family went way back.

The phone rang.

"Good morning! This is The Escapade, where styles and trends are everything. How may I help you?" Kailah forced a smile, hoping it would transmit a customer-friendly attitude through the phone line.

"Oh my God, I can't believe you went to work on your day off," Mona said, "especially since you were out all night."

"I really need the money," Kailah responded flatly. She folded her arms, as if Mona was standing right there in front of her. "And besides, I'm really not that tired. I'm really busy, though, so I'll see you when I get home."

"But wait, I—"

Kailah quickly hung up before Mona could get another word in. She hadn't figured out how she would be able to face Mona after what she'd done. Although she woke up feeling like she'd been run over by a truck, she happily told Sharon that morning she would come in to work on her day off just to avoid her best friend.

Kailah thought back to what had happened the night before. It was their last frat party, and it was the bomb. She couldn't believe what had taken place when Derrick motioned her away and into the back seat of his car. His windows weren't even tinted. There was a good chance that someone probably saw them. And as sick as it may sound, that made it even better.

The phone rang again.

"Good morning! This is The Escapade, where styles and trends are everything. How may I help you?" Kailah said in her perkiest voice. Her life had to get better.

......

Seven long years at University of Florida finally paid off. Mona's graduation date would soon be here, and she had to make final preparations. Her parents wanted to throw a huge bash back home in Los Angeles. Any reason to celebrate and invite the highest echelon of residents LA had to offer over to the house would please her mother. Bea Richards doted on her only child, relentlessly trying to control every aspect of Mona's life.

Mona's decision to attend college on the East Coast freed her from her mother's tight grip. Bea tried to convince Mona that moving back to LA would be a better career decision, but by now, Mona loved the taste of freedom and independence. True, her parents knew people in high places that could pull some strings. However, Mona's future goals were to set her own path in law and eventually launch a private practice in family law.

Being pretty and smart certainly went a long way. Growing up, Mona spent the majority of her time reading books and studying to maintain her 4.0 GPA. As a result of having rich socialites as parents, she excelled socially and received invitations to every party and event. Never really considering the girls she hung out with in high school to be meaningful friends, she found it unnecessary to keep in touch once she moved to Florida. Joining a sorority at UF brought new friendships, but the networking possibilities in the future were Mona's primary motive. Her relationship with Kailah had lasted and grown stronger in such a short period of time, which was a surprise to Mona since they came from very different worlds.

Mona taught Kailah how to survive in the world. Kailah had no class, still wearing bargain brand clothes, shoes, and make-up. Having no car, Kailah practically depended on public transportation to get to school and work. Mona eagerly took Kailah under her wing, allowing Kailah to move into her lavish loft-style apartment. Kailah, growing up in a tiny home in the country, didn't even know how to use a dishwasher or electric dryer.

After graduation, they would go their separate ways, promising to stay in touch. Mona found it hard to imagine what life would be like without her best friend. Kailah was the only one who knew everything about her.

"Mother, you're not listening to me. I'm simply saying that you and Daddy will probably feel more comfortable staying at the Hilton or Marriott, instead of here with me and Kailah." Mona had been on the phone for over an hour now. They were getting nowhere. She had just washed her shoulder-length hair and was about to blow dry it when the phone rang. She left her hair wrapped up in a towel. By the time she got off the phone with her mother, her hair would be a curly mess. Mona twisted her thin lips, dreading the thought of having to wash it all over again.

"I'm proud of my only daughter," said Bea Richards. "I want to spend some real time with you before you leave for Miami. You know, maybe we could do some shopping. I'll bet you need—"

"I know, Mother, but we'll have plenty of time to spend together," Mona said, cutting her off.

Mona talked for another twenty minutes or so before realizing she really needed to get back to the piles of dirty laundry she left lying all over the kitchen floor. This gave her the perfect excuse to end this more-than-extended phone conversation. Before ending the call, Mona had somehow successfully convinced her mother that staying at the Hilton would be best for all parties involved. She decided to go online and make the reservation as soon as she could get her last load of linens in the dryer.

What would her new life be like in Miami? Thomas & Clarke was the most prestigious black law firm in Florida, and exactly the steppingstone needed for her career as an attorney.

Since Bea Richards and Lois Clarke have remained close friends from childhood, it was no surprise that Mona would be offered a job. The salary offered *was* a shock, however, because it was the lowest. Mona had received lucrative offers from two other law firms in Miami. She pondered over this for weeks before making the decision to join Thomas & Clarke.

She pulled at her ear as she thought back to that warm day in April when she met with the partners of the law firm. She had almost missed her flight to Miami that morning because of a terrible accident on Main Street in downtown Gainesville.

"I understand, Mona, that you've received an offer from Beechum, Stowe, & Associates," said Lois Clarke, who sat directly beside Darren Thomas. The husband-and-wife team had been practicing law for twenty-five years. College sweethearts, they married right after graduation and started their law practice in Miami. Lois gave birth to two handsome sons, Robert and Louis. Robert, the oldest son, was a business graduate at NYU, and Louis was an artist studying in Italy. What the family didn't know was Louis' roommate, Benny, was also his lover.

"I have interviewed with a few law firms here in Miami and received several offers," Mona responded in her deep professional voice. Trying to remain in a calm and still manner was very difficult. Sitting right before her was her own personal mentor, Lois Clarke, dressed in a natural and wheat-colored wool-blend Donna Karan pants suit. A multicolored scarf accentuated her very long, thin neckline. Although she wore very little jewelry, it was of the finest quality. Lois took pride in her honey-colored ageless skin, and her make-up only enhanced her beauty with earth-toned colors.

Lois' stunning office was at least fifteen hundred square feet, with a breathtaking view of downtown Miami. The high-rise buildings reminded her of Los Angeles. As a child, Mona loved visits to the city to visit her dad at work; because her suburban lifestyle was such a contrast to the jubilant people she would see walking the streets. It seemed fresh and exciting. Mona looked forward to living in Miami. Going to college in Gainesville was a wonderful experience, but other than the school, it was a small country town. Miami life definitely appealed to her. Then again, any change would.

There were large framed African prints, or maybe even the originals, strategically centered on each wall. The mahogany executive-styled desk and chair matched the burgundy and evergreen classical furniture in the far corner of the office. Lois and Darren sat on the couch while Mona sat on the matching chair beside them. She took another sip of her coffee and then placed the mug on the coffee table in front.

"Thomas & Clarke is a reputable law firm, and I guarantee you will find no other private practice like ours," Darren Thomas said as he puffed out his chest. "We have some of the most prestigious clients both on a business and personal level." A dark, tall, handsome older man, Darren was bald and sexy. What a couple! They were still youthful, vibrant, and healthy. The third floor of the office building housed a full fitness workout center, and the couple encouraged other associates to use the gym as often as they desired.

Unlike Mona's parents, Charles and Bea Richards, the typical retired couple, had been traveling the world abroad for a few years, before Charles got bored and picked up a few of his old accounting clients. He worked in a tiny leased office on a part-time basis. In no time at all, the clientele grew and Charles was working fifty to sixty hour weeks again. This time, however, he made sure to take much-needed R&R breaks. Bea, who had been an interior designer for over thirty years, began to take up personal design of her own home. Needless to say, the home in Westwood, a suburb outside of Los Angeles, was involved in one remodeling project after another. The couple had to take temporary residence in their Beverly Hills apartment while the major construction went on.

"...And then there's, oh yes, Dottie Nichols. We were honored to represent her in the five hundred million dollar settlement against Warsung Industries." Darren Thomas rambled on and on about their law firm's most celebrated victories.

"What my husband is trying to say is," Lois rested her hand on her husband's arm, "if you decide to join this practice, you will be well on your way. Your family and mine go way back, and we will take excellent care of you."

Mona cleared her throat. "I'm most pleased and honored that you're giving me this opportunity to learn from you and begin my career with Thomas & Clarke."

"Well, I think this concludes our meeting," Darren said as he stood and walked over to kiss Mona's hand so delicately, portraying to be quite a gentleman. "If you will excuse me, I have a one-thirty with Ben Steiner. Good day, Ms. Richards."

Lois moved in closer to Mona and gently grabbed her hand. "Bea must be so proud of you, graduating with honors and all." She grinned from ear to ear. "I talked to Robert on Sunday and he asked about you, even though I know that's of little interest to you. I'm sure those young men are probably chasing you out of town."

Mona shook her head. "Actually, I've been faithful to one person for the past two years. His name is Derrick Green."

"Oh, sounds nice," Lois said as her cinnamon-colored eyes sparkled. "Take it slow, and the end results will be well worth it."

Mona nodded. She was taking things slow all right, saving her virginity for the man she would marry. Mona and Derrick had dated for over a year. Majoring in computer engineering, Derrick wouldn't graduate until the next semester in the fall. He planned to move back home, where he could be close to his parents, and work at a large computer company. Still, they were in love and set to handle a long-distance relationship, while both continued to pursue their own personal career dreams.

Could Derrick be the one? Patient and understanding, he never pressured her to have sex. That was what she loved most about him.

Lois stopped writing as she placed her pen on the notepad. "I have an early graduation present for you. Why don't you spend a few days in Miami at our condo on South Beach? What is your roommate's name again?"

"Kailah."

"Well, ask Kailah to drive down, and you girls have yourselves a pre-graduation break on Darren and me." Lois tossed her head, flinging her silky hair off her shoulders.

"I don't know what to say...Lois, I mean..." Mona hadn't actually said whether she would accept the job offer to work for Thomas & Clarke, and here Lois was offering the condo for the weekend. But then again, they were old family friends. Maybe this was personal and not business.

"Say nothing, but thanks," Lois said.

"Yes, of course. Thanks."

......

"Mona, you have to make the decision that's right for you and no one else," said Kailah. She sat in the living room on the couch listening to a Destiny's Child song on the radio, flipping through the April edition of *Ebony*, and wondering why she was listening to Mona, the brat.

What about me! Kailah thought with a sigh. *I haven't received an offer yet, not even a request for a second interview.*

Mona sighed. "I'm so confused with trying to decide what's most important, the money or the respect. I would be treated better at Thomas & Clarke. Under their leadership, I know I would be able to start my own practice after putting in ten years there."

Kailah looked up from her magazine and watched Mona trying to squeeze into a bright, yellow bikini. She had gained seven pounds in her last semester and thought no one noticed.

Mona looked at herself in the mirror. "Damn, I look good," she said out loud. "Girl, look at my breasts dangling in this top. Baby got front and back."

"Yeah, yeah, yeah," Kailah tisked. "I hope you get some sun and tan your high-yella butt."

Kailah and Mona were a physical contrast. Tall and very slim; Kailah was dark-skinned and always resented light-skinned girls, until she met Mona. Something that brought the two of them together meant more than just being sorority sisters. Mona really listened to Kailah and understood her.

Much surprise to Kailah was the fact that their friendship could possibly be on the verge of a total collapse. How did things end up this way? True, Kailah and Mona saw life from different perspectives. Mona, being an optimist, and Kailah, a cynic and pessimist. Maybe if Kailah had all of the privileges as Mona, then she would have the same superior complex and attitude. But she didn't. Kailah's outlook on life was based on reality, not fantasy. As the saying goes, "It's a man's world", but that didn't discourage Kailah. She could still make her mark and not have to rely on mommy and daddy to pull some strings for her either.

Mona put on a matching yellow wrap around her waist. Standing at only five feet two inches tall and slightly on the chubby side. She placed her Gucci sunglasses atop her head and grabbed her straw beach bag off the couch. "Let's go take a ride in my new Lexus on the beach. By the way, thanks for driving it down."

Kailah smiled. "Yeah, sure, no problem."

MIXED MESSAGES

She followed Mona out the door wearing a not-so-flattering red bathing suit. After spending the day cruising alongside the beach, Kailah felt relieved to finally get some rest. The six-hour drive on I-95 South to Miami had made her jumpy and irritable. The last thing she wanted to do was listen to Mona constantly complain about her perfect little life. Kailah had real problems. Having no idea where she would work or take up residence in less than a month had started to take its toll. Consumed in her thoughts, she twirled long strands of hair through her skinny fingers. When the phone rang, she answered on the first ring.

"Hello, gorgeous."

Kailah sucked her teeth. "Do you want to talk to Mona?"

"No, I wanna talk to you about the other night. I knew you were a freak. I got the goods on you, so you better treat me right."

"What do you suggest I do?" Kailah asked with a wicked grin on her face.

Kailah had Derrick right where she wanted him, eating out the palm of her hand. It wasn't easy getting him to notice, since he had fell flat-face in love with Mona from the moment he saw her. Playing on his weakness would eventually cause Derrick to stray. Therefore, Kailah took every opportunity to flaunt her tall, slender figure by strutting around him in the apartment in skimpy shorts and skirts.

In a way, Mona allowed it to happen merely through her own ignorance. She figured Derrick would never be interested in a dark-skinned girl. Months of celibacy could drive any guy crazy, especially a dog like Derrick. Kailah casually offered him a little sexual relief when she gave him oral pleasure at the kitchen table one night while Mona slept peacefully in her pink princess-styled bedroom. From that moment on, Derrick became the aggressor and chased Kailah to no end.

"I'll think of something," Derrick said after a long pause.

"Mona, Derrick is on the phone with his nasty self. You need to talk to your man, keep his no-sex-having ass in check." Kailah plopped back down on the chaise lounge facing the window.

"What is he talking about?" asked Mona as she grabbed the cordless from Kailah. "Are you telling Kailah dirty jokes again? You know she can't handle them," Mona said as she waved her hand in the air.

But I sure can handle sexing your man every night, Kailah thought silently to herself, laughing at her own inside joke.

Chapter 2
What Comes Around...

Kailah jumped at the chance to work for a small financial group in Chicago. Although, the mere thought of moving so far away from home did frighten her at first. Her close relationship with her mother consisted of long-distance calls that ended up in Kailah paying three-hundred-dollar phone bills every month. The costly bills resulted from lengthy conversations with her mother and talking to Mona, who happily took her rightful seat as the newest addition at Thomas & Clarke in Miami. Having to survive a long, cold, and snowy winter in Chicago, while Mona relaxed in the warmth of the beautiful South Miami Beach, didn't seem fair. That basically summed up her insignificant life.

"Are you settled into your place yet?" asked Mona.

Kailah rolled her eyes as she listened to Mona's endless bragging about staying at Darryl and Lois's condo on South Beach while she waited on her mother to fly down to assist her with finding a place of her own.

"Just about," Kailah answered, lying on her back in her barely furnished apartment. "So far, I've learned my way around downtown. Living here is nothing like Gainesville. Chicago is such a big city." Not used to the urban life, Kailah chose an older apartment building in Jefferson Park. The area reminded her of the small town where she grew up. An affordable neighborhood for middle-class families housed a few apartment buildings for singles just getting out in the world, like Kailah. That also meant women and men doing quite a bit of dating and wild parties thrown on the weekends.

"The windy city," said Mona. "Mother says Chicago has some of the best shopping and finest dining in the country. I can't wait to visit."

"Your shi-shi-poo-poo mother would say that," Kailah said. She continued painting her toes red. Kailah had found the perfect red dress to wear for the night. Short and sleeveless, the V-neck in the back added that special touch. She stood up to admire her slim, sexy figure. Kailah stared blankly at her own flat chest, wishing at that very instant she had Mona's size D-cup breasts.

Mona yawned. "I need to get some rest. I've got a long day planned with Mother. Her flight is due to arrive at eight in the morning."

"Yeah, I better get some sleep, too." Kailah pretended to yawn.

"I'll talk to you soon," Mona said sleepily and then hung up.

Kailah placed the phone back on the receiver and checked on the sirloin steaks in the oven. The table set with candles and the lights dimmed softly created the perfect ambiance. "Everything is just right," she said. "Salad's in the fridge. Now, I need to finish getting ready. Derrick will be here any minute."

Just as she added the finishing touches, the doorbell rang for the third time. Kailah put on her single pearl earrings and dashed for the door.

"Hey baby," Kailah said as she swung the door open. She stepped back to feast her eyes on the goods on Derrick from head to toe. "Getting a little impatient, are we?"

"Yeah, it's cold out here!" Derrick yelled. He removed his jacket as he strolled in. "Here, I picked up a bottle of wine on the way." He handed her a cheap bottle of Arbor Mist and landed a kiss on Kailah's big luscious lips. Then he whispered in her ear, "My sexual chocolate."

"I know you're hungry, so let's eat," said Kailah, easing out of Derrick's firm grip. She walked away, knowing he was staring and admiring her slim figure. Derrick was her frat brother at UF, and naturally, he would call her while in the city visiting his parents. They would get even closer every time he visited. After graduating, Mona and Derrick decided to end their relationship. While Derrick worked for a computer company in Springfield, living in different states had made it difficult to keep a long-distance commitment.

That evening, Kailah and Derrick took turns talking about work and how tough it was trying to make it in the real world. Derrick had experienced some degree of difficulty earning the respect of his fellow coworkers. Kailah watched and listened intently, with nothing but sincere empathy for him.

Derrick took one last bite of the steak. "Dinner was good, girl." His brown eyes opened wide. "You really know how to burn. A lot has changed since college."

"Thank you. It was all my pleasure," Kailah replied. They stared at each other across the table.

Thank God it was over with Derrick and Mona.

Kailah stood and seductively sauntered down the hall. Derrick followed closely behind. Kailah stood at the foot of her bed with Derrick behind her grabbing her butt. He undid the single top button to her dress, and the red material fell to the floor. He softly kissed her on the back of her neck down to her matching red thong, and then slid it down to join the dress on the floor. Still standing, Kailah turned around and spread her legs while he put his lips to her vagina from behind. She moaned as he helped her reach an orgasmic state. He pushed her on the bed and Kailah helped him undress.

Big and strong, Derrick was built just the way she liked them. Brother loved to workout, and so did she. Kailah lay down on her back as Derrick spread her legs and entered her. Tonight would indeed be most pleasurable.

......

"This is my favorite song!" shouted Mona as she turned up the volume of her car radio. She tapped her fingers on the steering wheel. "Sing, Luther, sing!" Mona had left the office at seven and was cruising home in her gold-toned Lexus ES 300, her graduation gift from Mother and Daddy. Mona pulled up in front of her townhouse and ran in the drizzling rain to check the mail.

"What? A letter from Derrick?" After entering the house, she shut the door behind her. Was Derrick writing to say that he regretted the break-up? She knew it. Maybe he wanted to get back together. Mona was greeted by the beeping of the home alarm system. Mother must still be out, she thought. Quickly, she ran to the keypad and pressed the code.

"I need a bubble bath," she said as she tiptoed through her new town home. No more empty spaces. Mother had been busy furnishing every corner in her two-bedroom townhouse. Once barren, Mona's new place now had lots of expensive fabrics, fine furniture, and exquisite art pieces and sculptures.

Ten minutes later, Mona slipped out of her clothes and slid into her garden tub. She could barely keep her eyes open. After an endless weekend with her mother, Mona couldn't wait to get back to work. With the Kravich case closing in on the trial date, she loved putting in the long hours at the office. She was now living the life she'd dreamed of while in college. Earning a six-figure income of her own, Mona thought it would at last give her the freedom and independence she craved from her overbearing parents. However, she was wrong. Mother made plans to stay a little longer than first expected. Something wasn't right at home with her and Daddy, but Mona didn't have time to worry about that at the present time.

......

A buzz sounded.

"Yes, Taneisha."

"Sorry to bother you, but you have a call from Ms. Mona Richards," Taneisha said in her usual loud crackling voice.

"Put her through," Kailah responded.

MIXED MESSAGES

Kailah picked up on the first ring. "I know this is important because you never call me at work," said Kailah. "So, what's up, girl?"

"You're not going to believe this shit, but I received a letter from Derrick." Mona's voice went up an octave.

"A letter?" Kailah felt her stomach twisting into a tight knot. Why in the hell would Derrick write Mona a letter? Did he want to get back with her? Maybe he felt guilty and wanted to confess he'd been sleeping with her best friend. No, Derrick was a dog. The last thing he'd want to do was spill the beans, especially since she'd been rocking his world for the past six months.

"Well, actually it's a wedding invitation!" Mona yelled. "He's taking this friend thing to another level. That fool actually thinks I would attend his wedding. Can you believe the bastard is marrying his little high school sweetheart from Chicago?!"

"No....I can't." Kailah's breathing was stilted. Tears welled up in her eyes. Hearing the news was a bitch. It couldn't be true. This must be a mistake. She grabbed a Kleenex from her desk to meet the first tear that rolled down her face, while the cheap mascara did its duty covering her face with black streaks after the stream that soon followed.

"Kailah, why didn't you tell me?" asked Mona. "You had to know he was seeing someone."

"I thought he was visiting his parents when he drove down to the city. At least, that's what he said the few times I talked to him on the phone." Kailah shrugged. "Maybe he didn't want the information to get back to you."

"What are you talking about?" Mona asked. "Derrick's parents moved to Ohio a year ago. Do you ever listen or pay attention to details anymore? And I thought *I* was being overworked."

"I guess.... I must have....uuhh ....forgotten or something." Kailah bit her lip. "Look, I have some loose ends that I need to tie up. I'll call you later tonight."

Click.

On the train ride home, Kailah remained in a daze. For the life of her, she couldn't understand why she felt so disturbed by the news about Derrick. She knew him to be a dog, and of course, Kailah knew she wasn't the only one he was sleeping with. Then again, Kailah thought they were friends, and she felt that deserved some level of honesty, if nothing else.

There were traits she disliked in Derrick...his conceited attitude for one. And then, he didn't fit in with the sophisticated men Kailah worked with. Derrick's frequent use of ghetto slang and hip-hop style of dress irritated the hell out of her. In college, acting, dressing, and talking like that was sometimes appropriate, but now Derrick needed to consider himself a professional. No wonder it took him so long to find a job.

Derrick did have potential, though. Kailah remembered that she didn't always have great style and taste. She could work with a brother; possibly help him out a little bit. Having a fine-ass body and being creative in bed made him well worth it. To be honest, Derrick had something to work with, and Kailah was addicted to the sex. She knew it to be a potentially dangerous situation, but still, she couldn't resist him when he would call and ask to come over at a moment's notice.

Once Kailah arrived home, she walked into her dark apartment. Not bothering to turn on any lights, she drifted slowly down the long hallway to the bathroom. Hearing the news about Derrick forced her to vomit repeatedly in the toilet, especially when she thought back to their last rendezvous two weeks ago.

"I'm gonna marry you, girl," Derrick had said as he placed Kailah's head on his hairy chest. "We're good together. You're good to me. Oh yeah, thanks for the thousand dollars. I'm a pay you back as soon as—"

"Shhh." Kailah put her fingers to his lips. "Baby, don't worry about it. I don't mind helping you out. I can't believe you haven't received a paycheck yet. What are those idiots at Micro-Comp doing?"

How could I be so dumb? Kailah thought. Disgusted with herself, she peeled off her silk blouse and skirt. Her panty hose were clinging to her sweaty skin. She grabbed her purple silk robe and didn't even bother to tie it before laying across her bed in complete darkness. Minutes later, she was fast asleep.

As the phone rang for the third time, Kailah extended her long slender arm out to the nightstand to lift the receiver.

"Kailah, girl, ooohhh, you are so late."

"Taneisha, I won't be in today. Reschedule my eleven o'clock with Mr. Terrence, and please-"

"No can do, girl," Taneisha said. "Mr. Terrence is here, and what a fine specimen he is. Why didn't you tell me, girl? I would've worn my best dress, or damn, at least shopped for one. You know I'll return a dress back to Anne Taylor in a heartbeat. Oh, let me stop. Joe is the best thing that ever happened to me."

"Shit, shit, shit!" Kailah exclaimed. "Taneisha, I want you to apologize to Mr. Terrence. Don't tell him I'm late. Tell him I...uhh...changed plans. Yeah...tell him I'll meet him at—"

"At Bacino's on North Sheffield!" Taneisha shouted. "Call me later, girl, and let me know how it goes. I'll see you this afternoon."

"Bye, Taneisha."

Chapter 3
Wedding Bell Blues

The A Train stopped at Harlem. Kailah tapped her foot nervously. The heavy-set woman sitting beside her got up, allowing Kailah enough space to sit and breathe comfortably. Three more stops until the airport. Mona had to be upset with her and worried to death by now. Her plane had arrived twenty minutes ago. Having every intention of leaving over an hour ago, the executive meeting lasted longer than scheduled and Kailah couldn't find an escape or a plausible reason to excuse herself. The moment the meeting ended, Kailah tore out of the building, not even stopping by her office to pick up her briefcase.

Excited the moment she learned of Mona's plan to visit, Kailah felt anxious. Why did Mona have to attend the wedding? Not looking forward to it, Kailah didn't want to see Derrick's face, let alone pretend to be thrilled for the happy couple.

Kailah massaged her throbbing temples. Taking a few days off from work added more tension. Kailah made sure all of her clients knew she would be away from the office, and Taneisha was more than capable of handling small problems or getting in touch with her if an emergency arose. However, Kailah was the type of person who always wanted to be at hand to oversee matters herself, and not depend on someone else to take care of it.

Kailah stepped off the train clicking her metallic DKNY heels loudly as she walked through the airport. Mona stood at the baggage claim area at O'Hare. Kailah ran towards her in a panic. Her slender arms were flailing in the air.

"You're not gonna believe this, but there was a little incident at work. Everything's okay now."

Mona grabbed Kailah and landed a big wet kiss on her cheek. "I missed you so much. I'm just glad you're here and

I'm here. I'm just so happy. It's been too long since I last saw you."

"Yeah, yeah, yeah," Kailah responded while wiping the red lipstick off her face. "I missed you, too, but damn. Don't get all mushy. People are gonna think we're gay."

"Who cares?" Mona yelled as she threw her arms wide open. "I want everyone at this airport to know I love my girlfriend." She laughed at the cold stares from others passing by. "Maybe I am being a little silly." She pulled her hands to her mouth and giggled softly.

"What the hell is wrong with you?" Kailah asked. This was not like Mona to be loud, obnoxious, and just plain ignorant. "Are you on something?" Kailah looked at Mona's blood-shot eyes. "Answer me."

"Well, I took two small, itsy, bitsy, tiny pills.... but it was only to relax me." Mona slobbered out of the mouth as she spoke. Her eyes had that fixated glossy look. "I guess it didn't help that I washed them down with two glasses of gin, too." She laughed hysterically.

"You're drunk. Let's go," Kailah said through clenched teeth. She picked up Mona's bags from the floor. "I'm going to kick your ass when we get out of here. So, just be prepared."

......

On the ride from the airport, Mona slept with her head rested on Kailah's shoulder. A few hours later, she lay in bed with her hand on her throbbing head as she remembered what happened hours before she arrived in Chicago.

"What time is it?" asked Mona. "My head is killing me!" Everything until now remained a blur. She didn't recognize the place as being her own. "Where am I?" She turned over and saw Darren Thomas lying close to her wearing a huge smirk.

"Good morning, Sunshine." His loud laugh haunted her.

What the hell is going on? This must be some kind of cruel joke. "What are *you* doing here? What happened last night?"

"I guess you don't remember, huh? All that pounding and banging, and you don't remember?" Darren chuckled to himself. "I get it. Well, I can play that game, too. It wasn't shit anyway. Get your ass up, whore, and find your way back to the yellow brick road." He turned over and pulled the covers over his shoulder.

The windows were open, blowing in a huge breeze from the beach. She finally realized she was in the condo where she'd stayed when first moving to Miami.

Mona grabbed her clothes and tiptoed out of the room. She dressed in the bathroom and slipped on the black evening gown from the night before. She needed to get out of there and fast. How was she going to explain this to her mother? Apparently, she had stayed out all night without as much as a simple phone call. Her mother would be worried to death. There was no time to think.

Mona took the elevator down to the first floor, pulled her cell phone out of her black-sequined evening bag, and began dialing very quickly. "Yes, I need a cab."

An hour later, Mona walked into her townhouse. The door to Bea's room immediately swung open. "Where have you been, young lady, and why didn't you call me to let me know that you were all right?" Bea tightened her lips. She zipped up her long lavender terry-cloth robe. "I've been so worried about you. I know you're a grown woman, but you're still my little girl. Miami's not the safest place for a pretty face like yours." She placed her hands on her hips. "So, where were you?"

"Mother, I really don't want to talk about it." Mona sat at the breakfast bar and plopped her head down on her folded arms on the counter. "Maybe later," she moaned.

MIXED MESSAGES

Bea rubbed her fingers through Mona's hair. "Okay, I can see you're very upset. Let me make you breakfast, dear. What would you like, honey?"

"Some coffee would be nice. I'm going to go take a bath," Mona said, turning to walk away, completely in a daze. She hoped her mother wouldn't notice. She ran her bath and sat perfectly still, feeling disgusted. By now, she could feel the soreness and realized she was no longer a virgin.

For the life of her, she couldn't remember what happened. Had she slept with her boss? What would she do? No one must know about this. She certainly wouldn't tell a soul, except for Kailah of course.

"Here we go," said Bea, juggling a cigarette and mug in her hand. "Just sit back and relax, honey. Mommy has everything under control." She sat on the edge of the tub and placed her French-manicured hand on Mona's forehead. "You have a slight fever. I'll be back with Tylenol."

Mona leaned back slowly as the water rushed into the tub. This was not the way she'd pictured this happening. It was supposed to be with the man she married...in a bed of rose petals...with champagne and soft candlelight...and Luther singing in the background.

Bea traipsed back in. "You have got to snap out of this, dear. Your flight to Chicago leaves in five hours. Judging by your appearance, you probably need some rest. I'll finish up with the packing you started before you left for the party. I know just the thing to get you to relax."

Bea returned a few minutes later. "Well, here take one. No, take two. This will help you get some rest. You'll feel so much better after a little nap."

Mona slept for what seemed like a lifetime. Awakened by the phone ringing, she could hear her mother's lurid voice outside her bedroom door.

"What do you know, she is awake." Bea handed Mona the cordless.

"Yes, this is Mona." She rubbed her warm forehead.

"Look here, Ms. Richards. We're not going to tell anyone about our little private party last night are we?" His tone sounded disturbed. "Don't get me wrong, I had a nice time with you, but that was it. I know you enjoyed me entering your little virgin territory, but you really need a little more practice before you can please a man of my stature."

And with those words, he hung up.

......

Kailah was in the kitchen preparing lunch when Mona dragged herself in and sat down. Removing a lighter and cigarette from her purse, she lit it.

"When did you pick up that filthy habit?" asked Kailah.

"Not sure," Mona responded with a quick shrug. "Don't worry, I'm not addicted or anything."

"Do me a favor and take it outside. The balcony is to your left." Kailah's voice was stiff.

Mona jumped up out of her seat and slammed the door shut behind her.

Kailah finished preparing lunch. Looking forward to having her best friend visit, she wanted Mona's stay to be pleasant. She couldn't believe Derrick marrying Angela had depressed Mona to such a pitiful state. Why did Mona want to attend the wedding anyway? What was she trying to prove with her boozing, smoking, and pill popping? Bea really had a negative effect on her. She had picked up all of her mother's nasty habits. Mona always hated her mother's weaknesses. Now look at her.

MIXED MESSAGES

Kailah shook her head. Like mother like daughter. The drastic changes the once perfect Mona had made in her life came as a complete surprise to Kailah.

Kailah placed the salad in the center of the table. Greek salad was Mona's favorite since her early college dieting days.

My, those were the days. The two of them would work out at the gym and finish up their afternoon with lunch at their loft apartment. Kailah worked evenings at the mall, and Mona always cooked dinner or picked up take-out because she never had a job while in college. Charles and Bea had established a very comfortable lifestyle, and there was nothing they couldn't provide for their only daughter.

Kailah, on the other hand, worked her way through college. The Carters were not wealthy, but a very proud working-class family. Henry and Anna Carter raised five children, four boys and one girl, in Micanopy, a small town outside of Gainesville. All of the things needed in life were provided: food, clothing, and shelter, but there wasn't much money left for anything else. Still, Kailah appreciated the little things her mother would do for her.

Anna Carter was a housewife and took care of the cooking and cleaning in their very modest home with only three bedrooms. She taught her children to be proud of who they were, to love the Lord, and always encouraged them to use spiritual guidance in order to succeed in life. Kailah's dad worked at a local factory and put in a lot of overtime. When home--which was very rare--he was very loving and devoted to his family. Those long work hours eventually aged him, and he was placed in a nursing home during Kailah's senior year in high school. She then attended college in Gainesville and lived at home for the first two years.

When Mona's roommate graduated and moved away, Kailah made the step out into some independence. All of her brothers, except Dinky, were grown and married with families of their own. Living with Mona was a great experience. They became very close friends, as well as sorority sisters. They stayed up late studying for exams or just talking about their problems. Mona, three years older than Kailah, studied law, while Kailah was a business student.

Now, they sat at the table eating and laughing together, just like old times. Along with the Greek salad, Kailah made turkey salad sandwiches and fresh lemonade.

"I miss lunches like this," said Mona, while she took her last bite of sandwich. Mayonnaise stuck in the corner of her mouth.

Kailah wiped it off with her napkin.

"Still messy, huh?" Kailah joked. "Nice to see that hasn't changed."

"What do you mean?" Mona asked. She took a sip of lemonade and cleared her throat. "I want to apologize to you, Kailah, for the way I behaved earlier today. I've been dealing with a lot these past couple of days...." Tears rolled down her pudgy cheeks.

Kailah grabbed Mona's shaking hand. "Don't worry about it, girl. I'm here for you."

Though the wedding bothered her, Kailah couldn't let on to her true feelings. She had to be strong enough for the two of them, because she knew how much Mona loved Derrick. Kailah was just in it for the sex with no emotional attachment. She squeezed tightly. "We're gonna get through the next couple of days. I understand what you're going through, and I'm here. It's those damn wedding bell blues."

Chapter 4
It Just Wasn't Meant To Be

"Is this our stop?" asked Mona as she kneeled over to look out the small window.

Kailah nodded. "Yep, we get off here."

With several shopping bags in hand, they stepped off the Blue Line train. The unpredictable and ever-changing climate in January brought cold drizzling snow. Good thing Kailah's apartment building was less than one block away, 'cause her dogs were aching.

Shopping with Mona turned out to be a contrite idea. Chicago's downtown was very busy with lots of cars on the street and people dressed in business suits marching in a fast pace, as if every moment counted for something. Mona complained the entire time about how dirty the city was. She turned her nose up at the graffiti that seemed to be displayed on nearly every wall and the potholes that were big as ditches.

Yet, that's not the way Kailah saw it. Without a doubt, Chicago was a variety city that could be as mellow as a simple jazz tune. Life there was very different from Florida. Rich in culture, music and arts were all around, causing never a dull moment to be found. Kailah enjoyed the entertainment at a nearby concert or festival in Grant Park. She wanted to invite Mona to visit for the much anticipated Budweiser Festival or "Taste of Chicago", but that seemed highly unlikely.

They reached Kailah's building and entered the double doors, then climbed two flights of wooden stairs to her apartment.

Mona placed the shopping bags on the floor beside the couch as she lay back and propped up her feet on the table. "I think we hit every department store in this damn city," she said while stretching her arms. "Lunch at Anthony's Pizza was

27

absolutely divine. I'm really proud of you, Kailah. You've become quite settled and familiar with this city already."

Kailah stood in the kitchen thumbing through her mail. She placed a bill from her father's nursing home on the refrigerator. Trying to take care of business in both Chicago and her hometown of Gainesville was tough.

"You know when I went home for Christmas, Mama was asking about you. She was happy to hear how successful you've become down in Miami."

Mona sat up. "Next time I'm in Gainesville, I'll be sure to go by and see Mama Anna. Your mother is such a lovely woman. I don't think she'll ever age." She laughed. "If anything, she looks younger with each year that passes by. I wish I had the opportunity to visit Mother, but she needs to go home first for me to even consider paying her a visit." She shrugged.

Kailah cocked her head. "I was beginning to wonder how her longer-than-expected stay was affecting you. Do you think it's really time for her to go back to LA?"

"Mother doesn't seem to think so," Mona responded as her gaze drifted downward. "Personally, it's been nice having her cooking the meals and cleaning up, but I can hire someone to do that for me." She put her finger on her chin. "I think I need to give Daddy a call."

"So, have you picked out an outfit for tonight?" Kailah asked, changing the subject. "I'm sure there will be lots of people at The Nubian. Friday's are always the most crowded, and then we can go to White Castle afterwards."

"I hate those reggae club scenes." Mona turned the corners of her tiny lips downward into a frown. "Maybe I'll just take a rain check."

Kailah sat on the couch next to Mona and put her arm around her friend. "Mona, my dear, you're here to experience the Windy City and have a grandiose time."

MIXED MESSAGES

Both girls fell out laughing because that is exactly what Bea would say, and exactly how she would say it, too. The line outside The Nubian was two blocks long. The music and bass was bumping for miles down the street, causing windows of the nearby ships to shake slightly. This was quickly becoming Chicago's hot spot on the Northside. Hot, however, didn't describe the weather. Both men and women were covered up with huge overcoats, gloves, and scarves to stay warm while they waited to get inside.

As they passed the window of a local sandwich shop, Mona caught a quick glimpse of her new hairdo, with light brown highlights, and gently placed a few curls back in place. She told Kailah keeping up with her weekly hair appointments was too difficult. Therefore, she asked her male "feminine" stylist to cut it short so she could sport her natural curly hair. The style allowed for easy maintenance.

Kailah wore her jet-black hair tightly pulled back in a long ponytail that hung down past her shoulders.

"How much longer?" Mona asked in a whisper as she shifted all her weight on the opposite leg.

Three white limousines pulled up in front of the building. "That must be the damn Chicago Bulls. Listen to those screams," Kailah said. The men wearing suits were barking and barely able to walk into the club.

Twenty minutes later, Kailah and Mona finally entered the club maneuvering through the large crowd. Kailah could hardly see what was in front of her because of the darkness. Dressed in a dark brown double-breasted pants suit and brown leather boots, Mona stomped her feet to the beat. A matching yellow and brown scarf covered her shoulders and was held in place with a nice brass-colored brooch. Kailah noticed her best friend had put on even more weight. The added pounds were probably from stuffing herself crazy over the lonely holiday season spent with her mother and working long hours at the office.

Kailah's black bodysuit showed off her nice slim figure. She knew she looked damn good, because four pairs of hands had felt on her butt within minutes of entering the club. Red, yellow, orange, and green lights came from the dance floor. She grabbed Mona's hand and headed in that direction.

An announcement came over from a microphone at the DJ's booth. "I would like to say something. Uh-huh. We're all here to announce that our brother, Derrick Green, will be tying the knot in just fifteen short hours, so his black ass needs to get all the single booty he's going to get tonight. So, ladies, let's give it up for the man of hour." More barking and ladies' screams came from the far left of the dance floor.

"I knew that was Derrick I saw!" Mona shouted.

"When did you see Derrick?" Kailah asked. She was ready to haul tail out of there. She knew that this was the moment Mona was waiting for: a chance to see him while he was still a single man. She kept saying that she didn't want to see Derrick for the entire week she was here. But Kailah knew Mona better than that. "Well, why don't go over there and give him some of your high-yella booty," she said smugly.

"I *am* going to walk over to wish him the best, and you're coming with me." Mona grabbed Kailah's arm and hurried over to the drunken frat boys from college. One brother immediately recognized his sorority sisters and told the others. The boys tried to compose themselves.

"Well, what do we have here?" Larry asked. "If it isn't your ex-girlfriend and her sexy-ass friend, Kailah. What's up, ladies?" Larry tried to put his hand on Kailah's butt, while another frat brother intercepted and grabbed it first.

Kailah slapped the shit out of both of them. All three of them started laughing. It was just like old times back in Gainesville.

Derrick appeared out of the crowd. "Hey, Red Bone," Derrick said, grinning from ear to ear. "Girl, I ain't seen you…shit…in months. How you doing?" He grabbed Mona's hand and kissed it ever so gently.

Mona smirked. "Good. And you look as if you're not doing so bad your damn self."

"Well, you know, the fellas wanted to throw me a little party." He paused for a moment and looked over Mona's shoulder at Kailah. She glared at him in return. "How long have you been here in the city?"

"My flight arrived just this Tuesday." She couldn't stop smiling. "Kailah and I have been rather busy. I would've called, but you know…I felt a little awkward."

"No need to explain. I understand." Derrick held her eyes as he took a sip of his drink. "You know I've been a little busy, too. Your coming up here lets me know that there are no hard feelings between us."

"No hard feelings. It was a mutual decision to end things." Mona nodded, then paused. "It just wasn't meant to be."

Later on that night, the phone rang and Kailah answered.

"You were looking good tonight at the club, Sexual Chocolate."

"Well, I guess that meant you were looking at something that you'll never ever taste again. And you better believe that," Kailah snapped. "What time is it anyway?" She raised her head, then squinted as she looked over at the clock on her nightstand. "Your big day is in just a few short hours."

"I can't stop thinking about you," Derrick whispered. "You can't tell me you don't think about those nights we spent together at your place."

"I also haven't forgotten about the money you owe me either, brotha, but you seem to have forgotten."

Derrick swallowed hard. "I told you I was going to pay you back, and I won't go back on my word."

"Your word ain't worth shit to me right now, Derrick," Kailah replied. "So, save it. I just wish you and Angela much happiness, because I am over it. And I've moved on to bigger and better things."

"So what are you saying?" Derrick asked. "You seeing somebody else?"

Kailah cocked her head back in utter surprise. He had the nerve to be jealous.

"I'm doing more than seeing. Good night, Derrick."

Kailah hung up.

The nerve of him. Derrick ignored her the entire time at the club. That's just like his ass to call her when no one else was around. Light-skinned women were the trophy prize for a shallow man like Derrick, who could care less about what a woman had on the inside, only her color on the outside. Most men considered having a white woman on their arm the most prized possession of all. Kailah didn't need a man like that in her life. She was definitely better without him.

Slavery taught blacks to hate their skin color, even though there are more colored people in the world. Nevertheless, an entire race of oppressed people believed black to be ugly and white to be beautiful. Men, black and white, worshipped a blonde beauty with blue eyes, to the point where women in this day of age dyed their hair and wore colored contacts in order to be looked at as the American Beauty. Those women who fell victim to what was considered the standards of society included many of her sorority sisters as well.

As a young girl, Mama Anna taught Kailah to love her deep mocha skin. Her daddy told her she was the most beautiful little colored girl he had ever laid his eyes on. He absolutely adored her. Kailah wanted nothing more than to make him proud. The last time she visited him at the nursing home, he told her so. Those were the qualities she looked for in the man she would marry. He would have to love, worship, and adore her, just like Henry Carter.

MIXED MESSAGES

Chapter 5
Get It Together

"Would you like me to take your dinner tray?" the Delta flight attendant asked.

"Yes," Mona responded as she massaged her temples. The meals in first-class were usually pretty good, but for once, she didn't have much of an appetite. Last night, Mona had held her hand over her mouth while holding the handset and listening to Kailah and Derrick on the phone alluding to the fact that they had been intimate. She wondered how long this had been going on. Hit with some serious blows to the heart and ego, she believed her life had been a total lie. Nothing was the same, and everything had changed...her innocence, virginity, and now her most cherished friendship.

How could Kailah do this? She looked out the window of the plane. She had loved her like a sister. Derrick disappointed her, but Kailah was supposed to be loyal. She trusted her. Hell, she needed a drink.

Her flight arrived two hours late, but Bea was still at the airport waiting for her. "Oh, darling I missed you so much." She pinched Mona's chubby cheeks. "Let's go get your luggage, and I want to hear all about your trip."

"Mother! I'm tired. I want to relax for the rest of the day before I go back to work tomorrow."

"Okay, dear," Bea said. "However, there is something I need to discuss with you on the way home."

Thirty minutes passed before Mona's luggage arrived.

"Good grief, I see you've added another piece to your luggage set since you've left," Bea said and pointed her index finger. "You wouldn't have to buy more clothes if you would lose a few pounds."

"I couldn't resist shopping, Mother." Mona laughed out loud. "I purchased a white silk blouse to die for. I'm going to start my diet this week. I promise to devote at least two afternoons a week at the fitness center on the third floor."

Bea's smile widened. "That's my girl."

As Bea drove off from the parking lot, Mona leaned back in her seat and stared up at the beautiful cloudless night sky. All day she thought about how she would gather enough pride and courage to walk into the doors of Thomas and Clarke. How would she go back to business as usual once she saw Darren Thomas again without killing him?

"Charles called last week wanting to know when I was coming home," Bea said. "He says he really misses me, and I must admit I miss him, too." Bea sat forward as she made a sharp turn onto the next street. "Well, I wanted to talk to you about it first. I want to make sure you'll be able to take care of yourself when I leave."

"I'll be fine, Mother." Mona sighed. "No need to worry. I'm a big girl, and I can take care of myself." She rested her head on the back of the leather seat. "And besides, I can hire some outside help to take care of the townhouse if I need it. Go home and take care of Daddy."

"Are you sure, honey?"

"I'm sure." Mona looked over at her mother and smiled. *That one little phone call to Daddy did just the trick.*

The next day, Mona sat at her desk reviewing the notes for her very first court appearance representing the Kravich family. Two knocks sounded as Lois entered and clutched the door.

"Gina wasn't at her desk, but I hope I'm not interrupting."

Mona kept staring at her notes wishing Lois would go away. "Oh, no... Not at all, Lois. I've been so busy. I really haven't had a chance to stop by your office. I apologize."

"Oh, no apologies needed." Lois took a seat in front of Mona's desk. Her Jackie O' styled navy dress and matching jacket looked stunning. "I've been a little worried about you, that's all. I was glad to hear that you took a little break from this case. Now, you're back and looking smashing, darling."

"Thank you." Mona spoke slowly while she nervously tapped her pencil on her desktop. "I'm on a diet, so... I have lost a few pounds,"

"Well, whatever you're doing is working." Lois moved in closer and placed her elbows on the desk. "You must share your secret," she teased.

Mona pretended to laugh back. "Oh, nothing in particular, just cutting back on the carbs. I've been meaning to come in early and use the gym on the third floor, but I've been staying up so late at night."

Lois threw her hand up. "Honey, you have to make the time. Otherwise, you'll never do it."

Mona looked at Lois sitting perfectly poised in the leather chair. All her life, she wanted what Lois had: the handsome and charming husband, wonderfully intelligent sons, prestigious career, and an extreme amount of hard-earned wealth. She had it all. Or so it seemed. The women at Thomas & Clarke respected Lois and did what she asked with no hesitation. However, when the boss wasn't around, they gossiped and talked about Darren's philandering behind at the water coolers and lounge.

Gossiping in the cafeteria would quickly come to a halt when Lois entered. Mona wanted to command that type of respect. By now, she realized "all that glittered isn't gold". The rumors about Darren Thomas had to be true. A smart woman like Lois had to be aware of her husband's infidelities. However, she never showed it, always together like the classic tailored suits she wore.

Another knock sounded at the door. Bea walked in. "Oh good, you're both here. Are we ready?"

"Ready for what?" Mona asked, cocking her head.

MIXED MESSAGES

"Before my flight left today, I thought it would be a good idea for us ladies to have lunch," Bea responded. "So, I called Lois and asked if she was free for lunch, and well...here we are."

Lois stood and slung her long hair to one side. "I'm in the mood for Italian. Let's go." She and Bea giggled like two young girls in grade school.

Mona grabbed her jacket and her purse to follow the two ladies out of her office and shut the door behind her.

......

"I don't know why I let Mother and Lois talk me into this." Mona looked at herself in the mirror as she straightened her skirt once more. This was her first date with a guy since Derrick. She adjusted the seam of her skirt. She had been too busy with work to go out socially or notice any guys. She avoided men like they were the plague. She tried to convince herself it was not really a date, but rather a night out with an old friend.

Robert, the eldest son of Darren Thomas and Lois Clarke, lived in New York where he managed a chain of retail stores. His parents were very proud of how successful he had become. Only in town for a couple of days, Bea and Lois thought it to be a good idea for Mona and Robert to hang out. Mona reluctantly gave Lois permission to give Robert her phone number. He called her three days later, and the date was set.

The doorbell rang.

Mona opened the door. As she stood there wearing a fitted pink chiffon sweater and matching pink skirt with a split, Mona hoped she had made the right choice, because Robert looked damn good in his silk Versace shirt and pin-striped slacks.

"Hello." She smiled and gave him a big hug. He smelled good. Calvin Klein. "Thank you for the flowers."

"You're welcome." As he entered, his eyes swept the room. Miles Davis played softly from the stereo. "You have a very nice place here."

Mona laughed from the kitchen as she searched for a vase. "Mother did all of the decorating, so I can't take any credit." She picked up her leather jacket and purse off the arm of the sofa. "So, what's the plan for this evening?"

"I was hoping we could eat at that seafood restaurant with the fantastic view of South Beach. Jack's."

Mona rubbed her hands together. "Sounds good to me."

At dinner, Mona and Robert didn't have a difficult time conversing with one another, considering they'd known each other since childhood. Mona couldn't get over how things had changed. In high school, Robert looked more on the geeky side with wide-rimmed glasses. Now, he'd traded them in for a soft pair of contacts, and he was so handsome with his nicely trimmed mustache, full beard, and low haircut. This went well with his medium cocoa-brown complexion.

After dinner, Robert and Mona strolled down South Beach to a nearby club to do some dancing. Mona hadn't danced with Robert since she'd visited him once at NYU when he was a student there.

On Saturday morning, Mona decided to sleep in late. She didn't feel very well, and her stomach was upset. Thinking back to last night brought on a slight grin. How nice it was to finally go out with a man!

Not haven't spoken to Kailah since she'd arrived back in Miami, she only assumed Kailah was too busy to call her. It didn't matter anyway, because the friendship was over. She had to work up enough nerve to let Kailah know.

Since her trip to Chicago for the wedding, Mona had lost twenty pounds. She simply started to focus more on work and stopped eating. Okay, she didn't exactly stop eating altogether.

But when she did eat, she would simply take a laxative to flush out her system. This was a trick she'd learned in college. The weight came right off.

She decided to take a mental day off. That meant no working at home, and she would receive some much-needed pampering. Gina had made appointments for Mona early on in the week at the styling salon and spa. She was going to have her hair styled, get a manicure and pedicure, and a massage at the spa.

The phone rang and Mona glanced over at the clock. It was eleven o'clock. She only had one hour before her hair appointment, so she would have to quickly get rid of whoever was on the phone in order to arrive on time.

"Hello, Mona speaking."

"Hey, this is Robert."

"Uh-huh." She was speechless.

"Well, I wanted to tell you that I had a good time last night," he said.

"I had a wonderful time, too," Mona responded. "Thanks for taking me out. I've been so busy all week. It was fun."

"Well, I know this is short notice and everything, but would you like to go catch a movie tonight? I'll even throw in dinner, but you have to promise to eat more than lettuce this time."

Mona laughed. "I ate more than lettuce. But, I promise."

"Okay, I'll pick you up at six o'clock."

"Six it is."

Chapter 6
Can't Mix Business with Pleasure

Kailah pushed through the rotating door of the eighteen-story office building. AND Consulting was a small firm located on the fourteenth, fifteenth, and sixteenth floors. Kailah eased her way through men and women dressed in blue and black business suits until she made it to the elevator. Only a few early birds were already in the office at this hour, and she was persistent on being one of them. Quickly earning her way into being one of the top consultants, Kailah spent long hours and evenings bringing in the most high-profiled clients.

For the past two months, Kailah worked on closing the Johnston Products deal. The review meeting was planned in one short week, and she still needed to make some last-minute revisions to receive final approval from Lynn Gleichman, Kailah's senior consulting officer, who was also a recent college graduate when first hired to work for the company. Speculation was she only received a senior position at AND because her father was the vice president of the company.

Lynn had quite the reputation before entering the doors at AND. Known as one to party hard and date older married men, Lynn actually lived in the home of a man old enough to be her father while he was off in the Caribbean with his wife and children. Lynn had no shame in driving his $70,000 BMW to work everyday.

Kailah passed Lynn's office and waved hello. While on the phone, she summoned Kailah into her office. She whispered, "I need to talk to you. Wait one second."

Kailah stood patiently while fumbling with her keys. *She acts like I don't have shit to do. All right, ten more seconds of standing here like an idiot and that's it.* Kailah looked down at her watch, counted to ten, and then marched out.

MIXED MESSAGES

When Kailah got to her office, Taneisha stood there pouring a cup of coffee with her long silver and black acrylic nails wrapped around the mug. She turned around and handed the coffee mug to Kailah.

"Just the way you like it, Boss Lady," Taneisha said with a big grin. Her gold tooth sparkled.

Taneisha grew up in the Robert Taylor Housing Projects on Chicago's south side in a single-parent home with two older sisters. At seventeen, she moved out of her mother's house and married her high school sweetheart, Joe Mitchell. Three months pregnant at the time, Taneisha was barely showing at the wedding. Six months later, she gave birth to Tyree and then her daughter Shyree followed.

Now, her children were nine and ten years old and making honor roll every grading period. Joe and Taneisha were proud of their children, and it looked like Tyree, who had taken up football like his dad, was quickly becoming the star player in the peewee division. Taneisha would leave early in the afternoons to take Shyree to dance lessons or Tyree to football practice, and she never missed a game. Kailah came along for the ride sometimes to support Shyree at her dance recitals or Tyree at his early Saturday morning games.

Taneisha was someone to be reckoned with at AND. Other assistants knew their place and when and how to step to her. "Don't get told," was the motto she lived by.

An early bird, she arrived at work around 6:30 or 7, before anyone else, but always managed to make up the time by taking extra-long lunch breaks to go gossip with the other assistants or mail room workers, or by leaving early to pick up the kids. Always professional, the clients loved her tenacity and crazy humor.

Being ghetto fabulous to the bone, Taneisha often spoke in slang and wore all the styles featured in the black hair magazines. One week, she would wear it short, then long, blonde, then burgundy, and then return the blue-black jet-straight hair back to curly. Being petite, she looked good in everything she wore. She was very much into wearing big-name labeled clothing, but never paid those high prices, choosing to shop at the warehouse or outlet stores. The white assistants at AND never knew the difference.

Kailah smiled back. "Thanks, girl, just what I needed," she said. "Do me a favor. If you see Lynn walking this way, warn me."

"Did you tell her off? That bitch is begging for an ass whooping!" Taneisha assumed a position like the Karate Kid. She slung back her weave ponytail. They both burst out laughing. "Girl, you're always letting her get to you, like she stole your man or something. Don't let her get to you."

"I know I shouldn't. I can't stand Lynn." Kailah slurped her coffee down.

Taneisha turned up her pointy nose. "I can't stand her either. Especially the way she flaunts her big ass around in those tight skirts."

Kailah nodded. "Yeah, her skirts *are* a little short and tight." Friday's outfit took the cake. Lynn strutted confidently into the office wearing a long, tight-fitted black skirt and a leopard skin low-cut top. The clients stared at Lynn's bosom so hard at the last presentation meeting they signed the contract without any hassle or questions. Of course, Lynn earned all of the credit for closing the deal and was treated to a celebration dinner by the senior partners. The rest of the team members got a cheap-ass wine basket with breads and cheeses.

The door swung open. "Excuse me, Ms. Carter, but I asked you to wait!" Lynn curled her lips. "You're so busy that you can't wait for a senior officer?"

"My apologies, Lynn. You were taking a long time, and I wanted to get an early start on finalizing the Johnston account."

MIXED MESSAGES

"The contracts are no good unless you have *my* final say-so," Lynn responded sternly. She placed her hands on her wide hips.

"I'm well aware of the proper chain of command, Lynn. I'm also aware of the fact that you haven't attended the last three late-night work sessions," Kailah said as she leaned back in her leather chair. "So, unless you want to finish preparing these contracts without my much-needed assistance, I suggest you take a better tone with me."

Lynn glared back and sucked her teeth. Kailah picked up a pen and pretended to work. Lynn spun around very quickly, slamming the door behind her. Kailah sat and stewed over the heated encounter. Knowing that it wasn't doing her any good to keep thinking about it, she decided to get back to work.

Two hours later, Taneisha buzzed.

"Kailah."

"Yes, Taneisha."

"Mr. Terrence is on line three."

Kailah took in a deep breath.

"Taneisha, would you please inform Mr. Terrence that I'm extremely busy, and unless he has an urgent or pressing matter to discuss with me, I will have to call him back."

Why didn't he just get the message? She wasn't interested in dating a client. Even though he was fine as hell! Kailah thought back to their first meeting at Bacino's.

"Thank you for meeting me, Mr. Terrence, especially with the sudden change in plans." Kailah greeted Keith Terrence with a strong handshake as he approached her table. "I apologize for not notifying you earlier, but—"

"No apologies needed, Ms. Carter. Let's just get to business. Shall we?"

Kailah cleared her throat. *Well, excuse me.* "Yes. I would like to discuss what Waltman Pharmaceutical's needs are, and how AND can meet those needs.

The blonde hair, blue-eyed waitress walked up to the table. "Hello. My name is Kimberly, and I will be your waitress today. Can I get you guys a drink?" she asked in a perky, nauseating voice. "What would you like?"

As they placed their drink orders, Kailah snuck a glance over at Keith Terrence. Dark-skinned with low trimmed hair and a goatee, he resembled Morris Chestnut. This was a clean brother. She admired his olive green business suit, which was perfectly cut to show off his muscular build. Damn, this brother looked good.

"Ms. Carter, what's good?" Keith Terrence asked.

"Pretty much everything on the menu. Bacino's is one of my favorite places to eat."

Keith Terrence replied, "I'm not a big fan of Italian cuisine. I'm sure I won't be placing Bacino's as one of my favorites." He smiled smugly as he took a sip from his glass.

"In that case, I'm sure you'll enjoy the house salad." She hated it when they sent black reps to meet with her, as if blacks were supposed to bond or something. She didn't have time for this shit. At the time, Kailah was still dealing with the disappointing news about Derrick.

Kailah's thoughts were abruptly interrupted when Taneisha put the call through against her request.

"What is it, Mr. Terrence?"

"I told you to call me Keith."

Kailah swiveled her chair away from the computer. "What can I help you with, Mr. Terrence?" She glanced over at the figure sheets on her desk.

"I know you're busy, Ms. Carter, so I'll be brief." Kailah's heart fluttered as she listened to Keith Terrence's deep, sexy voice over the receiver. "There's something I would like to talk to you about. I was thinking we could discuss it over dinner tonight."

Kailah paused for a moment. "I'm sorry, Mr. Terrence, but I'm way too busy."

"Okay."

Suddenly, a knock rapped at Kailah's door. "Mr. Terrence, I have someone at my door. I'll have to talk to you later. Bye." Kailah hung up quickly, walked over to the door, and swung it open.

Much to her surprise, Keith Terrence stood there with a cell phone in one hand and a huge bouquet of red roses in the other. She glanced over his shoulder and saw Taneisha doubled over her chair in laughter. Everyone else in the office rose from cubicles to watch the main event.

"Well, are you going to meet me tonight or what?" Keith asked. His smile revealed a nice set of pearly white teeth. "You're so beautiful, and I want to take you out for a night on the town. Your assistant has already told me you're busy with the Johnston deal, but you do need a break."

Kailah stood speechless.

"It's just one night, Kailah. I promise you won't regret it." He poked out his bottom lip, resembling an abandoned puppy dog that lost its mother.

How could she resist? "Okay. I'll take you up on your offer, Keith, but not tonight. What about Friday? I really need to stay late at the office tonight so—"

"No." Keith placed his arms on her shoulders. He slightly pushed Kailah back through the door to her office and closed it shut. "The offer is for tonight, Kailah. I know that I haven't made the best impression. I want to correct that. I'm very much attracted to you." He stared deeply in Kailah's eyes and licked his sexy pink lips. "Now, I'm not leaving until you say yes."

"Okay, you can pick me up at six-thirty, but don't be late." She smiled.

"I won't."

When Keith left, Kailah leaned back on her desktop and crossed her legs. *Who said you can't mix business with pleasure anyway?*

Chapter 7
Too Good To Be True

Kailah stood in the lobby of her apartment building awaiting Keith's arrival. Actually, it was a small entrance that reeked of cigarette and cigar smoke.

For over an hour, she struggled with what to wear. She finally decided her plum-colored sweater with her black leather pants and black leather boots would work. She wore her hair up in a wrap with loose curls dangling down to her shoulders.

"What's up, Kailah?

Kailah turned and smiled. "Hey, Jeff, long time no see."

"Got a hot date?" Jeff scanned Kailah from head to toe.

"Yeah, with Keith."

"Oh, Keith, the smooth guy you were telling me about when you came home with the roses."

"You got it." Kailah clicked her teeth. "Where are you headed tonight?"

"Over to a party with some friends. You should go with me sometime."

Kailah hesitated. *Is he asking me out?*

"Maybe I will."

"Okay." Jeff cupped his hands together. "Well, I'm off. Do me a favor and have some fun." He waved good-bye and left.

Every early Saturday morning, Kailah would exit her own apartment for a run only to see a different girl leaving her neighbor's apartment. Jeff, a single white guy, loved women and throwing wild parties. During the week, he was a young accountant, always dressed in executive-styled, well-tailored suits, who left as early as Kailah in the mornings. On the weekends, he wore black leather pants and stretch tight shirts to show off what he thought to be a great body. Kailah never complained, even when some nights would get a little rowdy. Jeff was a good neighbor, willing to lend a helping hand when needed, just right for Kailah who lived all alone and knew no one in the city.

A black Lincoln Navigator pulled up in front of the building and stopped. Keith jumped out with a dozen roses in hand. His brown fitted shirt showed off his muscular build. The dark brown leather-suede jacket to match and crème-colored silk pants looked very nice. Insecurity surfaced as Kailah wondered if she should have selected another outfit to wear. Keith walked with a confident brother-like strut. As he got closer to the building, Kailah pushed open the door and stepped out.

"It's about time!" Kailah exclaimed. "I was beginning to think you weren't going to make it." She threw her arms up in the air.

Keith caught her arms in mid-air and put them close to him. He snuggled up close to her. "I wouldn't miss this for anything."

"So where are we going tonight?" Kailah asked nervously. Their last meeting at Bacino's wasn't very pleasant. Kailah had already decided that if the brother started to act the fool, she would end the date right then and there, and ask him to take her home. Also, she would make sure to end their business relationship entirely, and refer him to another reputable consultant at AND.

"I thought we would go to a comedy club and grab a bite to eat. Qui Be Negroes is performing, and I thought you would enjoy it." He bit his bottom lip.

"I've heard of them." *This should go well,* she thought. Comedy was a cure for all ill feelings toward someone. Keith had a lot to make up for, being such a jerk the last time.

Keith opened the door of his SUV for Kailah and she stepped in. It was a steep step, so she needed a little personal assistance from Keith.

MIXED MESSAGES

Keith talked on the way about his pharmaceutical sales company and how difficult it was to get started. After graduating from Howard University in D.C., he came to Chicago to enter into a joint venture with a group of young black entrepreneurs like him. The increase of media advertising of prescription drugs helped his business soar, and now the beginning was only a blur.

"It was tough in the beginning. Loan officers aren't interested in young black entrepreneurs. So, I had to find other ways to raise money." He placed his hand on top of Kailah's, picked it up, and kissed it. "You are so beautiful."

Kailah seductively bit her tongue. *Sexy and charming.* She wondered if he was as good in the bed. This man now had her in the mood for some lovemaking.

"What about you, Kailah?"

"What about me?"

"How did you end up in the mean streets of Chicago?" Keith made a sharp turn onto Halsted Street.

Cafes, bookstores, and some of Chicago's liveliest clubs and restaurants on the Northside packed its tree-lined streets, also known as "Sweet Home Chicago".

"After graduating from University of Florida, I got a job with AND. I guess the rest is history."

"And here we are." He smiled coyly.

"I guess we are." They locked eyes for a moment.

"No." Keith chuckled. "I mean here we are... at the comedy club."

"Oh." Kailah turned away. She certainly didn't look forward to getting out of the warm SUV. It was tough for Kailah to get used to this freezing weather, having lived her entire life in Florida where the temperature was never lower than thirty degrees on the coldest winter day.

The valet approached the SUV and opened the door for Kailah. Keith handed the keys to the young boy, skipped around the back of the vehicle, and placed his arm around Kailah. As they followed the young black girl to their table, Keith was stopped by several people. Some were wealthy looking black men who could easily be found in *Ebony's* "Speaking of People" section of the magazine.

"I guess you're a popular guy," Kailah commented as Keith pulled out her chair for her to be seated.

"Not really." Keith shook his head. "You get to know people when you're out in the business circle."

As the evening died down, Keith asked if Kailah wanted to join him for cocktails at his place. She happily obliged.

Kailah sat on Keith's oversized sofa. She placed her wine on the glass table and let her eyes wander around the modern-styled loft apartment with hardwood flooring. All of the furniture pieces were brown leather. A huge window glass wall showcased a breathtaking view of The Loop, which is in the center of Chicago. The Wrigley and Tribune Tower had lights that cascaded on the streets, while the Chicago River looked serene and peaceful.

Keith reached out for her hand. "Come on, baby." Coltrane played in the background as Keith slid behind Kailah, placed his arms around her waist, and spun her around. "Dance with me."

They danced seductively, teasing one another. Keith's hands roamed over Kailah's body. She liked it. She put her arms on his broad shoulders so Keith's hands would have easier access to her body. He began to slide his hands underneath her juicy cheeks.

Ooohhh, this feels so good. He smells so good. Brother knows how to work his hands. I wonder what else he can work.

Without asking, Keith escorted Kailah up the black spiral staircase to his bedroom. He kissed her on the lips so softly while cupping her breasts in his hands.

"I want to make love to you, Kailah."

"Me, too." She could hardly speak.

MIXED MESSAGES

Then he pulled his shirt over his head. Kailah ran her hands over the ripples in his chest. He quickly pulled her close and began to unzip the back of her leather pants. He slid her pants down to her knees. Kailah stood in her plum-colored lace bra and panties.

"You are so beautiful." Keith's warm breath danced circles in her ear.

She lay on the bed and watched while Keith undid his belt. He unbuttoned and unzipped his pants, and Kailah watched intently while the silk pants slid down Keith's muscular thighs to his calves. He leaned over, kissing and sucking passionately on her neck.

"Hhh-mmm," Kailah sighed.

He held her closely with his strong arms. Kailah wrapped her slender arms around his neck as he guided himself inside of her. She moaned in pleasure.

Very slow, but forceful Keith knew exactly the spots on Kailah's body to make her tingle, and he hit every one. Kailah explored sexual spots on Keith's body, too. When she got on top and took control, his loud grunts let her know that she was doing it right.

He is just too good to be true.

Chapter 8
It Was Good While It Lasted

Kailah walked into the office to find a huge basket of flowers on the center of her desk. Taneisha stood reading the small card that had accompanied the arrangement.

"What in the hell do you think you're doing?!" Kailah folded her hands across her chest.

Taneisha stumbled, almost falling to the floor. "Damn, you scared me."

"That'll teach you to stop snooping in my office. Now get your ass up and out."

Taneisha passed Kailah and snapped her fingers. "You wouldn't even have your little basket if I hadn't let the delivery guy in. So, think about that."

"Okay, I'll think about it." Kailah shut the door in Taneisha's face. Then she screamed, "I did."

Kailah sat down at her desk, reaching over to smell the beautiful wild tropical floral arrangement.

Her phone buzzed. "You're going to give me the juicy details, right?"

Kailah shook her head in disbelief. "Of course, girl."

Kailah then dialed her best friend's number while she jotted down notes with her free hand.

"Mona speaking."

"I was beginning to think I was going to get your voice mail again."

"I've been busy." Mona's voice sounded stiff.

"So have I," Kailah responded. "But I always take out time for my best girlfriend."

"We are *not* the same people," Mona said. "Very different."

Something was up with Mona. Kailah just wasn't sure what. They hadn't talked since Derrick's wedding. Maybe she should have called sooner to see how she was dealing with everything. Kailah didn't have time to play the guessing game, so she decided to be direct. "What the hell is with you, Mona? I've never known you to be so cold."

"I've changed. I guess you could say I've had a bit of a revelation."

"I'm listening."

"About people who are supposed to be your friend, better yet, your sistah!" Mona yelled. "Then they stab you in the back and sleep with your man."

"When…" Kailah was stumped for words and slumped over in her seat. "How did you find out?"

"*That* is not important," Mona replied. "The fact is you were sleeping with Derrick. I know about it. And I no longer consider you a friend."

"Please, just let me try to explain."

"Explain! There's nothing you can say to me. I don't want to hear it. You've always been jealous of me. Always wanted what I had. I should've known better than to be friends with a trifling sistah such as you!"

"Okay, bitch." Kailah snapped. "I'm not gonna sit here and let you trash me like that. Better think again." Kailah sat back in her seat to catch her breath. "No one ever liked your snooty ass, and I was the only one to feel sorry for you and befriend you. Always acting like you're better than everybody else just because your mommy and daddy got a little bit of money. That don't make you better."

"I never thought of myself as being better," Mona stated.

"If you want to go way back to the start of things, I was the one who expressed interest in Derrick in the first place. Next thing I know, a week later, he showed up at our apartment to take you out for lunch."

Mona chuckled. "I told Derrick that you liked him, and he told me he was not interested in your little skinny self. He said

53

he wanted a woman with a little meat on her bones like me. I can't help it if he wanted me and not you."

"Obviously, he was interested in me," Kailah said as she clutched her chest. "He just wanted a token bitch like you as a trophy girlfriend."

"Well, I don't have time to pass insults back and forth. No, I haven't called you, and don't intend to ever again."

"Is that the way you want it?" Kailah asked.

"That is simply the way it is. Good day, Ms. Carter."

•••••••

"Baby, you should have heard the awful things she said to me." Mona moved in closer to Robert's chest. They were lying on the bed in her townhouse. Robert had been spending a lot of long nights at Mona's place. At first, Mona was a little uncomfortable with the mere thought that she was even slightly attracted to Robert. But why shouldn't she be? He was her age, unlike his old-ass father. He was very nice, gentle, and sometimes romantic. Some girls would consider him strikingly handsome with a body that some brothers would kill for. She wasn't a virgin anymore, so why the hell not? All those years of saving herself for the right guy to come along, shit, she didn't know what she was missing. With Robert, sex was so damn good. He made her reach climactic levels she'd never imagined possible.

"It's all over now." Robert kissed Mona on the shoulder. "Now she knows exactly how you feel. I just hate to see your friendship end this way."

"Friendships come and go. I'm not bitter, and I have no regrets." Mona shrugged. "It was good while it lasted."

Robert kissed Mona on her forehead.

"What movie are we watching tonight?"

Mona leaned over the coffee table and picked up the videos. "*Sleepless in Seattle* or *You've Got Mail.*"

Robert revealed his dimpled smile. "So I guess that means it's a Meg Ryan night."

"Yep." Mona folded her arms.

Robert slid the tape in the VCR. "Okay, I choose the e-mail movie."

"Goodie." Mona clapped her hands softly as Robert placed his arm around her on the couch. Mona kicked up her feet and crossed them on the table.

Mona found it difficult to enjoy the movie. It hurt like hell knowing she was at odds with her best friend. Having her heart sliced in two weighed heavy on her, consuming her thoughts all the time. She desperately wanted the pain to ease away. Mona resisted the constant urge to pick up the phone and make things right. The good part of her tugged at her conscience, urging her to place the call, but then she would hang up, believing that Kailah should be the one to apologize. Mona was the innocent victim, or more like the fool for placing so much trust in one person. How could she trust again?

And why hadn't Kailah called her anyway? Didn't she still care? Getting over this fallout wouldn't be easy, but Mona knew that with time she could eventually get through it. Staying busy with work and having Robert around helped a great deal.

Mona ran her fingers down Robert's arm, kissed it softly, and then she laid her head on his shoulders. He had a way of making her feel safe and protected.

Soon, she drifted off to sleep.

Chapter 9
Things Are Gonna Get Ugly!

Mona stood at the bar drinking an apple martini and wearing a silver crepe dress with a front slit. The matching jacket was embroidered with sequins. Lots of people were drinking, mingling, and having a good time at the victory celebration Darren Thomas and Lois Clarke were throwing. Mona started tapping her silver heel as soon as she heard her favorite jazz tune blasting from the speakers.

As Mona danced alone at the bar, Robert leaned over and whispered in her ear. "If you wanted a dance partner, all you had to do was ask."

"What happened to chivalry?" Mona asked. "Why do I have to ask for a dance partner? The handsome gentleman should appear from the crowd, escort me to the dance floor, and sweep me off my feet."

"Wake up from your dream, okay, and fast forward to the year 2003." Robert threw his hands up. "What's up, girl? You looking good with yo' fine ass. Why don't we get on the dance floor and you can show me how to back that thang up!"

Mona laughed as she put down her drink. "All right, I'll dance with you, but keep your hands off of my ass."

They pushed through the crowd of people. Mona never realized the Thomas family knew so many people and had so many clients. Just then, "Sending You Forget Me Nots" by Patrice Rushen began to play. All people, middle-aged and up, rushed to the floor. Mona and Robert were right in the mix and dancing hard.

Mona felt a pair of eyes on her. She did a full turn and caught a brief glimpse of Darren Thomas. Darren and Lois were also dancing to the old school jam. Mona pretended she didn't see them and kept on dancing. Moments later, she saw Darren storm off the dance floor with Lois following in heavy pursuit.

MIXED MESSAGES

"I haven't had that much fun in a long time, Mother," Mona spoke into her cell phone while driving home from the party. "Well, I'm just pulling up in front my house. I'll call you first thing in the morning. Kiss Daddy for me."

Mona removed her keys from the ignition, grabbed her purse, and stepped out of the car. As she hurried to the door, she heard something fall on the ground. She swung around to find her lipstick rolling down the driveway.

Shit, that cinnamon brown lipstick was my favorite color, too. Oh well, it was getting low and about time for me to replace it anyway.

As she turned around to keep walking, she bumped into Darren Thomas. Her arms flailed in the air as she stepped back. "Why are you here?"

"I want to talk to you," Darren responded. He grabbed Mona's arm. Mona pulled back, but his grip only got stronger. "Are you trying to keep things in the family? First, you fuck me, and now my son."

"Get your hands off of me!" Mona struggled to get away from Darren's grip. "I don't know what you're talking about! You need to go away. Now!"

"I'm not going anywhere, bitch. We need to come to a little understanding." He placed his fingers in between Mona's legs, right up the split of her dress. "Stay away from my son, or I'll kill you."

"Mr. Thomas, please, just leave," Mona cried. "You've been drinking. You don't know what you're—"

"Shut the hell up, you whore! Why are you crying? I just want to talk to you."

Mona kicked Darren's leg and tried to free her arms again. "Let go of me!" She kicked him in the groin and ran away. She shook while she unlocked her front door and ran inside. Right behind her, Darren forced his way in, too.

"Look at what you made me do!" Darren's face was turned up in anger. "I just wanted to talk to you and you do this to me! You ain't nothing but a whore!"

He slapped her across the face with the back of his hand. Mona fell to the floor and scooted over to the end table, trying to reach for the phone. Darren pushed the table over and the receiver fell off of the hook. He turned her over and kneeled down. He snatched her stockings off and then her panties. Fondling her with one hand, he pinned Mona down by her chest with his elbow. Once he had managed to pull his pants down, he roughly entered her.

Stop! Please don't do this! Mona silently screamed.

Darren groaned and moaned. He breathed his alcoholic breath into Mona's face. Finally, he got up and zipped his pants. He walked out of her townhouse, leaving the door wide open. Slowly, Mona crawled over to the phone and dialed 911 through her tears.

......

"Is that everything, Ms. Richards?"

"Yes," Mona responded. "Officer, I've told you everything that happened last night."

"Okay, Ms. Richards. Here's my card." The short stocky officer placed it on the stand next to Mona's hospital bed. "If you remember anything else, please don't hesitate to call."

"I won't, Officer Daniels. Thanks for your help."

The officer adjusted his belt as he exited, and Mona dozed off to a peaceful sleep shortly after he left.

Not long after drifting off to sleep, a heavy-set black nurse tapped on her shoulder. Mona put her hand on her head and tried to sit up in the bed. The nurse helped her by propping up her pillow.

"Thanks." She tried to smile, but her jaws hurt so much.

"You need me to get you something, honey?"

"No, I'm okay."

The nurse left as Bea entered with Charles following closely on her heels.

"Oh my God, Charles, look at our baby." Mona's face was black and blue from all the bruising. Bea gently stroked Mona's head.

Charles pulled a chair up alongside the bed for Bea, and then squeezed Mona's hand. "How you doing there, Babycakes?"

"I'm okay, Daddy." Tears rolled down her face. "I'm so glad you're here."

Bea patted Mona's leg. "Of course, we're here, Sweetie. Mother is going to take good care of you."

"And I'm going to take care of Mr. Darren Thomas, too!" Charles yelled. "I hope the police find him before I do."

"Charles, would you please stop? You don't even know what really happened," Bea corrected. "I'm sure that once the police take a statement from Darren, this will all be straightened out."

"No, I'll be the one straightening things out." Charles cracked his knuckles. "Things are gonna get damn ugly around here if I get one second alone with him."

......

"Mr. Thomas, do you have anything to say?" A reporter put a microphone in Darren Thomas' face as he and Lois Clarke were leaving the courthouse. A mob of reporters and cameras waited on the courthouse steps.

He stopped and looked into the camera. "I'm not guilty of such a crime. There was no crime committed against Ms. Mona Richards. I was heavily under the influence of alcohol, and Ms. Richards seduced me. I'm guilty of giving into her flamboyant woes, not of rape."

A female reporter then stuck her microphone in front of Lois. "Lois Clarke, how do you respond to the allegations made by the victim?"

Lois composed herself and cleared her throat. "I wish the affair never happened. Still, my husband and I will survive this. I believe my husband, and Ms. Richards is lying."

Darren placed his arm around his wife. "My wife is the real victim, not Mona Richards. Not a day goes by that I'm not praying that my wife and family will find a way to forgive me of being involved in such an adulterous affair." He began to cry. "Please, please, no more questions."

The couple walked quickly away. The mob of people followed until Darren and Lois jumped in the back seat of the black limousine.

He is such an actor. Lois, the real victim? Then why am I the one lying in the hospital? Damn liar.

Mona used the remote control to turn off the television set, then turned over on her side and closed her eyes.

MIXED MESSAGES

Chapter 10
What Are Friends For?

Kailah walked into the doors of the hospital and placed her sunglasses on top of her head.

Bea stood outside of Mona's room speaking with the doctor. She looked at Kailah and grabbed her hand as she approached. "Thanks so much, Dr. Adams. Kailah, I'm so glad you came." She gave Kailah a big hug. "Mona's going to be so happy when she sees you."

I don't know about that. Kailah was surprised to get a call from Bea the night before, and upon hearing the shocking news, she booked the next flight to Miami. On the plane, Kailah went over all sorts of scenarios in her head. What would Mona say now that they would be face to face? They hadn't spoken to one another after the nasty quarrel on the phone several weeks ago. It didn't matter, though. She had to be there for her. Mona was like family.

Bea walked in with Kailah. "Look, who's here."

Mona looked up at Kailah and tried to force a smile. Kailah couldn't believe what she saw. Mona's face was pale white with black and blue bruises. She looked helpless and barely able to move around in the white hospital gown. Mona had lost a considerable amount of weight, too. "I came as soon as I heard. How you doing?"

"Good. The hospital staff is taking great care of me. It's nice to see you." Mona reached over for the remote on the bed stand so she could turn on the television. "I'm sorry we couldn't see each other under better circumstances."

Bea's cell phone rang, and she quickly snatched it out of her purse. "Hello." She nodded and placed her hand over the receiver. "I'm going to take this call out in the hallway while you girls continue to get caught up." Bea exited, closing the door shut behind her.

"I don't know why you wasted your money to fly all the way to Miami, because I never invited you here," Mona said, folding her arms.

Kailah placed her hands on her hips. "When I received the call from your mother, I felt that was all I needed." She walked over to the window, pulled the curtain back, and looked out. From the fourth-floor window, Kailah could see the red convertible she'd rented from Avis. She had rode along the beach earlier that morning to get her thoughts together and work up the courage to drive to the hospital. She still wore her bathing suit underneath her strapless, pastel blue sundress. "I didn't know I had to wait for a personal invitation. I just wanted to make sure you were okay and see it for myself." She knew it. Mona hadn't told her mother a damn thing about their falling out. No wonder Bea called. She knew she shouldn't have come.

"Besides the fact that I got my ass kicked, I'm fine as you can see," Mona stated emphatically.

Kailah decided not to respond, because she actually felt Mona was handling her surprise visit better than expected. She really missed Mona. Many times she had dialed the number just to hear Mona's voice mail and hung up. So much was happening in her life, and she really wanted to share it with Mona...especially about Keith. Things were happening so fast.

Kailah walked over to the right side of Mona's bed. "Look, I didn't come here to argue with you. The truth is I miss our friendship. While we grew closer over the years, I've always thought of you as a sister. Our friendship shouldn't fall apart over some guy. It means more to me than that."

"I think you should have thought of that before you began to sleep with my boyfriend!" Mona exclaimed. She lowered her voice. "It's the deceitful lies and sneaking around behind my back that makes me feel so betrayed by you."

MIXED MESSAGES

"I'm sorry for hurting you, Mona." Kailah's hands shook nervously as she struggled to fight back tears. "I never meant to hurt or betray you. I regret the day I ever met that muthafucker named Derrick. He took advantage of me, financially and emotionally."

"If Derrick took advantage, then you deserved it. What comes around goes around. You really disgust me. Now, get the hell out of my room. I don't ever want to see you again." Mona turned off the television and flipped over on her side.

Kailah slumped over and hung her head low as she walked toward the exit door. She covered her face shamefully as she passed the lounge area where Bea sat heavily involved in her phone conversation.

......

"How's your salad, dear?"

"Delicious," Mona said as she swirled a piece of lettuce in the dressing of the Caesar salad.

"Is that all you're going to eat?" Bea looked across the table at her daughter and reached for Mona's bruised hand. "I mean, I hear the food here is the best in the city, and all you want to eat is lettuce. I think you're taking this dieting way too seriously. This is the first meal you've eaten in over a week."

"Mother, I'm eating all the time." Mona rolled her eyes. "You're just exaggerating." She hadn't had an appetite since leaving the hospital. She'd been an emotional wreck with all of the reporters camped outside of her townhouse and the endless calls requesting interviews and pranks. In the restaurant, people seated close by kept looking over at her table and whispering. She cast her eyes downward and excused herself from the table to go to the restroom.

Now she knew why such a state of hysteria existed in the restaurant. On the way to the ladies room, Mona noticed Robert sitting at a nearby table.

Shit! What the hell is he doing here? Great! Mona quickly passed his table, making a point to look in the opposite direction. Out of the corner of her eye, she watched Robert as he rose from his seat to follow her.

"Mona…Mona…please, stop."

Mona stood in her tracks and held her breath as she let Robert catch up to her. How handsome he looked in his navy blue sports coat worn over a white polo shirt and khakis. She couldn't believe how much she'd missed him.

"What do you want?" Her guard was up.

"I just want to talk to you," he said, gasping for air.

The last time I heard that, I was raped, beaten, and left for dead. "Look, we have nothing to say to each other. I haven't heard from you in weeks."

Robert took a step back and placed his hand behind his head. "What do you expect after all of these trumped-up, bullshit rape and assault charges against my father?"

Mona held her hand to her head. "Oh, I'm not even hearing this shit right now!" She closed her eyes and took a deep breath. "Believe what you want to believe, but stay the fuck away from me."

As Robert tried to step closer, Mona lunged backward.

He paused for a second.

"Don't do this, Mona. You're tearing my family apart, and only you can make it right. Our families go way back. You don't know what you're doing and—"

"If your family is going through turmoil, it's because of your father, *not* me. I'm not going to stand here and allow you to make me feel responsible for anything." Mona glanced over to Robert's table to see his date frown and fold her arms. "I suggest you get back to your date before she leaves you to finish your meal all alone."

Robert peered over his shoulder, and she signaled him back to the table. "Just think about what I said," he said before walking away.

Once he returned to the table, Robert appeared to be apologizing to the lady who was gorgeous enough to be a supermodel. Hell, she probably was. Jealousy crept in where love still resided in her heart. Mona couldn't begin to understand what she had done to deserve so much gut-wrenching pain. Just weeks before, Mona would have been the one sitting across from Robert. Life had certainly taken a drastic turn.

When she finally reached the ladies' room, she walked into the stall and sat down on the floor with her head facing the toilet. Ramming her thumb down her throat caused the vomit to come up instantly. She suddenly felt relieved as her pain was purged.

With the sound of women's voices approaching, Mona stood up slowly, flushed the commode, and exited the stall. Suddenly, she began to feel dizzy and couldn't hold herself up. As she grabbed the door for support, one of the ladies ran over to her.

"Miss, miss...are you all right?"

"Yes, I just need to sit down for a moment." Mona collapsed on the floor.

Chapter 11
Redemption Leads to Salvation

"I should be there shortly, Mama."

"Child, just be safe on them roads, because they are dangerous," said Anna Carter. She always worried about her children while they traveled. "I'ma be praying you arrive here safely."

Kailah veered her rental car into the left lane on I-75. "I know you will, Mama. See you soon." Her eyes were puffy. The way Mona treated her hurt very deeply. She had taken off time from work in a moment's notice to fly down to Miami to see Mona. For the life of her, Kailah couldn't understand why she insisted on being so damn mad. Derrick was married to some other woman, and things simply didn't work out in their relationship. Clearly, she had underestimated Mona's feelings for Derrick.

Kailah knew that Mona would be upset to learn that her best friend had a sexual relationship with her ex-boyfriend. However, after several months had passed, Kailah couldn't imagine Mona carrying a grudge for this long. Nobody's perfect. Mona's self-righteous and judgmental attitude allowed her to take things too far. It wasn't like Mona didn't have faults, but somehow, she managed to focus on everyone else's imperfections and not her own.

Moving on in life without Mona would be difficult, but there were no other alternatives. Kailah felt disappointed in her best friend for not being able to forgive and let go. One would think that best friends would never allow a man to come in between and ruin the relationship. If that's the way Mona wanted it, though, so be it. Kailah gave it her best shot and now dealing with the consequences of her actions was brutal. She had definitely learned her lesson. Never be a fool again. Kailah's sexual escapades had cost her a cherished friendship.

MIXED MESSAGES

Kailah's chest felt heavy like a ton of weights rested on her heart. How did this happen? How did she let another person get so close? No sense in pretending. A piece was missing and chances are no replacement would ever fill the empty void.

Kailah turned onto the long, bumpy, and dark dirt road, having no trouble navigating her way. All of her fondest childhood memories flashed right before her. She pulled in front of the house and parked under the huge oak tree in front of the yard. Kailah blew the horn, popped the trunk, and jumped out of the car to gather her luggage.

The outside light flicked on and the wooden screen door creaked opened. "Is that you, Kailah?" Mama Anna asked as she walked down the concrete block steps.

Kailah stuck her head out from behind the trunk of the car. "Yeah, Mama, it's me." She walked toward her mother with both hands filled with luggage. Mama Anna put her arms around Kailah's neck. Kailah tried her best to embrace her mother and hold back the tears, which she could no longer do.

"I knew something was wrong with you, child," Anna said, rubbing Kailah's head. "Mothers always know when things ain't right with they children."

Once they were inside the house, Kailah tiptoed down the hallway to the kitchen. The old wooden house hadn't changed one bit since she was a child. Mama Anna stood at the stove fixing Kailah a plate of food.

"Smells like collards."

"Fresh from the backyard garden." Anna placed the plate on the large wooden table that barely fit in the small kitchen. Kailah poured a glass of freshly squeezed lemonade, and then sat down. She rubbed her belly as she eyed the plate full of macaroni and cheese, collard greens, smothered pork chops, and cornbread.

Kailah raised her eyebrows. "You expecting company?"

Mama Anna laughed and tossed her hand in the air. "This is leftovers from Sunday. Your brothers came over with their wives and children. Then Don took a plate over to the nursing home for Henry."

Kailah rubbed both hands together as her eyes feasted on the meal. "Mama, you know you can throw down. Thanks."

"Make sure you say your grace now," Mama Anna added. "Food is no good if you can't thank the Good Lord for it."

Kailah nodded. "Yes, Mama."

While eating her dinner, Kailah filled her mother in on all the latest events. She talked about the end of the friendship with Mona, but didn't tell how she'd slept with Derrick, only admitted to dating him without telling Mona about it. Those parts were worth crying about. She laughed as she told her mother about her steady relationship with Keith.

By this time, the two of them were seated in the living room like old friends. Before Kailah knew it, she was driven to tears again as she spoke of the hospital visit to see Mona in Miami. "I know I did wrong, Mama. I just don't know why she won't forgive me."

"Sometimes, it takes time," Anna said. "You just can't expect a girl to forgive you just like that. And you been with her man. You was wrong, Kailah." She sat forward in her father's old accent chair with rich tapestry upholstery and rested her hand on her hip.

Kailah pulled up her blanket to cover her shoulders. "Mama, I told her it was a mistake. I was practically begging her to forgive me."

"Just give this thing some time." Anna stood up to leave the room, then paused and looked back at Kailah. "What you need to do is pray to the Good Lord. Ask for His forgiveness. He will make a way."

With that said, she disappeared down the dark hallway.

MIXED MESSAGES

After her steamy shower, Kailah slipped into her pajamas, climbed in bed, and grabbed the book she had placed on the nightstand earlier.

Kailah couldn't concentrate on reading, so she lay in bed staring up at the ceiling, allowing her thoughts to drift off.

Kailah's blurred vision kept her from seeing anything in front of her. Her speech slurred every time she tried to speak.

"Come on, Kailah. We're almost there. You can do it."

"I can't…I can't see…I need to go home and just—"

"I'm going to take you home. I just need to go get my keys."

"Okay, Jake."

Jake, a white guy in Kailah's finance study group, had invited Kailah and Mona to his frat party. Mona decided right away that it wasn't her type of party and left. Kailah felt obligated to stay for at least an hour, and Jake offered to give her a ride home.

Kailah had one drink and felt as though her head was going to drop at any moment. Jake helped her down to his room to get his car keys to take her home. He fumbled for a moment and then opened the door.

"Come on in, Kailah. I'm not going to bite you," he joked.

Kailah followed the now shadowy figure into the open doorway. As she entered, another voice spoke in the room.

"Who was that?"

"My roommate. Now just sit down for a minute while I look for my keys. I know I put 'em somewhere on my bed." Jake reached over and kissed her, and Kailah kissed him back.

"Aaahh, I knew you liked me." Jake kissed her again. "You want to do something?"

"Do what?"

"I've never fucked a black girl before. Let's do it." He started kissing and groping Kailah all over. She tongued him hard while he pulled up her denim skirt and slid her silk panties down her legs.

Minutes later, Jake was inside her. It felt so good that Kailah began to move her hips back and forth.

"That's it, baby. Shake that big ass for me." Jake was breathing harder and harder. His strokes got faster and faster until he collapsed on top of her. Then he got up.

The other voice in the room then spoke. "Now you have to give me some of that sweet black pussy." Seconds later, Kailah felt him enter her, too. He was rougher than Jake, pouncing hard on top of her over and over again. Kailah screamed in agony. It hurt like hell. The guy pulled Kailah's long legs up in the air and tightly cupped his hands on her butt.

Kailah could hear Jake in the background cheering as his friend pulled his penis out just in time to squirt all over her body and face. They were laughing, and then silence followed. Not having the strength to get up, she fell asleep.

She was awakened a few hours later by the sorority girls who stayed in the dorm room where she was sleeping. They helped her shower, get dressed, and called Mona to pick her up. Kailah had never been more embarrassed and ashamed of her actions. She swore to never drink again.

***

Kailah sat up in bed. She hadn't thought back to that incident since it happened four years ago. Kailah placed the book back on the stand and rolled out of bed. Kneeling down on the floor, she closed her eyes to say a prayer. She began to cry and ask God to truly forgive her for all her wrong doings: For the way she treated her best friend and dealt with Lynn at work, for sleeping with Derrick and all the other men when she knew it wasn't right, for the foul language she spoke, for gossiping and talking about people behind their backs. It all came out. She couldn't take it anymore. The pain was too much.

Kailah cast her eyes upward, knowing God forgave her that instant. She immediately got up and ran down to her mother's room. When she turned on the light, Kailah saw her mother sitting in the rocking chair praying. She sat down next to her mother as she did as a child, and they prayed together. That night, Kailah repented for all her sins and took the Lord Savior into her life.

Just before Kailah went to sleep, she made one final attempt to reach Keith.

Kailah waited for him to answer the phone.

"You have reached the voice mail of Keith Terrence. I am unable-"

Kailah hung up in disbelief. Where could he be at four o'clock in the morning? Crazy thoughts ran through her head, but she quickly dismissed them. There was no sense worrying about it now. She'd find out soon enough.

Her flight would be leaving in just a few short hours, and she still needed to return the rental car. She said another quick prayer, turned off the light, and dozed off to sleep moments later.

......

A knock rapped on the door.

"You may enter," Lynn said cheerfully.

"Hello. Did you miss me while I was away?" Kailah asked with a grin.

"You weren't gone long enough," Lynn responded, not bothering to look up. "Where are the figures for the Phillips account? You told me you would get them to me by Thursday."

Excuse me? Today is only Tuesday, and she's tripping over the Phillips account. Kailah could tell her a thing or two, but she took in a deep breath and decided to take another approach. "I know I told you I would get the figures for you, but guess what?"

"I'm waiting."

"I worked on them while I was in Florida." She placed the file on Lynn's desk. "I also took the liberty of having them couriered over to Randolph Phillips this morning." Kailah grinned at Lynn. This went along with her new attitude. She was going to put a little more time and energy back into her career.

Lynn stood up waving both hands in a frenzy. "I can't believe you sent those final calculations without my final approval! That's it! I've had it! I'm going to the top executive about this one, and your ass will be written up by the end of the day!"

Kailah couldn't believe it. Since when did Lynn need to look over paperwork? This floozy didn't even have a clear understanding of all the figures, adjustments, and contracts.

Kailah took a seat. "Lynn, it seems I have clearly stepped over my bounds by sending over the figures without your final approval. However, I was just trying to make things easier for you. I apologize. I was wrong." Kailah looked for the stunned expression to appear on Lynn's face. Seconds later, Lynn's mouth was locked still.

Kailah continued. "I promise it won't happen again. If you feel you must write me up for that, then do what you have to do."

Lynn leaned back in her chair, taking her small black-framed glasses off her desk and placing them on her face. "I will… will accept your apology. Make sure it doesn't happen again."

Kailah rose and straightened the wrinkles out of her skirt. She walked out of Lynn's office and shut the door. While resting her head on the back of the door, she began to laugh to herself. *When all else fails, kill 'em with kindness.*

......

"Baby, you should've seen the look on her face when I apologized." Kailah leaned up from the bed to show Keith. They both laughed. "I wish I had a camera to snap a picture of those big red lips drooping."

Keith grabbed Kailah's face and landed a kiss on her cheek. "I must admit I'm very proud of you. Joining my church was a major step, but you've taken things a step further with this kindness thing."

It certainly felt good to be back in Chicago where life was normal. Keith had greeted her with an armful of roses and balloons at the airport. She wanted to snap at his ass for not returning any of her phone calls, but quickly changed her mind when seeing his handsome face.

Realizing how much she missed her man outweighed feelings of anger. After everything she'd gone through with Mona, Kailah needed the pampering Keith would be more than willing to afford her. Anxiety and pure excitement shot through her body. Her first night back was every bit of extreme pleasure, making it difficult to return to work early the next morning and deal with Lynn.

Kailah kissed Keith back passionately. "I love you, baby. Thanks." She placed her hand inside of Keith's silk boxers and rubbed his hardness. Keith climbed on top of her and slowly spread her legs apart, massaging them as she moaned deeply.

Keith gave Kailah soft kisses on her neck. Then he whispered in her ear softly, "There's something I want to ask you."

"Uh huh, what is it?" *This is no time to carry on a conversation,* Kailah thought to herself. Kailah felt the need to express her love in a more meaningful way.

"Will you marry me?"

Kailah opened her eyes to see a three-karat diamond ring on Keith's pinky finger. The marquis swirl ring had lots of baguettes and clusters surrounding the diamond.

"Oh my God! Yes! Of course, I will marry you." She grabbed his face and kissed him passionately.

The lovemaking was going to be even more special that night.

Chapter 12
Forgive and Let Go

"Excuse me, Lois. There is a Ms. Hightower here to see you. She says it's urgent."

"Yes, I've been expecting her. Send Ms. Hightower in." Lois stood and walked over to greet her visitor. She had just gotten back in her office after working out on the third floor, and was still wearing her sweats.

They shook hands and Lois walked around to sit back in her leather executive chair. She patted the white towel around her neck and her face gently. "Good afternoon, Ms. Hightower. Please take a seat."

"I must tell you Mrs.—"

"Just call me Lois."

She appeared to be quite nervous as she kicked her leg. "Okay, Lois. You can just call me Natalia. I must admit that I felt I would successfully gather all the incriminating evidence against Ms. Richards you needed for your case."

"I don't understand," Lois said, frowning. "I hired you to conduct a full investigation on Ms. Richards, and I was told you were the best. So, what is it you're trying to tell me?"

Natalia cleared her throat. "Let me get straight to the point. I was unable to locate any incriminating information from Ms. Richards' past. I decided that I would follow her around and make some personal notes on my own. Perhaps, I would learn something to help you. That's when I…uhh … I…"

Lois leaned forward. "Now is not the time to stutter!" She regained her composure. "That's when you *what*?"

"That's when I saw your husband, Mr. Thomas, passing by Ms. Richards' residence one night."

Lois tried to hold back her laughter. "Run that by me again. You saw *my* husband? You must be mistaken, Natalia."

"I'm not mistaken. Your husband was driving his black Mercedes, and I decided to follow him. He then drove to a condominium on South Beach. I presume the condo is owned by the two of you."

"You're the damn investigator. Don't you know?" Lois wasn't sure if she wanted to hear the rest. Just when she thought she would be putting an end to Mona.

Natalia continued. "Thirty minutes later, a young lady pulled up in a tan convertible. I just confirmed by walking on the first floor in this building that this woman is the front receptionist here."

No. Not Myra. It couldn't be.

"Well, Myra Smith went to the same condo numbered 4304B at 7:30. I finally saw her speed off in her car at 11 o'clock that night."

Lois sat quietly in her chair. No words could express the way she felt. Her body felt cold and numb all over.

"Now what I need to know is if you are in further need of my services. I'm confident that if I dig a little deeper, I'll be able to get some dirt."

"No thank you, Ms. Hightower." She stood. "Your services will no longer be needed. I'll make sure you are well compensated. Good day." Lois held the door open while the private investigator made a quick exit.

That night, Lois Clarke threw a vase across the room at Darren Thomas. He ducked, the vase hit the wall, and he took off running down the hall.

Lois yelled down the staircase, "I could just kill you. You no-good, two-timing bastard." She fell to the floor and let out an agonizing cry. Darren's car roared loudly away from their home.

How could he do this to her after all these years? Thirty years she'd spent with this man, and he'd been lying to her. She could actually wrap her hands around his neck and strangle him.

MIXED MESSAGES

......

Kailah handed the bridal magazine over to Taneisha. "Here it is. Look, look, look. Isn't it beautiful?" Kailah asked with both her hands up to her mouth. She was so excited to be sharing this news with Taneisha, she could hardly contain herself. The princess gown with a hand-beaded bodice and beaded train appeared absolutely stunning.

"Girl, this is some dress," Taneisha responded, bending over Kailah's desk to stare at the magazine. "How much are you spending for this?"

"Enough."

Kailah never felt comfortable discussing high-priced ticket items with Taneisha. She always felt guilty, because of the salary differences of an executive and executive assistant. And Kailah already knew that Taneisha felt like she just had money to waste, because she always spoke so harshly about the other executives at the firm. Kailah appreciated their friendship and never wanted this one issue to come between them. Discussion of money matters and pay was a surefire way to strain a relationship with even the best of friends. Mama Anna had told her this as a child.

She changed the subject. "Keith and I sat down last night and picked a date for the wedding in June."

"That gives you one year to get all your plans together." Taneisha smiled so big, her brown eyes looked Chinese. "I'm so happy for you." She extended her long arms out to give Kailah a big hug and kiss.

Kailah hugged her back, but she was desperately wishing to be sharing this moment with her best friend Mona. Kailah decided earlier that week to try her hardest to renew the friendship. And now she had exactly one year to do it.

......

"I think we're making some great progress here, Ms. Richards." Dr. Knight swiveled from left to right in her chair. "It's even better that we're getting to the source of your pain. We'll explore that even further on your visit next week."

"I'm feeling much better…healthier… ready to conquer the world." Mona got up from the orange lounge chair.

Dr. Knight gave her a big hug. "Take care, dear." Dr. Knight was a tall, slender black woman. Her shoulder-length brown hair curled over in a flip style. Mona admired how youthful and vibrant she looked, while in her mid-forties.

Mona walked out of Dr. Knight's office over to the receptionist's desk to pay for the visit. "Rona, every time I come here, you're sporting a new hairstyle."

"Well, you know, girl, I have to keep up with the latest." Rona began to play with her blonde braids. "See you next Tuesday. Don't forget, I'm still going to set you up with my cousin in Tampa as soon as he comes to town."

"Bye, Rona." Mona started to giggle. "I'll be waiting on my Prince Charming at home while I'm watching reruns on another Friday night."

Mona exited the small office building, dressed very plain with her blue denim baseball cap to match her denim overalls. Anyone from her past would not even recognize her. But still, it didn't matter to her anymore. She felt like an improved person who was beginning to love who she was becoming. Not the insecure girl who always tried so desperately to gain the attention and approval from her mother and others she knew.

Since Mona's second return from the hospital, she lived her life as a recluse. The Darren Thomas scandal was being broadcast over all of the local television networks and papers. The media became dauntingly fixated on the upcoming trial. Darren Thomas followed the advice of his attorneys to accept the plea bargain after reports began to surface about his philandering with other interns and associates at Thomas & Clarke. He wouldn't serve one day in jail, but be placed on probation for a year and 300 hours of community service would be tacked on to the sentence.

Mona followed through with a lawsuit against Thomas & Clarke, while accepting a settlement of close to a quarter of a million after her attorneys took their share.

Lois filed for a divorce, vowing to take Darren to the cleaners. Initially, she wanted to split all their assets and holdings right down the middle. However, once she learned that her husband showed up at a social gala with his new, young blonde bimbo on his arm, Lois had a change of heart. The entire Thomas family was embarrassed when confronted with the truth and now refused to speak to the media. Mona found that surprisingly ironic, considering the fact that they were once using the media to destroy her.

At home, she had two new voice messages.

"First message sent today at eleven o'clock a.m.:

Hello, dear. It's me, Mother. I wanted to let you know my plane arrived safely. I'm on my way over to Lois'. God, she is having such a difficult time with this divorce, so I'll probably end up staying the night over there. That's what best friends are for, right? I'll be over to see you first thing in the morning. Ta-ta, love."

Mona pressed delete.

"Second message sent today at one forty-seven p.m.: This is my fourth time calling this week. It's urgent tyou call me back. Some latest events have come up. Well, I guess that's all I have to say. Bye."

It was Kailah. Mona deleted the message.

......

Bea pulled into the paved circular driveway in front of Lois' four thousand square-foot gated home and was greeted at the door by the plump housekeeper.

"Good afternoon, Mrs. Richards."

"Hello, Maria."

"Mrs. Thomas has been expecting you. She is upstairs in her bedroom. Can I get you anything?"

"Brandy will do me just fine. Thanks, Maria." Bea walked up the marble stairs to Lois' bedroom. The door was barely cracked open, and a foul smell drifted beneath her nose. She turned up her pointy nose and stuck her head inside.

"Lois."

No answer.

The long drapes to the window were drawn, but the wind blew them wildly in the air. It was very dark. A light came from underneath the door in the bathroom. The door was unlocked, so she entered. Lois sat in the tub with a cigarette in her hand. She turned around and scowled.

"Is that how you greet your best friend these days?"

"I didn't know I had anymore friends left. Everyone is treating me like an outcast," Lois muttered. "It seems like everywhere I turn, I keep finding out Darren has just about fucked them all anyway. Damn whores."

"Never mind them. I'm here. Always have and always will. And I never fucked your husband."

Lois laughed. "You never liked light-skinned men anyway. Neither did I until I met Darren's tired ass and fell in love with him."

Bea held up her hand. "I remember. I was there, too."

"Right."

"You two were quite the couple. I was so envious, until I met Charles. We never had what you two had, though."

MIXED MESSAGES

Lois pointed her cigarette. "Be glad. Charles is a good man. Darren is a snake. He slimed his way in my life, and now that bastard has found a way to slime out."

Lois sat up in the tub and clumsily tried to get out. Bea reached over to help her, grabbing the cigarette and throwing it in the bath water.

"Leave these cancer sticks alone. They'll kill you."

Lois snarled. "Huh. You should talk. So will pills and alcohol. But, I don't see you giving those up."

"Shut up before I drop you like a bad habit." Bea held onto the towel, noticing her friend had lost several pounds. "Now, let me do something with your hair. It looks like it hasn't been brushed in ages."

......

Kailah strolled in from her lunch break, tossed her briefcase on her desk, and flopped in her chair. Less than a minute later, Taneisha stuck her head in.

"Anything happen while I was out?" Kailah asked.

Taneisha came in and handed Kailah a stack of yellow message slips. "Your mother called. She said it wasn't urgent."

Kailah placed the slips on her desk and picked up the phone. "I better call her first."

"Okay, but she said it wasn't important," Taneisha restated before leaving.

"Hey, Mama, is everything all right?"

"Yes, child. You sound so distressed." Anna Carter took a deep breath. "Everything is fine. Stop your worrying. Just like when you were a little itty-bitty girl. Always worrying about grown folks' business when there was nothing you could do about it." She started to laugh.

Feeling a little ridiculous, Kailah laughed right along with her. "You never call me at work. So, I was a little concerned. That's all."

"I just wanted to let you know I got a call from Mona today."

"Oh, yeah." Kailah fidgeted in her chair.

"Well, we got to talking for a long while. Then we got on the subject about you."

Kailah leaned back further in her chair. "So what was said? Does she want to talk to me? She hates me, doesn't she? I knew it."

"See, there you go again. Jumping to conclusions! If you supposed to be a Christian, you need to show a little more faith in the Lord. I did not teach my child to give up so easily, even in the worst situations."

"I know, Mama, but—"

"But nothing. If you know, then act like it and stop all that crying."

How did Mama know she was crying? Kailah grabbed a Kleenex out of the box on her glass-topped desk and began patting her face dry. "Okay, Mama, go ahead."

"Mona agreed to talk to you. She said you can call her tonight."

Kailah jumped out of her seat and started to jog in place. *Yeessssss! Thank you, God! To God be the glory!* She sat back down and regained her composure. "No problem, I'll call her tonight, Mama."

"I reckoned you would. Good afternoon."

"Good-bye, Mama. Oh, and uh, Mama?"

"Yes, child."

"Thank you so much for talking to Mona. I don't know what you said, but I know it was you."

"It was God. And don't you forget it."

MIXED MESSAGES

......

Kailah took the short red cotton FUBU dress off the rack and held it up in front of her. "How does this look?"

"Good, girl. You know how I love me some FUBU."

"It does look cute on me. I'm gonna go try it on." Kailah handed Taneisha her bags. Taneisha browsed at the rack with discounted silk blouses.

Minutes later, Kailah came out in the dress. It fit her perfectly.

"Yeah." Taneisha nodded. "You gotta get that."

"Just perfect for the Miami sun." Kailah twirled around and danced a jig in the full-length mirror.

"Sure is. I don't know why you ever moved from Florida in the first place."

"I've lived there my entire life. It was time for a change."

"I guess you're right." Taneisha held up a bright orange bikini. "This would go good with your complexion."

Kailah looked at her smooth dark mocha-colored arm as she reached out for the hanger with the bikini. It *would* look nice on her. Then she remembered the last time she was at the beach with Mona. They had so much fun that weekend before their graduation. How she missed those times.

Kailah sighed. Mona had been through a lot this year, and she had only added to her misery. Determined to regain all the time lost, it was her personal commitment to make life easier for Mona. This was a second chance. She wouldn't mess up this time.

The first phone conversation was very awkward. Mona didn't have too much to say. After a few more talks, Mona finally began to come around. Kailah was thrilled to have the opportunity to talk to her. She hadn't realized how much she truly missed having a friend as close as a sister. Of course, Taneisha helped to fill that void. But there was a history between her and Mona…something that she would never have with Taneisha.

Even though Kailah and Mona were very close in the past, Kailah realized their friendship would probably never reach that level again. Over time, Kailah learned when you love a man, as much as she loved Keith, the thought of another woman sleeping with him disgusted her. Let alone her best friend. At first, she couldn't understand why Mona became so irrational when learning about her sexual relationship with Derrick. Kailah was ignorant of being in love and committed to a man.

However, being in a relationship with Keith completely transformed Kailah in so many ways. For once in her life, she actually knew how it felt to think of someone other than herself. Kailah always thought Mona to be rich, spoiled, and self-centered, but that simply wasn't true.

The spoiled one was Kailah, having grown up in a home with four brothers and parents that doted on her. Kailah learned quickly how to be manipulative and conniving in order to have her way. Through her Christian walk, she learned more about herself by reflecting on her past and connecting it to the present. Even though she still had a lot of growing up to do, Kailah felt grateful that she no longer was the same person as before. She hoped that she could somehow convince Mona of this.

Taneisha and Kailah purchased sandwiches and freshly squeezed lemonade in the mall. Kailah went to the restroom while Taneisha found a table in the busy food court. When she came back out, she caught a glimpse of Taneisha waving through a large crowd of people.

"This was close," Kailah said as she sat down in the chair. Her tight pair of stonewashed jeans fell just below her waist. The tight-fitted cotton tee was fit enough to expose her navel.

"I just about had to curse out them guys over there. Shit, you know I had to let them know they wouldn't be sitting here."

Kailah laughed. "You were going to curse them out, huh? Girl, you know you're crazy."

Taneisha snapped her fingers. "Better not forget it. I come from a family full of crazy muthafuckers."

Kailah chuckled. She wished Taneisha didn't curse so much. She was such a beautiful woman, but when she opened her mouth. Ooohh! The beauty would somehow vanish.

"Yeah, I know, especially your Aunt BeBe. She's psycho."

"Now, if you think BeBe is crazy, you should meet my Uncle Seahorse. He'll cut ya just for looking at him funny." Taneisha laughed and took another bite of her sandwich, leaving a dark red lipstick stain on the wheat bread.

"No, I don't need to meet anymore of your kin folks. I'll take your word for it."

"Okay." Her penciled eyebrows rose and fell twice as she used her napkin. "'Cause you know we having another cookout next weekend."

"Well, I guess I'll miss it, because I'll be on my trip."

"Oh, yeah." Taneisha stroked her fingers through her long platinum blonde ponytail. "I can't believe you're going without Keith...with his fine ass. Don't leave him for too long. You might find another woman dipping in that deep dark chocolate. You better be glad I'm married."

Kailah cocked her head to the side. "Don't play. Or I might have to cut ya'."

"All right, all right, I'm messing with you. You know how Keith gets on my nerves. He's too prim and proper for me. You know I only put up with him because he's your man."

Kailah took a sip of lemonade. "Keith ain't going anywhere. I'm not even worried."

"Well, at least it's just for a week."

"Yeah."

Chapter 13
I Do?

Mona opened the door to her home.

Kailah stood silent, not believing how much Mona had changed. Her hair was very long, past her shoulders. She almost looked Hispanic.

"Are you coming in, or are you just going to stand there and stare?" Mona placed both hands on her hips. She was dressed very casually in a pink knit top and dark denim jeans.

Kailah frowned. She thought she would be able to fight back the tears. It was just so hard to believe. After all her prayers, her life was really coming together. .

Mona grabbed two pieces of Kailah's luggage and pushed her into the townhouse. "There you go...one step, and then another. See, you're getting the hang of it. Two more steps. You're in!" Mona shut the door quickly.

Kailah turned around and hugged Mona, sobbing like a baby.

After an hour of making small talk and catching up on each other's lives, Mona helped Kailah unpack in the guest bedroom.

"Do you remember Katrina Hutchinson?" Mona held up her picture and started laughing. They were sitting down on the floor in Mona's bedroom listening to an old Smokey Robinson CD.

"Oh, yeah." Kailah stood up. She stuck her chest and butt way out. She began to strut across the floor. "All these girls at UF just hate me, see, 'cause I'm fine," she said in a high-pitched, stuck-up voice. She stopped and held one hand out for a high-five. "That girl wasn't a bit more fine than she was pretty, with that puppy face. Every time I saw her, I thought about that puppy chow commercial."

Mona laughed even harder and slapped Kailah's hand. "I know it. We used to trip over that girl. I wonder what she's up to."

"Probably swearing up and down the women on her job are jealous of her, 'cause she's just so fine."

Mona bent over and grabbed her stomach, fighting to stop the laughter, while Kailah stared at herself in her red silk pajamas in the mirror on the door.

"Today has been the best. I'm really glad you came," Mona said. "I missed you terribly."

Kailah turned and knelt down beside her. "I prayed hard for this. I'm glad you were able to find it in your heart to forgive me and accept me back into your life. I know it must have been hard for you."

"Well, if I can forgive my mother, then I can forgive you."

"Throughout this whole ordeal, I also learned that once I repented for my sins, God forgave me. The hardest part was forgiving myself. Once I did that, I was free from all the pain and guilt." Kailah closed her eyes as she held Mona's hands.

"I know exactly what you're saying. Through my therapy sessions, I'm learning how to forgive others and release all the anger. It drove me to almost killing myself before I realized that I wanted to live. I still have so much living to do." Mona let go and readjusted the pillow she was resting her back on.

"I guess we both had some growing up to do," Kailah said, giggling. "And just think of how we thought we were so mature after we graduated from college. Our life was only just beginning. The Bible says that when we are first saved, we are then babes in Christ. I've learned so much these past few months. The Lord is so good. Mona, I hope that one day you will be able to accept Lord Jesus into your life."

"Perhaps one day." Mona shrugged. "So are you ready for the big day? Your wedding is only three weeks away now."

MIXED MESSAGES

"The closer we get to the actual date, the more nervous I get." Kailah placed both hands on her face. "Keith is such a good man. Sometimes I feel like I'm not deserving."

"You two deserve one another," Mona replied with a slight smile. "He certainly seems like a nice gentleman. I can't wait to finally meet Mr. Keith Terrence in person."

Kailah looked stunned. "So you are coming then?" She laid her head on the pillow on the floor.

"Yes, silly girl," Mona said as she grabbed her pillow and lay beside Kailah on the floor. "I wouldn't miss it for the world."

......

"Keith certainly has good taste in his automobiles," Mona said as her eyes swept around inside the Lincoln Navigator. The vehicle had a beige interior with leather seats and every luxury item top-of-the-line vehicles came with. "How does this navigation system work anyway?"

"Well, you simply type in the address of your destination, and the directions will appear on the screen." Driving very slowly, Kailah turned into the dark parking garage housed underneath Keith's apartment building. "I wonder what Mama's up to. She was just trying to squeeze all six sweet potato pies, two cakes, and banana bread in the oven before I left."

Mona grinned. "Sounds good. What else is on the menu for the rehearsal dinner?"

"Well, let's see." Kailah quickly spotted a parking space and zipped in. She opened the door and walked around to the back. "Mama has planned her own soul-food fest. Let's just say this. My side of the family is going to get their grub on, and Keith's parents are going to be shocked a pig has that many parts that are edible." The thought frightened her because she really did want to have the dinner catered. Though, to suggest such a thing to Mama would have crushed her. It was like old times, however, watching her mother prepare a big dinner in the kitchen at Keith's apartment.

Mona limped in her tight navy blue pumps after Kailah.

"I can't wait to sit down. What floor is Keith's apartment on?"

"The sixth floor."

When the two of them stepped out of the elevator, she noticed Mr. and Mrs. Terrence patiently waiting for someone to answer the door.

Kailah tried her best to straighten her dress before she approached the older couple. "Hello, Blake and Juanita. How are you doing?"

"Just fine, Kailah." Mr. Terrence walked over to give Kailah a hug. Juanita stood in the same place and gave a quick smile in her direction.

"I would like to introduce my best friend Mona. She just flew in from Miami."

"Nice to meet you, Mr. and Mrs. Terrence."

Kailah fumbled with the keys for a few seconds. Once she had finally pushed open the door, they were immediately greeted by the aroma of fried chicken coming from the kitchen.

"Did you invite the caterers over, Kailah?" Juanita asked.

"Actually, my mother is cooking tonight. Everything will be catered tomorrow." Kailah tried to keep up with Juanita, who headed straight to the kitchen. Kailah's four brothers were picking up large dishes covered with aluminum foil from the table. Mama Anna was nowhere in sight. "Where's Mama?"

"Karen took Mama over to the park about twenty minutes ago," Donovan, Kailah's oldest brother, said. He and Karen had been married for eight years now and had four children; one child was Karen's from a previous marriage. "We're just trying to get the last of these dishes, and then we're on our way over there, too."

MIXED MESSAGES

"Okay, well, I'm going to get dressed, and I'll be there in less than an hour." Just when they began to leave the kitchen, Kailah suddenly stepped in their path. "Where are my manners?! Guys, I want you to meet Keith's mother, Juanita. Juanita, these are my brothers, Donovan, David, Donald, and Roy."

All of them said a quick "how do you do" and left. Kailah spotted an open bottle of wine on the counter and poured herself a glass. She could hear her brothers speaking to Mr. Terrence and Mona while they went to exit through the front door.

"Well, you certainly come from a large family." Juanita walked over to the refrigerator, eyeing the glass in Kailah's hand. She helped herself and poured a glass, too. "I see that you have everything taken care of. Blake and I simply wanted to stop by and see our son before we drove over to the rehearsal dinner. Where is he?"

"I haven't seen Keith since—"

"I thought I heard that lovely voice in my kitchen." Keith brushed right past Kailah over to Juanita and gave her a big hug, then kissed her on the cheek. "Mom, you look fabulous."

Juanita grinned from plump cheek to cheek. "Well, thank you, son."

It looks like she's dressed as if she's going to a funeral to me. Who the hell wears black to a rehearsal dinner? Lord, forgive me. Kailah cleared her throat.

Keith looked over. "Oh, hey baby. When are you getting dressed?"

Kailah smiled coyly. "I'm going right now." Kailah poured the remaining contents of the wine bottle into her glass and exited the kitchen, storming up the stairs and then down the hallway to Keith's bedroom. Her pastel pink dress was already laid out on the bed, along with her slip and stockings. Her dyed-to-match pink satin strap shoes still lay in the box on the floor by the bed.

Mama Anna must have come in and prepared her attire for her. A small card was perched on the bed. She slowly opened it.

My Dearest Kailah:
Tomorrow is a special day that the Lord has made. I pray that this marriage is everything you dreamed it would be, and that God puts a special anointing on this marriage.
Mama

Kailah put the card down and broke out into an ugly cry. *Oh Mama, why couldn't you be here right now? I can't do this. I don't know what to do.*

Mona burst into the room without knocking. "What's up with your soon-to-be mother-in-law?" she asked just above a whisper.

"I know, I know." Kailah shook her head from side to side. "She hates me."

Mona rubbed her back.

"Shhhh, you don't want everyone to hear you." Mona handed a box of Kleenex to her. Kailah snatched out a tissue and blew her nose loudly.

"I can't do this!" Kailah felt like her stomach was going to explode. Lightheaded, she cried like a baby.

Just then, a light knock came at the door. "Everything all right?" Keith asked.

When no one answered, Keith knocked on the door again. "I said, is everything all right in there? Kailah, it's getting late. We're all waiting out here for you."

"Kailah, go ahead and take your shower," Mona said. "I'll talk to Keith."

Feeling so drained by the anxiety, Kailah stood and wiped her face. Thinking she was ready for all of this, now she wasn't so sure. As she stared in the mirror at the familiar creature with black streaks of mascara running down her cheeks, she

MIXED MESSAGES

overheard Mona talking to Keith. She figured taking two Aleve would help with the excessive pounding of the strong migraine.

Tomorrow, she would be a married woman and that meant her life would only get better. No woman wanted to have a mother-in-law that hated her. She sought comfort in knowing that even the worst situations could change for the better. God's hands are over everything. All things work for the good. Now, all she had to do was look beautiful and enjoy the moment.

Chapter 14
Newlyweds

"Are you comfortable?" Keith asked, rubbing Kailah's foot that lay across his lap. His newly decorated place looked almost like a new apartment once Kailah added her special touch of interior design. African art, statues, and masks hung on every wall, table, and counter.

"Baby, that feels nice." Kailah opened her eyes and looked over at Keith. "Why are you so good to me?"

"Because," Keith placed Kailah's foot down and slid in between her legs, resting his left arm on her shoulder, "you're my queen, and you should be treated like royalty." He kissed her behind her left ear as Kailah let out a deep sigh.

Keith glanced at his watch and his eyes grew wide. "I know just the perfect item for tonight, but I'm going to have to make a quick run to the store. Why don't you slip into something more comfortable while I'm gone?"

Kailah's eyes lit up at the mere thought of what Keith needed to make the night better. He had piqued her curiosity. "Okay, baby. Don't take too long now." Kailah jumped up from the couch and quickly ran up the stairs toward the bedroom. A few seconds later, she heard the door shut.

Taking a hot, steamy shower alone was not her idea of a romantic night. Surprised Keith hadn't made it home yet, she watched a rerun of "Any Day Now" on Lifetime as she finished her cup of hot tea. When the show ended, she checked the clock once more. Kailah dialed Keith's cell phone for the fifth time, and again no answer.

As she turned over on her side in bed, she exhaled slowly. She didn't like this, not one bit. It wasn't the first time her husband had disappeared for hours. A question of whether or not she could trust her husband entered her mind.

MIXED MESSAGES

"Sorry for taking so long." Keith leaned over Kailah in the bed.

"What time is it?" Kailah asked, trying to reach over to look at the clock on the nightstand. Her vision was slightly blurred, so she couldn't really see anything clearly.

Keith intercepted her arm and began kissing on her back. Kailah still wore the little purple teddy with matching panties that she had put on earlier that evening. Turning her over on her back, he undid the ribbon to expose her breasts and licked both of them very seductively. Kailah placed her arms on his head as Keith worked his way down to her navel.

Keith poured strawberry-flavored oil on Kailah's stomach and commenced to teasing her skin with long strokes of his tongue.

"Oohh, baby, you taste so good."

Still sleepy, she moaned softly. Once she was fully awake, Kailah began gyrating her hips up and down as Keith gave her more oral pleasure. Her grabbing him by the head made Keith go wild.

After making sure Kailah was fully aroused, Keith turned her over onto her side and entered her from the rear. He grabbed her hips as he thrust harder than he ever had before. Kailah moved her head from side to side while Keith jerked. Moments later, they both reached their climax.

......

"Just when I thought it couldn't get any better." Kailah shared the details that took place last night on the phone with Mona.

Kailah worried if she spent too much time talking about her marriage. Immediately when she woke up that morning, she thought to call Mona to tell her about it, like when they were in college. And why not? Kailah used to listen to Mona go on and on about Derrick and their perfect little courtship.

It felt good for Kailah to have a wonderful man to talk about, but at the same time, she didn't want to appear to be gloating. Tables had turned, and Mona was now the one without a man. Not absolutely sure if Mona was truly happy for her, it made her feel slightly uneasy.

But then again, Kailah had to remember that Mona's personality differed from hers. Mona's honesty about her feelings would show, and she didn't have a problem expressing them. Kailah had to deal with her own insecurity in realizing now that she was happily married, past friendships had somehow vanished. Women at work and at the gym didn't necessarily feel as enthusiastic as she did. Kailah wanted to make sure that didn't happen with Mona, because she truly loved her and wanted the friendship to grow.

"Makes me want to run out and get married. Keith sounds like Mr. Perfect," Mona commented.

"He is. The list goes on and on." Kailah stood in the kitchen cooking breakfast. "Dang, I just burnt my finger!" She screamed, sticking her finger in her mouth.

Mona laughed. "Dang? Is that the best you can do?"

"I've been trying so hard to cut back on my profanity. Now, you know I've always cursed like a sailor." Kailah scraped the remaining scrambled eggs onto Keith's plate. Moments later, Keith strutted in the kitchen and kissed Kailah on the lips. It was so passionate that she had to put the phone down while Mona rambled endlessly.

"Morning," Keith whispered softly in her ear.

Kailah picked the phone back up to find Mona still talking about her new job.

"—I love teaching. I feel like I'm really connecting with the students. The only problem is the pay. It's ridiculously low. I'm thinking I may have to get a second job to help cover my financial expenses. I don't want to call Mother or Daddy and ask them for help."

"What about your settlement money from the lawsuit? Surely you have enough left." Kailah took out a carton of orange juice from the refrigerator, then set it down on the table. Keith placed his hands inside her purple silk robe, gently caressing her breasts. She playfully smacked his hand away and waved her finger at him.

"I'm using that to cover my therapy costs."

"Well, I know that you're probably going to say no, but if you need to borrow money, I can loan it to you," Kailah said, knowing Mona would never accept a handout. "You can take as long as you need to pay me back."

Mona could barely get the words out of her mouth. "Even though I hate to admit it, I may just have to take you up on your offer."

"Let me know, and I can have it wired over to you within twenty-four hours."

"Okay. Thanks a lot, Kailah."

"Anything for my best friend. I love you, girl."

"Well, there's something else I want to talk to you about." Mona hesitated a moment. "I met someone."

"What?" Kailah took a bite of her sausage. "Who?"

"His name is Davis. You know the receptionist at my therapist's office?" Mona asked.

"Yeah, the ghetto receptionist with the blonde braids."

"They're purple now, but anyway, Davis is her cousin and he lives in Tampa. Rona gave him my phone number, with my permission of course, and we've been talking for a little over a week now."

"It sounds like you're interested in this guy. Am I right?" Kailah asked, already knowing the answer.

Mona chuckled. "Yes, you're right."

"Tell me more about him so I can get excited, too." Kailah finished her breakfast while she listened intently.

"Davis Simpson is his name. He's thirty-seven. Lives in Tampa and works as a computer engineer. He's a devout Christian. He has two daughters from—"

"Hold up. Did you just say that Davis has two kids?" Kailah was a little surprised. "How do you feel about that?"

"I'm fine with it."

"Maybe it's because you're not thinking clearly. The last thing you need is a man with baggage, and I'm not talking about his kids either. I'm talking about the mother. Baby Mama Drama. I know you heard the song and saw the video."

"Oh, come on now. You're being ridiculous. All I'm doing is talking to the man. I'm not marrying him, Kailah." Mona took in a deep breath.

"I just want you to be careful. We sistahs have to look out for one another," Kailah said.

"Good looking out for a sistah. Hey, I don't mean to end the conversation so quickly, but I have some errands to run today before my appointment with my therapist."

"Uh-huh, yeah, sure." Kailah knew Mona was only trying to end the discussion about Davis. "Well, keep me posted about your new Mr. Wonderful Dad!" Kailah laughed.

Mona laughed, too. "Whatever. Good-bye."

"Bye, girl."

Chapter 15
Not My Husband!

"Hello," Kailah answered.

The phone went dead.

"Not again," Kailah said.

"Everything all right?" Keith questioned as he traipsed in the room wrapped in a towel.

"That's the second hang up today. I guess all of your old booty-call girlfriends don't know you're married yet." Kailah shot Keith a dirty look as she walked past him.

While passing, Keith reached out and grabbed her. "Wait just a minute. We need to talk about this. I know that look on your face."

Kailah tried to pull her arm away. "You better get your hand off me, Keith. I don't want to talk about this right now."

They began to scuffle until Keith finally let go. He held both hands in the air as a gesture of surrendering.

"Okay, baby. Please, come sit down on the bed." Keith winked and reached out his hand in a gentleman fashion in the direction of the bed.

Kailah hesitated for a moment, pushed Keith's hand out of her way, and plopped on the bed. Keith followed her.

"Baby, remember we discussed this when you came up with this genius idea of moving into my place because it was bigger?"

"Yes, I remember. However, we've been married for almost six months now, and I didn't expect these calls to still be coming at this point. I never dealt with this when we were dating. And we dated for a year and a half before we got married." Kailah picked at her fingernail.

Keith took her right hand and kissed it softly.

"Dating and living together are two different things." He put both of his hands on her face and kissed her on the

99

forehead. "Kailah, I love you. Let's not fight over this petty stuff. I was saving this for later, but something tells me I should discuss it now."

Kailah cocked her head. "What?"

"I'm thinking that this place might be too small for us when we decide to have some kids. And plus, the city is no place to raise children. So, I called a real estate agent to find a few houses for us to check out."

Kailah clapped her hands. "Baby, you mean we're going to move into a house? Oh my God, I have to call Mama. No, I'll call Mona first. What will I do about decorating? This place was just a rehearsal for the big thing. 'Cause you know I want a big house, Keith, like the ones in the magazines. Are you listening to me?"

"Uh-huh, yeah, I'm listening." Keith anxiously rubbed his hands across her breasts, and then reached over to kiss her softly on the lips.

Kailah grabbed his hand and kissed it. "I love you."

They kissed while Keith forcefully pulled her sweater over her head. Then he reached behind to undo her bra, throwing it to the side. Next, he peeled her panties off in one quick motion.

"Do you want me to turn off the lights, or do you want to do it with the lights on?" Keith asked.

Kailah turned over on top of Keith, removing his towel. "Leave them on.

Around 2 a.m., Kailah tossed back and forth until she could no longer sleep. Keith slept peacefully on his side facing her. Her stomach growled nonstop, so she dragged herself downstairs to the kitchen with the intention of fixing herself something quick to eat, but soon, she began to think about the phone call from earlier.

MIXED MESSAGES

I wonder if... She walked over, grabbed the phone in the kitchen, and pressed *69. Listening for the next prompt, she pressed 1 to dial the number back and waited while it rang.

A woman's voice answered, "Keith, where the hell are you? I've been waiting all night for my fucking medicine."

Kailah was stunned. "This is Keith's wife. What medicine are you talking about?"

The dial tone sounded. Kailah dialed the number back, but changed her mind and placed the cordless phone back on the base charger.

What the hell was she talking about? What medicine? None of his clients ever called the house. The woman called his name, though. She did say Keith.

Kailah massaged the back of her neck, trying to loosen the tension. It was at that moment she decided she would phone Taneisha first thing in the morning to let her know she would be taking the morning off. Some investigative work needed to be done. She was going to get to the bottom of this... and real soon.

......

Kailah nervously pulled up in front of Waltman Pharmaceuticals in her silver Volkswagen Passat, a newly purchased gift from Keith. He didn't want Kailah catching the train anymore because he felt it wasn't safe. She spotted a parking space down the street and pulled in. With a clear shot from her rearview mirror, she waited. Looking at her watch, she expected Keith would be coming out any minute to meet her for lunch. She had set the date that morning while pretending to get ready for work.

Keith stood at the edge of the street, waiting for an opportunity to cross. He ran over, jumped into his Lincoln Navigator, and pulled out onto the street. Kailah ducked down as the SUV passed her.

Kailah took in a deep breath. *You can do this.*

She opened the door slowly and climbed out. Hurrying across the street, Kailah opened the brown wooden door to the small business office. The middle-aged receptionist at the front desk immediately recognized Kailah and waved while she was speaking with a client through her headset.

"Hey, Demi," Kailah spoke softly and then proceeded down the small hallway toward Keith's office. She opened the door slowly and closed it, trying not to alert Seth, one of Keith's partners, whose office was directly across the hall. She didn't even bother turning on the lights.

Okay, now what? She sighed deeply. Her stomach was tied up in knots.

The filing cabinet seemed as good a place as any to start looking.

......

Kailah nervously fidgeted on the couch when Keith strolled in the front door. He folded his arms. His eyes were fixed on her with an intense gaze.

"I tried to call you today at your office after you stood me up for our so-called lunch date," he said while attempting to make eye contact.

Kailah looked the other way. Then, she grabbed the remote control and turned off the television.

"And so what happened? I had an emergency meeting that I couldn't get out of." Her stomach was doing major flip-flops.

Keith let out a grunt and spun Kailah around to face him. "Emergency meeting, huh? In my office, right? What the hell were you doing snooping around in my office, Kailah?"

Kailah's mouth locked in fear. "I... I...called that number back... and..."

"And what, Kailah? Damn it, I'm asking you a question, and you better answer me. Now!"

"Please, Keith, just let me go!" Kailah hollered.

MIXED MESSAGES

Keith forcefully pushed Kailah away. He stood up and walked toward the other side of the table. "You know, don't you?" He placed his hands on his face while pacing back and forth. "Answer me!"

"Know what, Keith?" Kailah yelled back at him. "That you're a goddamn drug dealer. Yeah, I know! Fucking pharmaceutical company, my ass! Your company is a front for a hustling drug-dealing business!" She headed toward the stairs. Keith ran after her as she sobbed hysterically.

"Shhh, baby, please calm down." Keith pulled her into his arms.

"How could you keep this from me? You're a liar. I trusted you."

"Baby, please. Just let me explain." Keith wouldn't let go no matter how hard Kailah fought.

"I don't want to hear any explanations from you. Now, let me go. I'm leaving you. I want nothing else to do with you. You make me sick." Kailah struggled to pull herself up the stairs, but Keith grabbed her by the legs and wouldn't release her. She had already packed her bags and made plans to stay with Taneisha if she needed to.

Keith finally released his tight grip and buried his head in his hands, breaking down into tears. "Please, don't leave me. Baby, baby, please don't do this."

Kailah turned to look at him at the foot of the stairs. Never had she seen him this vulnerable and emotionally distraught. And because a part of her felt sorry for him, she went back and sat down on the step he was sitting on. Keith put his arms around her and squeezed tightly, never wanting to let go.

Chapter 16
The Dating Scene-Take One

Mona pulled up in front of the hotel, got out, and handed her keys to the valet. Nervously, Mona swung open the door to the lobby and spotted the phones on the right.

"Hello."

"Hi, Davis?"

"Yes, this is Davis. Is this Mona?"

Mona smiled. "Why, yes, it is." She loved the sound of his heavy voice. It resembled that of group member Michael from Boyz II Men, whose voice could seduce any woman. Hell, not just in the bed, but anywhere the brother saw fit to make love.

"I'll be down in a minute," he said.

Okay, girl. I know you haven't had any in awhile, but don't have sex on the first date.

Mona gained her composure, straightened her sleeveless black dress with the split up to her thigh, and sat down on the couch in the guest waiting area. She really wanted to look sexy tonight, so she had a manicure, pedicure, and a facial to help her relax.

Davis had the entire weekend planned, starting with dinner at an Italian restaurant.

"You must be Mona." So deep in thought, she didn't notice the strikingly handsome gentleman in front of her. He was light-skinned with very low cut and wavy hair, and his soft and thick eyebrows defined the most beautiful green eyes she'd ever seen.

"I am." Mona nodded. "Nice to meet you, Davis."

Davis reached out his hand towards Mona to help her up from the chair. "I'm honored to make the acquaintance of such a beautiful young lady."

His smile shows nice pearly white teeth. He is absolutely the most gorgeous man I've ever laid eyes on. How in the hell am I going to get through this date without letting him know that?

Every woman had to play hard to get, but it seemed Mona was already caught and ready to have this man's babies.

As Davis opened the door, Mona caught his eyes fixated on her as she walked out. Her diagonally cut dress seductively revealed her very large breasts.

Davis handed the valet his ticket. Trying to calm the butterflies in her stomach, she said, "So, Davis, how was your drive down from Tampa?"

Davis smiled. "Not bad. Not bad at all."

The tall and slender valet pulled up in a white Jeep Cherokee and opened the door to help Mona in while Davis jumped in the driver's seat. Davis was decked out in crème-colored Dockers, a matching polo shirt, a black suede shirt-styled jacket, and black suede shoes.

On the ride along Washington Avenue, Mona didn't say a word. The busy nightlife in Miami was full of locals and those vacationing to escape the cold weather up north. The crowd was especially thick in South Beach where the narrow palm-trees lined the streets. Young people stood crowded on the sidewalks of Bash and Niva, alongside several jam-packed nightclubs. A tall man, jamming to his music, roller-skated past them at a traffic light. One man dressed in a bright orange-striped suit performed on a tall unicycle for a small crowd. The bright lights reminded her of Las Vegas, minus the casinos.

"Are you always this quiet?" Davis asked.

Mona nodded. "No, not always."

"You're a lawyer, right?" Davis asked as they sat waiting for the traffic light to turn green.

"I was a lawyer at a law firm here in Miami. Now, I teach a class at the University of Miami." Mona hoped Davis wouldn't ask details about her past. She didn't want to drudge up any memories of Darren Thomas. Not yet, and probably not ever. "Do you like what you do?"

"I enjoy my work. Computer engineering provides me with the challenges I need to stay interested in my work. The company I work for is great because the people make it a nice place. They are serious about the work and teamwork is emphasized."

Mona's eyes were fixed on his small, sexy lips as he spoke. When he finished, he looked at her, and she quickly turned the other way to pretend like she had been gazing out the window all along.

Davis continued. "I think it's important to enjoy every aspect of your life, career and personal. Don't you agree?"

"Oh, yes, I agree," Mona responded. Once again, the butterflies were back.

Davis parallel parked from Margutta's, got out, and opened the door for Mona.

"Thank you." She reached for his hand and stepped down slowly. As soon as the cool February breeze hit her, she suddenly remembered she had left her shawl in her car.

"You're very welcome. My, you're shivering. Wait one minute." Davis opened the back door and pulled out a pastel yellow sweater. "It's my daughter's, but I think it will fit you."

"Yes, thank you." As they crossed the street, Mona placed the sweater on her shoulders while Davis put his arm around her.

With this being one of the most popular Italian restaurants in Miami, Davis had made reservations earlier in the day. Therefore, they didn't have to wait long to be seated.

Davis held out her chair for her as she sat down. "You are such a gentleman, Davis. Thanks."

"It's my pleasure. Besides, this is our first meeting, and I want to make it special for you." He took his seat and picked up the menu, then ordered wine for the two of them. Within minutes, the waiter was back to take their orders.

Mona cleared her throat. "How old are your children?" she asked, attempting to make small talk.

"My older daughter, Tori, is fifteen. And Keisha is thirteen."

Mona's eyebrows rose. *Is he older than what I thought? He damn sure doesn't look as if he would have a fifteen-year-old daughter.* "Oh. How often do you get to see them?"

The waiter returned, placing their plates in front of them.

"Every chance I get, which usually means on the weekends. However, I talk to both my girls on the phone every day." Davis paused to eat a fork of anti-pasta. "I make it a point to stay involved. Whether it entails going to dance recitals, soccer games, or swim meets, I'm there. I never miss anything."

"I'm sure your daughters appreciate it. They're lucky to have a father like you in their lives." Mona said while cutting the large pieces of lettuce into smaller ones.

Mona listened intently as Davis continued to tell stories about his daughters. Mona loved the way his face lit up while he told her about Keisha breaking her arm during a soccer game, and how she was only concerned with whether her team had won the game or not.

"She has my competitive spirit," Davis added, looking at Mona with a slight grin. "Are you enjoying your evening so far?"

"Yes, I am." Mona wiped her mouth with the cloth napkin. "The salad was delicious."

When the waiter approached the table to discuss the dessert menu, they both declined and headed back to the hotel.

"Would you care to join me at the bar for a drink?" Davis asked while they were standing in front of the hotel. He gazed deeply into her eyes, as though searching for an answer.

Okay, Mona, you had a really nice dinner. The conversation was good. He said all the right things, and was heavy on the complimenting, too. Remember your agreement. No sex on the first date. Say goodnight and be on your way.

"I would love to."

They entered the hotel and Mona knew deep inside this was not the way she'd planned this evening to go. She also hadn't planned on this man looking so damned fine. And she also hadn't planned on him being so charming either.

Davis held Mona's hand and led her to the bar.

......

"And nothing happened?" Kailah asked.

"No."

"I can't believe it."

"I can't believe it either. I won't lie to you. I was tempted."

"You know what that means, don't you?" Kailah said. She sat at her desk thumbing through some paperwork. The work was piling up, and Kailah had been spending a great deal of time at the office trying to get caught up. Also, this provided an excuse to stay away from home as much as possible. She avoided her husband like the plague, and when they saw each other, she kept the conversation to a minimum. They hadn't had sex in three weeks.

"What does it mean, psychic Kailah?"

"You really like him. You're interested in pursuing a serious relationship. That's what it means. That's why you're being stingy with the coochie."

Mona laughed. "I won't deny it. I do like him. That's why I'm driving to Tampa next weekend to meet his girls."

"Already? Don't you think you're moving a little quickly?"

"Maybe, but Davis really wants me to meet Keisha and Tori." Mona coughed a few times, and then continued. "I didn't want to say no. Besides, I want to meet them."

"Okay, whatever you say. I want you to share all the details when you get back. Don't leave anything out. 'Cause I'll know if you do." Kailah looked over at the clock. Her meeting would begin in five minutes. "I gotta go, but happy birthday. How does it feel to be twenty-nine?"

"Like I'm one year away from being thirty. Thanks for sending the money, too."

"You're very welcome."

Kailah turned the key and opened the front door to her apartment, flicking on the closest light as she entered. Keith hadn't made it home yet. Finally being able to relax, Kailah made a turkey and cheese sandwich. Then she walked into the living room with a plate in one hand and a glass of grape soda in the other.

Surfing channels with the remote, Kailah finally found a _Fresh Prince of Bel Aire_ rerun. As the front door slowly opened, she thought to herself that she shouldn't have gotten comfortable on the couch. Kailah wasn't in the mood for talking after putting in twelve hours at the office.

Keith strolled in the door, his eyes lingering on Kailah for a moment. "Hey, baby."

"Hey."

"I heard you laughing all the way down the hall." Keith sat down on the couch. "That Will Smith is a crazy cat." He took his shoes off and put them beside the table.

"Yeah, he is." She took another bite of her sandwich.

"What time did you get in tonight? I wanted to take you out to dinner."

"Yeah, Taneisha told me you called. Sorry, I was way too busy. Where did you eat?"

"I didn't. I had some business to take care of."

Kailah sucked her teeth. "I bet you did. Street hustling is a twenty-four hour profession." Kailah picked up her plate and glass and walked into the kitchen to wash the dishes.

"Well, at least now you want to talk about it," Keith said.

"Keith, the only thing I want to talk about with you is when are you getting out of this business and going legit. Otherwise, until you say that, there is nothing to talk about. I'm a professional, and I thought *you* were when I married you. I'm scared something terrible is going to happen, and you're going to end up in prison or dead. Then I'll be left here to pick up the pieces. How will I be able to show my face at AND? Huh? Answer that question for me."

"Baby, you're throwing a whole bunch of what if's at me. You shouldn't even concern yourself with AND." Keith slapped his hand against his chest. "Hell, you don't even have to work. I make more than enough to provide for us."

Kailah jerked. "I don't care about your money."

"Oh, you don't? You weren't saying that when I was taking you out to the most expensive restaurants. You didn't care when I bought you a new car." Keith scratched the back of his head. "Let's see, Kailah. You've been spending thousands of dollars going shopping every weekend…you and your girl, Taneisha. I see the diamond tennis bracelet and the new jewelry up in here. You buying Donna Karan and Versace suits to wear to work now. I've never seen you in none of this shit when I first met you. So, don't act like you don't care about the money."

"Keith, you don't understand. It's like I'm living a lie. What if the members of our church found out about this?" Kailah threw her arms up in the air. "I would be so ashamed. I enjoy going there. I'm getting more and more involved in the children's ministry. Being a member of the congregation has changed my life for the better. I know I have some things to work on, and the Lord is dealing with me, but this is too much for me. I can't do it."

"Nobody's asking you, Kailah. You're my wife, and I love you." Keith pulled Kailah into his arms. "I'm not going to let anything happen to you. And nothing's going to happen to me. That street thing got started when we needed the money to start our own business, when no banks would give us a loan. We have legitimate clients now. Andre, Seth, and I are moving up and in the process of cutting those old ties loose. It's just going to take us a little time. That's all. I promise you, baby. Pretty soon, this will all be over."

Kailah put her arms around Keith. She did miss him. He was her everything. The conversation did put her mind more at ease. But still, she would believe it when it happened. She needed proof.

As Keith kissed her softly on the neck, Kailah didn't put up any resistance. Three weeks was too long to go without sex in a marriage.

She unbuttoned her blouse and then removed her bra. If the marriage was going to last, then she had to trust and believe in him completely. She stripped out of her pants, while Keith enticingly watched her.

Keith had been good to her. It had been tough for him. She knew how much he valued her love. Both of their parents were still married, so it was important for them to remain together and somehow make it work.

Once she was completely naked, Keith performed a private strip show for her that she would not soon forget.

***

The next morning, the alarm buzzed.

Keith reached over to turn it off as Kailah entered from the bathroom.

"What are you doing up before me?"

"I have to go in early. We're sealing the deal on the Kipper account today, and I want to get in early and review the final contracts. Oh, and that reminds me." Kailah walked over to Keith, who was still lying in the bed, and gave him a kiss.

"What's that for?" he asked.

"There's another reason why I got up so early." Kailah wrapped her arms around his neck and then rubbed her hands down his chest.

Keith raised his thick eyebrows. "Oh, there is?"

"Yeah, I had to get up and pee on a stick."

"A pregnancy test?" Keith rose up and placed his back against the headboard. "Are you pregnant, baby?"

She grinned. "Yes."

Keith grabbed her and landed a big kiss on her cheek. "I love you so much." He ran his fingers across her lips, then kissed them. "I'm going to take good care of you and my son."

Kailah traced a pattern across his muscular chest. "I know. But, how do you know it's a boy?"

Keith threw his hands up. "Believe me, I know. "'Cause I'm the man!"

Kailah sucked her teeth. "Yeah, right."

Chapter 17
Too Close for Comfort

"What are you talking about, Davis? Spending the evening watching black exploitation videos is not what I consider a romantic date." Mona placed her last few clothing items in her suitcase. "Besides, I have this absolutely stunning red dress that I'm planning to wear this weekend. Otherwise, I wouldn't have spent two hundred dollars that I don't have to buy it. And red is my signature color, if I must say so myself." She laughed.

"It was just a joke. Come on, you had to know I was joking," Davis responded. "I don't even own any videos of the sort."

"Of course not."

"The girls are so excited about meeting you. I must admit, though, I'm a little nervous. You're the first woman in my life to meet them, besides my ex-wife."

Now why did he have to say that? If he's nervous, then how does he expect me to feel? She walked into the bathroom to grab her make-up case.

"Are you there?" Davis said from the other end of the phone line.

"Yes, I'm getting a little sidetracked. That's all. I think I'm about ready to head out," Mona finally said, not wanting to respond to his last comment.

"Okay. Drive safely, and if you get lost, call me. You can reach me on my cell."

"I will."

"I can't wait to see you again."

Mona smiled. "Neither can I."

After Mona did one final check to make sure she had everything, she hopped in the car to head to Tampa.

That evening, Mona collapsed and stretched out on the couch at Davis' home.

"I'm worn out."

They had spent the entire afternoon at the mall with the girls. Keisha picked out every scantily clad top or dress she could find in the stores. Wearing less clothing meant one could be as sexy as Beyonce Knowles or the women in those hip-hop videos. While Keisha was checking out the stores, Tori checked out the guys. She wasn't the least bit interested in spending time with her dad and his new girlfriend at the mall when there were phone numbers and AOL screen names to collect. Finally, Tori asked if she could have some cash to shop alone and catch up with them later. Davis only agreed at Mona's urging.

They were just getting back to rest for a few hours before heading out to dinner. Immediately, Tori and Keisha rushed in to see who would be first on the computer. Seconds later, Keisha came back into the living room.

"Daddy, Tori's on the computer, and I really want to use the phone to call Mommy. Can I use the other line in your office?" Keisha was definitely Daddy's little girl.

Short and a bit on the chunky side, she wore her hair like all the girls her age, with the pastel-colored butterfly clips. The constant whining and complaining was beginning to get on Mona's nerves. Whereas, it didn't seem to bother Davis at all. He just about gave Keisha anything and everything she asked for with very little hesitation. Now Tori, on the other hand, resembled Davis. Tall and slender with wavy long hair past her shoulders, Tori asked for very little, wishing mainly to be left alone. Both girls had been blessed with beautiful green eyes like their dad.

"Sure, baby," Davis responded. "Let your mom know that I need to talk to her before you hang up."

"Okay, Daddy." Keisha happily disappeared down the hall.

MIXED MESSAGES

"Do you want me to get you anything?" Davis asked from the kitchen as he opened a can of Pepsi and took a gulp.

"No thanks."

Davis walked over to the stereo and turned up Musiq Soulchild's CD. Davis wore a pair of dark-colored khaki shorts and a yellow polo. Mona stared at his physique out of the corner of her eyes. Davis smiled warmly over at Mona and sat on the couch beside her, grabbing her feet.

"Here, let me give you a foot massage. I know you must be tired from all the walking at the mall." Davis held her left foot and worked his fingers around them. When he finished with the left foot, he kissed it, and picked up her right foot.

"This is relaxing." Mona laid her head back on the pillow. She'd never had a man this attentive to her needs. She'd made a mental note to be sure to brag about it later to Kailah. It had always bothered her that Kailah was able to nab a good man, especially with Kailah's history with men to boot. Even Kailah herself admitted she had lost count.

Davis began to work his hands up Mona's leg and slowly up her thigh inside her blue denim skirt. Just when Mona started to relax, he quickly removed his hand when the sound of footsteps sounded from the hallway.

Keisha plopped down on the couch beside Davis. "I didn't know you had this CD. It's my favorite." She giggled and cuddled up next to him. Davis hugged Keisha back and kissed her on the cheek.

"You're off the phone already? Now, why didn't you tell your mom I wanted to talk to her?"

"I did, Daddy. Mommy said she had to run, and she would call you later."

Davis sighed. "I bet she will."

As she pretended to be napping on the couch, Mona thought to herself what had he meant by that last statement.

"Don't worry, Daddy," Keisha said. "I didn't say anything about Mona. I wouldn't want Mommy to get mad. I like your new girlfriend. She's pretty, and she's nice to me."

Get mad? Now why would Doris get mad when they have been divorced for over two years? See, this was the shit Kailah had warned me about. She'd make it a point to ask Davis about it later. Right now, she was feeling tired and needed to get some sleep. Once the girls were asleep, she and Davis would have the rest of the night to do whatever. And whatever that was, she needed to be well rested and ready for it.

However, whatever never happened. When they got back from dinner, the girls didn't show the slightest sign of being tired. Tori suggested on the ride back home that Davis stop by Blockbuster Video to rent a couple of movies. So after arriving home, Mona soon found herself standing over the counter in the kitchen emptying a bag of buttered popcorn into a large plastic bowl. Keisha and Tori were already seated on the couch watching the previews, and Davis was in his bedroom on the phone returning Doris' call.

"Enjoy." Mona placed the bowl on the front table and watched as Keisha took a huge handful and began to munch loudly on the popcorn.

"Uuhh, girl," Tori responded. "That's why you're fat now. Always eating like food's gonna go out of style or something."

"Shut up!" Keisha screamed, grabbing another handful, this time eating louder than with the first.

"Would you quit smacking in my ear? Damn—"

"Ooohh, you cursed. I'm gonna tell Daddy."

Tori elbowed Keisha in the side. "So...go tell him, Piggy. I don't care."

Keisha crossed her arms and pouted. "Wait 'til Daddy comes back. You're gonna get it."

"Get what?" Davis appeared from around the hallway with a frazzled look on his face. He stood waiting for an answer.

MIXED MESSAGES

The girls were silent. Tori turned toward Keisha and scowled.

The fighting had been nonstop. First, they argued over which radio station would be played in the SUV on the way to the mall. Then, it was what store they would go to first. At dinner, Tori complained about Keisha's obnoxious eating habits. At Blockbuster, they couldn't agree on one movie, so they both ended up getting a movie.

Lastly, they argued over which movie they would watch first. Davis finally ended the heated debate by saying the movie he picked would be watched that night, and the girls could watch the movies of their choice after church tomorrow.

Being an only child, Mona always wanted a baby sister. But, she had no idea sisters fought like this and could be so cruel. Her friendship with Kailah was Mona's only relationship that could even be considered sisterly. Kailah was the only girl in her family, so they always had that bond.

Mona finally said, "The girls got into a little discussion, but it's over now. Let's sit down and enjoy the movie."

Davis shook his close-cropped head and sat on the floor in front of Mona, letting out a heavy sigh. Mona knew his exhale had nothing to do with Keisha and Tori either. She began to massage Davis' shoulders while he watched the movie.

"Just relax. Let me take care of you," she whispered softly in his ear.

......

"Are you planning on getting out of bed anytime soon? The real estate agent will be here at eleven o'clock."

Kailah rolled over and sat up. She was still nauseated and had a migraine that wouldn't stop. Being three months pregnant, she still couldn't shake the morning sickness. Taneisha had been a huge help at the office by scheduling all of her meetings after lunch. Usually by that time, Kailah would have hauled herself into AND. By no means was she getting behind in her work, because Kailah had no problem staying late in the evenings to get caught up.

The only person who had a problem with it was her husband. Keith expressed that he felt she was spending too much time at work and not getting the rest she needed. At every urging, he told Kailah to cut back on the number of accounts she handled.

However, Kailah wasn't ready to give up her climbing status at AND. Her superiors depended on her, and she didn't want to let anyone down, especially herself. Determined more than ever to take Lynn's undeserved position as Senior Consultant, Kailah was winning the favor of every member of the board, including Lynn's father. She made it plainly obvious to everyone that Lynn had no business running the department and steps had been strategically orchestrated by Kailah to show it.

Of course, Lynn only hurt herself by showing up to meetings late because she hadn't checked the revised schedule. With Lynn not being prepared for presentations, Kailah was asked time and time again to take the lead. Now the board members expected Kailah to present all proposals before their most-respected clients.

No way was Kailah just going to hand her clients over to another consultant at AND. She knew plenty of women who were able to handle motherhood and still climb to the height of success at the same time. Of course, all of these women had a dynamite nanny to help out at home with the kids, cleaning, and cooking. She didn't see why she had to be any different. The only problem was Keith. His mother had instilled in him the crazy notion that women gave up their careers to stay home and raise the children. This was no surprise to Kailah because he had made her aware of this long before they were married. He let it be known that he wouldn't have a problem carrying the financial burden.

MIXED MESSAGES

Kailah had no doubt that he could. That is until she learned of Keith's shady business dealings. As far as she knew, Waltman Pharmaceuticals hadn't severed those ties yet. Therefore, in her opinion, Keith's financial future was not secure.

She was going to be a mother now and was more determined than ever to build her own little nest, separate from Keith's, so she would be prepared if anything happened to him. What if the FBI got wind of Keith's illegal dealings, arrested him, and seized all of his assets? Or worse, what if the IRS became involved? Kailah would be left with nothing. A business-savvy person such as her needed to prepare for these types of events. This was her profession. She was her most important client, and she needed to handle her own financial affairs just like she handled her other clients' accounts: by always thinking ahead.

Kailah stepped out of the shower, her stomach sticking out just a hair. She rubbed her stomach and smiled.

"Today, we're going to make an offer on a house that you are going to live in. It's a beautiful two-story home in an exclusive neighborhood with a huge backyard for you to play in. Wait until I fix up your nursery. We are going to be so happy there. I just know it."

Chapter 18
A New Arrival

"What time is the movie?"

Davis looked down at his watch. "Seven-thirty."

Sitting at the vanity Mona carefully placed her hair in a French twist. She had asked her hair stylist, Lisa, to demonstrate a few hair tricks that she could do on her own at home. Living on a strict budget didn't leave a lot of room for her usual hair expense of two hundred dollars a month, which would include a touch-up relaxer, a style and cut, two wash-and-sets, and a deep-conditioning treatment. The ritual was to get in her office early every Thursday morning at Thomas and Clarke so that she could leave mid-afternoon to make her regularly scheduled hair appointments. Now, Mona could only afford to go once a month for a touch-up relaxer, style, and cut. By cutting back on her visits, she had managed to cut her bill in half.

"I don't mean to rush you, but if we don't leave within the next five minutes, we're going to be late for the movie," Davis said, standing in the doorway of the bathroom.

Mona stood up. "Let's go, then. I wouldn't want you to have to sit in the back with all the black folk again," she muttered.

"What do you mean by that comment?" Davis asked.

"Nothing." Mona grabbed her brown sandals and sat down on her wicker chair to fasten the buckles.

"Mona," Davis followed her down the hallway to the door, "do you want to tell me what this is about?"

"We can talk about it later, Davis. Really, I'm sorry," Mona said as she locked the door to her townhouse. They walked down the driveway, and Davis opened the door for her to climb into the Jeep Cherokee.

MIXED MESSAGES

"Now, what has you in a foul mood this evening?" Davis asked as soon as he backed his Jeep out of the driveway.

Mona didn't want to bring up the discussion on the way to the movie, but at the same time, she wanted to get it off her chest. "I overheard you today."

"Overheard me? When?"

"While you were on the phone with Doris today. You told her that you still loved her."

Davis was silent.

"I'm sorry you had to hear that," Davis finally responded. "I'm having some problems with Doris, but it's nothing that I can't handle. You just have to trust me."

"What kind of problems?" Mona asked. *Trust? I've known him for all of eight months. What makes him think that is enough time for me to trust him?*

"I don't want to talk about it right now. I'm bound to get upset all over again just thinking about it."

"Davis, if you want me to trust you, then you have to open up to me and let me know what's going on."

Davis slammed his fist on the dashboard. "I said to just leave it alone. Damn." He clenched his teeth.

"Okay." Mona nodded as she watched the people walking through the parking lot. One family rushed as fast they could toward the movie theater. Mona assumed they were trying to get to the new Disney movie premiering that night. She laughed to herself as she saw the husband leaving his wife behind to drag their screaming toddler across the street, completely oblivious to the fact that her two boys had run out into the street without even looking to catch up with their father.

While they were walking towards the theater, Davis put his arm around Mona. "Do you want me to get you some popcorn or soda while you find us some seats?"

"Sure."

"I want to sit closer to the front. I had a difficult time hearing the movie the last time."

"Okay." Mona chuckled silently to herself. *You mean, you had a difficult time hearing back there with all the black folk talking in your ear.*

No one spoke a word in the SUV on the way back to Mona's place. As soon as they entered the townhouse, Davis immediately headed down the hall towards the bathroom. He never liked to use public bathrooms. Noticing the light blinking on her answering machine, Mona pressed the play button. Keith's excited voice sounded through the speaker.

"Mona, Kailah wanted you to be the first to know. Kamryn was delivered at six this evening. She weighed six pounds three ounces. You can reach me on my cell phone when you get in. Oh yeah, and Kailah's okay. She handled it like a true champ." Mona could hear Kailah in the background coaching Keith on what to say.

"Who was that?" Davis asked as he turned on the lights in the kitchen.

Mona was deep in thought. "Oh, that was Keith. He called to tell me that Kailah had the baby tonight."

Davis came out of the kitchen holding two glasses of red wine, placing both glasses on the table. "That's good news."

"I know. I was just a little worried because she went into labor two weeks before her scheduled C-section."

"How's the baby doing?" Davis placed his hands on Mona's shoulders.

"Fine. She weighed six pounds three ounces."

"That's small, but I'm sure she'll be okay."

"I hope so." Mona yawned. "I'm really tired."

"Tired? I was hoping we were just getting started," Davis said as he began to nibble on Mona's ear. He pulled her mouth close to his and kissed her softly. Then he cupped his hands on her large breasts. Mona responded freely to his touch as Davis unbuttoned her blouse and unhooked the bra to free her caramel-colored breasts. His eyes widened at the beautiful sight that was before him. Mona held him and breathed heavily as he slowly devoured them. Davis then took off his shirt, and Mona rubbed her hands across the soft, curly hairs on his chest. As he slid in between her legs, she could feel his penis stiffen, which made her juices start to flow.

When Davis went to unzip her pants, Mona was suddenly stricken with fear. "You know, I'm really tired," she said while grabbing his hand and yawning. "I think I need to get to bed." She pushed Davis away and fastened her bra back on.

"Well, can I join you?" Davis looked over at her like a desperate little puppy.

Mona couldn't believe he was pressuring her into a sexual relationship. She really thought she wouldn't have to deal with this, being involved with a man who claimed to be saved. She felt safe with Davis, but over the past two weekends they spent together, the demands were becoming stronger. Mona didn't feel at all comfortable with that. She wanted to have sex, but there was a mental block she just couldn't get past.

"Not tonight. It's too soon. I'm not ready yet."

"You're not ready?" Davis said, running his fingers through his wavy hair.

"That's right."

"You know, I've been very patient with you, Mona, but you're not even meeting me halfway. How long do you think I'm supposed to wait? Another eight months?"

"I expect you to wait as long as needed. Anyway, what's all this talk about you being such a Christian man? I thought you of all people would understand that sex before marriage is a sin."

"Mona, I don't need you telling me anything about being a Christian. When was the last time you went to church? When was the last time you went to see your therapist? The real issue is you don't want to get over your rape. You want to remain the victim. You want me, your friends, your parents, and the rest of the damn world to bow down to you and kiss your ass like your ass is made of gold or something."

Mona leaned over on the bar and rolled her eyes. "What the hell are you talking about, Davis? You don't know anything about what my life has been like for the past year. You have two daughters. You should understand. Just picture a man beating one of your daughters senselessly and then raping her. Then imagine her later learning that she's pregnant and then forced with the decision to have an abortion because she doesn't want nothing to remind her of that terrible night." She pointed at Davis. "Until that happens to you, you don't know anything about what I've been through. You can't imagine how you make my skin crawl every time you get near me. I hate it! I want to be there for you, Davis, because I really do love you. But, I just can't!"

Mona stormed out of the room and down the hallway, locking herself in the bathroom.

Davis ran after her, knocking on the door. "I didn't know. You didn't tell me all of this. I'm so sorry."

In the darkness, Mona sat trembling on the cold floor.

......

"Thank you, Keith," Mona said as Keith placed a cup of coffee on the table in front of her.

"He's been helping out a lot around the house. The doctor says my body needs four weeks to heal."

"I'm glad to hear it," Mona responded as she watched Kailah rock Kamryn gently to sleep. "Is she asleep yet?"

"Almost. I can tell she's sleeping when she starts purring like a little kitten. It's amazing how much I know about her already, and she's only a week old."

Kailah rubbed her baby's back softly. She couldn't believe this little person lived inside of her stomach for nine months. Being a mother was the most rewarding experience, even though she endured a brutal labor. The pain seemed a blur compared to the sudden joy she felt whenever she saw Kamryn's chubby pink face sucking on her tiny fingers.

Mona nodded.

Keith walked back into the living room, planting a kiss on both Kailah and Kamryn. "How are my two favorite girls? Hey, honey, I need to leave for a couple of hours to take care of some unfinished work at the office. You know I haven't been there all week. Are you going to be okay?"

"Sure, baby. We'll be fine."

"All right, I won't be long." Keith grabbed his leather jacket and headed for the door. "If you need anything, just call me on my cell."

"I will. Don't worry, Mona will help out."

"Yeah, okay." Keith nodded. "Bye, Mona."

"Bye, Keith."

Seconds later, Mona heard the garage door buzz open and then shut.

"Keith certainly seems to be a changed man."

"Yes, he is." Kailah tried to get up with the baby in her arms but felt a sharp pain in her side. "Mona, can you get Kamryn and put her down for her nap?"

Mona reached over to pick up the baby. Kamryn whimpered for a few seconds but calmed down once Mona held her firmly in her arms.

"I absolutely love what you've done with the house," Mona said as she came back down a few minutes later. Her eyes

sparkled with excitement as she studied the Charles Bibbs'
paintings on the wall.

"Yeah, it turned out pretty nice. Of course, it cost a pretty
penny."

"I imagine it would cost some money to decorate a thirty-
five hundred square foot home." Mona sat down beside Kailah
and propped her feet on the table. "So, what have you decided
to do about work? When are you going back?"

"Well, I decided to take a six-month leave of absence. That
should give me enough time to find a suitable nanny and adjust
to the demands of motherhood and my career."

"What does Keith have to say about your plan?"

"I haven't told him yet."

"I guess you have six months." Mona smiled.

"I'm not worried about it. This is my life and my career.
I've worked too hard to build it to what it is today." Kailah
tossed her hand. "Please, I'm not worried about Keith."

Mona sat silent for a moment.

"That's a good attitude. Different than the one you had a
few months ago."

"Well, I was pregnant at that time. I let my emotions get
the best of me, but I'm over it now." Kailah picked up the
remote, surfing the channels. "There's nothing coming on
tonight. You want to rent some movies?"

Mona frowned. "No thank you."

"Oh, still upset about the time you rented movies with the
girls, huh?" Kailah laughed. "That's what you get, trying to win
the Stepmother of the Year Award."

"Shut up." Mona picked up a pillow and hit Kailah across
her stomach with it.

"Oooww, girl, I'm hurting there." Kailah scowled.

"Good." Mona pointed her finger at Kailah. "That's what
you get for trying to win the Mother of the Year Award."

"You're cold, Mona, but I love you anyway."

MIXED MESSAGES

"I love you, too." Mona wrapped her arm around Kailah's neck and kissed her cheek. "You know you're my girl."

......

Keith entered the restaurant and was immediately greeted by the maitre d'.

"Hello, Mr. Terrence. Your party has already arrived. Let me show you to your table."

"Thanks." Keith followed him to the table where Andre and Seth were sitting with a few of their first and most loyal clients. All of the men were well dressed in dark suits. Keith wore a navy blue suit with a light blue collared shirt to accent.

Keith nervously straightened his jacket.

"Here's our man now. He's a new dad. Give the man his props." Andre stood up, reached over, and hugged Keith. Everyone else at the table began yelling and clapping at the same time.

"Thanks, man." Keith unfastened the buttons on his jacket as he took a seat in the empty chair next to Seth.

"Now, we can get back to our toast. Hey, pour my man some champagne!" Andre waved his hand to signal the waiter.

The young waiter immediately rushed over to the table to fill Keith's glass, then placed the bottle in the ice bucket.

All five men held up their glasses while Andre motioned his hand to silence the group. "A toast to our biggest year where we have doubled our profits and here's to an even better year! Here, here." All men agreed and clanked glasses.

Seth leaned over on Keith's shoulder. "You all right, man?"

"Yeah, I just got a lot on my mind."

Seth rubbed his hands together and smiled revealing his dimpled cheeks. "I know how hard it is adjusting to a new family. But, I tell you, I've never been happier. Trinity and the kids are everything to me. I would die for them."

Keith remembered the day Seth made the big announcement of his and Trinity's engagement. It was a meeting similar to the one they were sitting at right now. That was seven years ago, before the three of them had gained their success. At the time, Keith thought Seth was crazy for wanting to give up the single life and be tied down in a marriage.

Now, he couldn't imagine living one day without Kailah. She was his world, and everything revolved around her happiness. Things wouldn't be right between the two of them until he could convince his partners to handle only legitimate clients at Waltman Pharmaceuticals. He just wasn't sure how much time it would actually take.

After dinner, Andre walked with Keith to the parking lot. "Let me holla at you for a second."

"Sure, what's up man?" Keith asked.

Andre made small talk until everyone left. Then he leaned on Keith's Lincoln Navigator and said, "Just when everything is getting good, why you wanna make things difficult?"

"Man, I don't know what you're talking about." Keith laughed.

"Naw, see, you know damn well what I'm talking about. Seth already told me you're asking about when we going legit and shit."

"Man, we always agreed that we would drop some of our clients once we got to where we needed to be in this business. Don't act like you don't remember." Keith slapped his hand across his chest.

"We too deep in this shit now. We can't drop anybody, without some fool dropping us. And I ain't going out like that, even if I have to drop you myself."

Keith bristled. "What you saying? You gonna rat me out? You care more about this money and business than you do your own boy?"

MIXED MESSAGES

"What I'm saying is we got a good thing going. Don't mess this shit up, Keith." Andre threw his hands mid-air. "Or else, I'm going to have to make good on my threat."

"Oh, so you're threatening me now?" Keith pushed Andre. "What's up, nigga?"

"This is what's up, fool!" Andre pulled out a 35mm from his waist and cocked it directly in Keith's face.

Keith's blood went stone cold. He stood paralyzed in fear. Thoughts of his wife and daughter flashed through his mind.

"Yeah, I could take your black ass out right now." Andre quickly looked around and then put the gun away.

Before Keith even realized it, he had struck a hard blow to Andre's jaw. "Man, don't ever do that shit again."

Andre grabbed his jaw and started to laugh. "All right, man. You're still my boy...my partner. All I'm saying is give this thing a little more time. I want to drop these fools just like you, but it ain't that easy. We need more time."

Andre and Keith gave each other a brotherly hug right before Keith opened the door to his SUV and climbed inside.

"See you in the office tomorrow morning!" Andre yelled back as he jumped in his white Lexus and sped off.

Keith watched as Andre drove away, then he rested his face on the steering wheel and took a deep breath.

This shit is never going to end. And I know just what I have to do.

Chapter 19
Ain't That Just Like a Man?

Kailah fed Kamryn while rocking back and forth in her glider. The walls in the nursery were a pastel mint green with angels and ferries she had painted on herself. It was a safe and dreamy haven that would relax any mother nursing her baby. When the phone rang, Kailah answered on the first ring.

"Hey, are you busy?"

"Hey, Mona. How was the trip to Hawaii?"

"Everything you said it would be when you went on your honeymoon. Mother was being her usual unbearable self, but I enjoyed spending time with Daddy."

"I'm just glad you managed to take a break. After everything you've been through, you really needed it."

"Yes, it was very relaxing." Mona sighed. "The trip allowed me to take my mind off some things."

"Now, don't forget about my baby on the sixteenth of September."

"You know I wouldn't miss my goddaughter's christening for the world."

"What time is your flight arriving, so I can be there to pick you up?" Kailah asked as she burped Kamryn on her shoulder.

"Oh, no, don't worry about it. I'll catch a cab. I don't want you to bring the baby to the noisy airport."

"Kamryn will be fine. I can't have my best friend catching a cab from the airport. I'm going to pick you up, and that's that." Kamryn burped, spitting up milk in the process. "I swear this girl spits up on cue. Hold on while I change her shirt." Kailah pulled a shirt off a hanger in the closet. Filled with dresses from corner to corner, Mona was to thank for her contributions. Mona was also the one to blame for the fifteen pairs of baby shoes that adorned the closet floor.

"I'm back." Kamryn made cooing noises in the background.

"Everything okay?"

"She's fine. What about you? How are you doing?"

"Good," Mona said.

"What about you and Davis?"

"Over," Mona muttered under her breath.

"What?" Kailah said in disbelief.

"Yes, he called me the night before I left for the trip to tell me that he can't do this anymore."

Kailah frowned. "Can't do what anymore?"

"Be in a sexless relationship, I guess. He wasn't very clear. But, I pretended to understand and let him off the hook."

"I don't understand. I thought you were past that 'no sex before marriage' rule back when you became involved with that guy Robert."

"Well, I was until the rape. I just can't bring myself to do it."

"And why not?"

"I just keep having this mental block, and I clam up. I can't explain it." Mona breathed heavily into the phone.

"What does your therapist say about all of this? I mean, you're paying her enough money. I'm sure she has some suggestions." Kailah placed Kamryn on her lap and began to bounce her around.

"Well, that's the thing. I haven't been going. I thought I was better."

"Excuse me if I'm wrong, but not being able to have a physical intimate relationship with the man you love doesn't sound like you're over it to me. So, what's the real reason? You don't want to get better?"

"I can't afford it. When the settlement money ran out, I was left with no choice but to cancel my visits."

"That's too bad." Kailah rubbed her daughter's back softly. "What are you going to do now?"

"Well, I'm going to get a second job. But, as for Davis, I don't need him. I need a man who is willing to stand by me no matter what."

"I see what you're saying. Ain't that just like a man, though? I know Keith wouldn't have stuck around that long if I wasn't giving it up. All I can say is Davis must really care about you."

"Not enough," Mona said.

Kailah sucked her teeth. "Maybe you're the one that didn't care enough. I mean, you weren't willing to do what you had to do to make the relationship stronger. You have too much pride...always have."

"Maybe." Silence filled the line for a moment.

"I think you should call him," Kailah said. "How hard is that? Don't ruin a good thing. Davis is a good man."

"He really is. I'll give it some thought."

"Do that. Well, I better go get dinner started. Juanita's still upstairs taking a nap, and Keith and his Dad will be back from the game soon."

"Okay. By the way, how's the visit from the in-laws going anyway?" Mona asked.

"As well as can be expected. You know Juanita hates me. So every opportunity she gets to fire an insult, she usually does with no hesitation. I'll just be glad when I can relax in my own house again."

"I'll bet. Well, it can't be any worse than having my mother as an in-law." Mona's voice went up an octave.

"Actually, I'll take Bea over Juanita any day," Kailah responded. "Take care of yourself."

"Of course. See you in two weeks."

Kailah placed the cordless phone on the counter, then took out the steaks Keith planned to grill when he got back from the game with his dad. She glanced over her shoulder to check on Kamryn bouncing away in her baby bouncer that she had placed on the floor by the sliding glass doors in the kitchen, so she could keep an eye on her while preparing the vegetables for dinner.

Soon, Juanita came in the kitchen while Kailah was peeling the potatoes.

"How was your nap?" Kailah asked in a cheerful tone. "You managed to get a couple of hours of rest in this afternoon."

"Actually, I did." Juanita reached for a knife and began dicing the onions. Kailah watched as she hacked away on those defenseless onions with her long red manicured nails. "We got in so late last night that I was just exhausted from the flight."

"I know a thing or two about exhaustion. The other night, Kamryn had Keith and me awake till well after midnight. She just would not fall asleep." Kailah laughed.

Juanita tossed her head back in an indignant manner. "That problem would be remedied if you set proper nap times and put my granddaughter on a schedule. Didn't your mother teach you anything about raising a child?"

Kailah kept on peeling the potatoes, placing them in a bowl and rinsing them off in the sink, ignoring Juanita's sarcastic remark.

"Keith tells me you're planning to go back to work soon," Juanita continued as she began to dice the green, red, and yellow peppers.

"I do plan to resume my work at AND, but not for awhile." Kailah hoped her response would be enough to end the conversation. She already knew what Juanita thought of working mothers.

"That's the problem with our youth today. Mothers are so concerned with their own careers that they are hardly making any time for their children. Whatever happened to sacrifices?"

Does this woman ever quit? She is about to push me too far. She doesn't even want to go there with me. I don't want to have to tell her about herself, but if she says another thing—

"I was barely able to cut up these vegetables with these dull knives in here. Where is your sharpener?"

That's it! "Please, excuse me. I think Kamryn needs to be changed. And you know I have to stick to that schedule." Kailah scooped up Kamryn and quickly exited the kitchen. She stormed up the stairs and headed for her bedroom. She closed the door and locked it behind her. Where were Keith's migraine pills?

An hour later, there was a knock at the door.

"Baby, open the door."

Kailah opened it. "Hey, how was the game?" She went back to playing on the floor with Kamryn.

"The Bears lost." He reached over to kiss his baby girl.

"Figures."

"What's with you? My mother says she was helping you prepare dinner, and then all of a sudden, you left her to do all the work by herself."

"That's not what happened. Kamryn's diaper needed changing." Kailah tried to avoid eye contact with Keith.

He grabbed her by the arm. "So, my mother is lying?"

"Keith, let go of my arm." His grip tightened. "Your mother is always insulting me. I've had enough of her put-downs for one day, so I came upstairs. Now would you let go of my arm, Keith? I'm not going anywhere."

Keith finally let go. "What is it with you and my mother? You know how she is. I don't see why you can't find a way to just get along with her." Keith undressed and slipped into a pair of lounge shorts and a t-shirt.

"Your mother hates me. I'm doing my best to try and get along with her, but I do have feelings." Kailah's face shriveled up. "I haven't done anything to that woman. Why can't she just

134

find a way to try and be civil towards me? I'm this close to losing it with her and giving her a piece of my mind." She threw her hands up in frustration.

Keith came up behind Kailah and put both his arms around her. "It won't come to that. Baby, I didn't realize my mother was upsetting you like this. I'll go talk to her."

"No, Keith. That wouldn't be right." Kailah wiped the tears from her face. "I need to do it."

"Okay, if you think that's best. I love you, baby. Well, I'm going out on the deck with Dad and start grilling those steaks. I'll take Kamryn outside with me. You go talk to Mom." Keith walked over and picked up the baby. He kissed Kamryn on the cheek as he left the room.

Kailah looked in the mirror at herself. *You look a mess.* She pulled out the long, powdered blue dress and placed it on the bed. Then she took out a matching bra and panty set and went in the bathroom to run a shower. A steamy shower would do her a world of good.

After Kailah got out of the shower and dressed, she walked down to the guest bedroom and knocked on the door.

Juanita opened it. She looked as if she had showered and changed also, now wearing a sleeveless denim dress.

"Can we talk?"

"Yes, young lady." Juanita curled up her lips. "And I have a few things to say to you in return."

Kailah didn't like the sound of that, but she wanted to get this off her chest. "I just wanted to let you know that I'm delighted to have you here. I want you to enjoy your stay here. I know this is an awkward situation, being that we live so far away. Therefore, I would really like for us to take advantage of this time to get to know one another a little better. I realize we never really got the opportunity to do so before the wedding."

Juanita clutched her chest in complete shock. "I must admit the marriage proposal and then the wedding a year later did catch us by surprise. I guess I never *did* have a chance to get to know the woman my son chose to spend the rest of his life with."

Kailah folded her arms. "I think what you're trying to say is Keith never even bothered to ask you. I know that. I realize I'm not the type of woman you pictured your son married to, but he's my husband. You don't have to like me, but I think you should respect me like any other stranger on the street. I don't feel like I've done anything to deserve less than." Kailah turned around and left the room. On her way down the stairs, she patted herself on the back for handling the situation like a Christian woman should.

She walked through the sliding glass doors and stepped onto the wooden deck where Keith and his dad were. Keith stood over the grill while Blake sat in a chair holding a giggling Kamryn.

"Let me get her for you." Kailah leaned over to pick up Kamryn.

"No, no, Keith already tried earlier. You think I'm too old to hold my own granddaughter. Well, I'm not. Plus, she likes her granddaddy. Now, sit down over in that chair. Relax. All you young people are just too uptight these days."

"All right, then." Kailah went back inside to check on the roasted potatoes and vegetables in the oven.

"It sure does smell good down here. I'm starving." Juanita walked in and picked up the bowl of salad.

"Me, too." Kailah followed Juanita out on the patio, while carrying the hot dish.

"Just in time, ladies. The steaks are ready," Keith announced.

"I need to go get the plates and silverware," Kailah said.

"I'm coming, too," Juanita said as she followed Kailah back into the house. "You know, I never told you how beautiful this home is. I know you and Keith are going to be very happy living here."

Kailah looked over at Juanita and smiled. "I think so, too."

......

Mona stepped out of the shower. The bathroom filled with the fragrance of raspberry from her Bath & Body Works shower gel. She smoothed on the raspberry body cream and entered her bedroom naked. Maxwell's latest CD played on the stereo. Mona put on her sage green silk gown with matching panties and sat down on the bed. Her hair was still wet and wrapped up in a towel. She grabbed September's edition of *Ebony* and found an article to read.

As she thumbed through the magazine, the conversation she had earlier with Kailah replayed in her mind. Maybe she should call Davis, just to let him know she made it back safely from her trip.

She picked up the phone and quickly dialed the number.

"Hello, Simpson residence."

"Hello, Tori. Is your dad there?"

"Uh-huh. He's here. How you doing, Ms. Mona?"

Mona smiled. "I'm fine. How's school?"

"It's good. I got a boyfriend. His name is Terry, and he is *so* fine. Please don't tell Daddy. He will trip. Here he is."

"Hello, Davis speaking."

Mona held her breath as she savored the sound of his voice. "Davis, this is Mona."

"One moment."

A woman's loud voice sounded in the background. All of a sudden, there was silence. She assumed Davis must have walked into another room and shut the door.

"I'm relieved to hear your voice," Davis said. "How are things?"

Mona twisted her lips. "Good. I just got back from my trip and wanted to let you know I made it home safely."

"I'm pleased to hear that. I've been busy with the girls this weekend. You know how tiring that can be."

"Yes, I know. I didn't want to keep you. I can tell you have company. I heard the woman's voice in the background," she snapped.

"Well. That was...Carol...a friend of mine from work. She was just joining us for dinner."

Mona sighed. "I see. Well, I won't keep you. Goodbye, Davis."

"When will I hear from you again, Mona?" Davis asked. "I would like to talk to you soon. I've missed you. Carol is just a friend. There's nothing between us."

"It's none of my business, Davis. Bye."

Davis grunted. "You didn't answer my question."

"I guess we'll talk whenever you decide to call, and when you're not busy with Carol," Mona said, snatching the towel off her head.

"Why do you have to act like that? Carol is a friend. You're the woman I love."

Mona sucked her teeth. "Oh, really? Well, if you loved me so much, then why haven't you called me in over two weeks?"

"I thought I was giving you the time you needed. You said I was pressuring you."

"You had me believing that I was the one that didn't love you enough." Mona ran her fingers through her hair. "When the truth is, you just found yourself an easy lay, so you dump me and jump in the bed with her. I guess you didn't have to look very far, since the bitch is right there on the job. Lucky for you."

"I'm not going to argue with you. You left me with no choice but to go forward with my life without you. I'm not going to apologize for that."

"I don't expect you to. You're not the man I thought you were, so I'm better off without you." Mona slammed the phone down, ending their conversation.

Moments later, the phone rang back. Without hesitation, Mona lifted the receiver and placed it back on the base, hanging it up again. This time she kept the phone off the hook. She wasn't in the mood to talk.

After a couple of hours, Mona woke up suddenly and sat straight up in bed. Realizing she'd left the phone off the hook, she reached over to put it back on the base. Then hard knocking came at the door. *Three o'clock in the morning! Who in the hell could that be?* Suddenly, the phone rang, startling her.

"Yes."

"Mona."

She rubbed her eyes in an attempt to fully awaken herself. "Yes, this is Mona."

"I've been trying to call you since you hung up on me the second time."

"It's late, Davis. Call me back in the morning."

"I can't do that," Davis said.

"What do you mean?"

"I've been knocking at your door for the past hour."

"What?" Mona sat straight up. "Are you crazy?"

"Something like that. Would you just open the door, please," Davis pleaded.

Mona got out of bed and peeked out her vertical blinds. Davis' Jeep Cherokee sat in the driveway. She hurried into the bathroom to wash her face and brush her teeth. Then she ran down the hallway and opened the door. Davis stood in blue jeans and a black leather jacket.

"Are you going to invite me in?"

Mona's eyes lingered for a moment. "What are you doing here?"

"Let me in first, and then I'll explain."

Mona stepped aside as Davis entered her townhouse. He walked over to the couch and took off his jacket.

"Don't get comfortable."

"Mona, please."

"What?"

"I love you. When you called me tonight, I was so relieved to hear your voice. I miss you so much."

Mona folded her arms.

"My choice to end the relationship was not the right decision. I made a mistake. I wanted to do what was right for you. I love you, and I can't live without you. I can't breathe without you. I need you and only you. That's what I drove all the way down from Tampa tonight to say." Davis grabbed Mona and pulled her close to him. He gazed directly into her eyes. "Don't tell me no, Mona."

He kissed her tenderly on the forehead.

Mona melted right in his arms. This time, she wouldn't be able to say no. She wanted him, too. She'd always wanted him. That was no secret. Until now, she never had a real connection to a man. But then after the brutal attack, Mona believed she would *never* feel again. She didn't even know what it was like to feel...until now.

Davis slid the spaghetti straps of Mona's gown off her shoulders. He then slid the gown down past her thighs and onto the floor, doing the same with her panties. He kissed her passionately. Mona reciprocated, unable to move. Davis took off his shirt, and then picked her up and carried her into her bedroom.

As he finished undressing right in front of her, Mona watched intently. He then crawled in bed with her and began to kiss her wildly. He rubbed her right breast with his right hand and put his left hand on her butt. He slid her down closer to him and spread her legs open, grabbing her thighs.

MIXED MESSAGES

Mona entered a world of once denied oral pleasure and closed her eyes. Grabbing Davis by his curly hair, she moved her hips to meet his lips.

"Yes," she cried out.

Davis licked and sucked all over her stomach and supple breasts. Davis slipped a condom on his well-endowed penis and entered her with one strong thrust. Mona let out another a sharp cry as he held her closer.

"It's okay, baby. I'm not going to hurt you," he whispered in her ear. "Just let go."

Mona felt herself relax and opened her legs wider so that Davis could enter her more freely. She released all of her fears and pain, and received so much more in return. Each thrust was stronger and even more intense than the last.

He moaned and groaned her name in pleasure.

Minutes later, Mona couldn't hold back anymore, and she experienced the first orgasm of her life with a man. Davis reached ecstasy closely behind her.

Afterwards, he held Mona close in his arms.

Chapter 20
God Bless the Child

"Hello."

"Hey, it's me. I just wanted to let you know that my flight number is 1472, and we're scheduled to arrive at six-twelve Saturday morning."

"We?" Kailah sat up in her bed. Keith started to wake up, but Kailah kissed him and coaxed him back to sleep.

Mona chuckled. "I want you to meet Davis."

"Well, I guess that means you two are a couple again."

"Better than ever. I took your advice. You were right. I wasn't trying hard enough."

"Glad you listened for once," Kailah said. "What about your problem?"

"What problem?" Mona laughed even harder.

Kailah raised her eyebrows and smiled. "Well, I see. I'm just going to take my little self back to sleep, and I'll see you Saturday."

"You do that. Bye."

"Good night."

......

"Anyone care for a slice of apple pie and some vanilla ice cream?" Kailah asked as she stuck her head in the family room where Keith and Davis sat on the leather couch watching the football game.

"Yeah, baby, hook me up. And can you put some caramel syrup on my ice cream, too?"

"Sure. What about you, Davis?"

"Yes, I would like it the same way. Thanks."

Kailah walked back into the kitchen where Mona sat at the table holding Kamryn.

"You know you can put her down. She's been asleep in your arms for almost twenty minutes now."

"I know, but I just love holding her."

"Me, too." Kailah smiled as she watched Mona with Kamryn. Kailah wanted the same happiness for her, because she knew Mona had never experienced that kind of endearing love from Bea. Maybe Davis would turn out to be Mr. Right, and they would soon marry. He certainly seemed like a nice guy. Not to mention he was so damn cute.

"Kamryn's christening at the church was very touching. I couldn't stop crying."

"I noticed," Kailah said. She walked over and sat down at the circular table beside them. "My little girl looked beautiful in that pretty white dress."

Mona perched her thin, soft pink lips. "Well, it took me over a week to find the right one. I had it especially ordered for my goddaughter. Nothing's too good for her."

Kailah flung her long, black hair with honey highlights over her shoulders. "I appreciate all you do for her. I know that money is tight for you."

"Yes, it is. She's worth it, though."

Kailah sat up straighter and rubbed her jaw. "So, how are things with Davis? I really think he was made for you."

Mona giggled. "You think so?"

"Yeah, you're glowing, girl. I haven't seen you like this in a long time. He must be putting it down." The crème-colored, double-breasted pantsuit was the best she'd seen Mona dressed in since college. Lately, Mona could care less what she was wearing, and half the time, Kailah wasn't sure if Mona even combed her hair.

"He is." They both burst into laughter. As if on cue, Davis walked in, and they started to laugh even harder.

"If I didn't know any better, I would think you two were in here talking about me."

Keith walked up behind Davis, wearing a red and white Chicago Bulls t-shirt and a pair of black and red mesh shorts. "Or talking about me." He reached over and gave Kailah a kiss. "Baby, where's the pie?"

"Oh, I'm sorry. We just got to talking, and I forgot all about it."

"Uh-huh. Now that I'm here, I'll fix it myself. Hey, Davis, man, you want me to fix yours, too?"

"Sure." Davis sat at the island as Keith cut two huge slices of pie. "So, who do you think is going to take it all the way to the bowl this year?"

"Man, this might be the Bucs' year!"

Davis nodded. "I'm hoping it is. Man, they always get so close, but never go all the way. It would be nice if they pulled it off."

"They just might take it!" Keith yelled, startling the baby and causing her to wake up and whimper.

Mona picked her up to try to quiet her down, but Kamryn didn't stop.

"Here, let me get her." Kailah reached over and grabbed her. "She probably needs changing. Your daddy and his big mouth." She stuck her tongue out at Keith.

"My bad. You want me to help?" Keith asked.

"Just go watch your game. I got it. I need to change out of this dress anyway." Kailah disappeared up the stairs.

While leaning over in her black slip, Kailah changed Kamryn's diaper. Mona entered the room eating a slice of apple pie.

"It amazes me that someone so tiny can smell this bad." Kailah tossed the soiled diaper in the diaper genie.

Mona turned her pointy nose up. "Now that's one smelly diaper."

"Tell me about it." Kailah went in the bathroom and washed her hands. Kamryn lay on the bed laughing and kicking her feet in the air.

"I'm glad you came in here. There's something I wanted to talk to you about," Kailah said. "Go close the door."

Mona shut the door and climbed on the other side of the bed. "What is it?" she asked as she took a final bite.

"Mr. Calbretti wants to meet with me tomorrow morning. He says he wants me to come back to AND immediately."

"Why? You still have three more months of leave left." Mona scratched her head.

"Well, it seems Ms. Lynn Gleichman was demoted, and they want me to assume her position as Senior Consultant." Kailah couldn't remove the smug look off her face.

"Have you discussed this with Keith? I mean, what does he have to say about all of this?"

Kailah looked straight ahead with no emotion. "We talked about it. He told me how he felt."

"And, how does he feel?"

"Keith wants me to stay home, and I've agreed to do so. I'm going to return back to AND in six months on a part-time basis only."

Mona twisted her lips. "So, you're basically going to turn down the offer for the position you have dreamed about for a lifetime?"

"Yes, I am. And you know what? I don't feel bad about my decision either. I wanted to be Senior Consultant so badly because I felt I deserved it. However, the other reason was because I didn't want Lynn to have it."

"Well, the top execs at AND also feel you deserve it."

Kailah gestured with her hands as she spoke. "You don't get it. Part of my problem is that I'm always competing with other women. That's the reason why I almost lost you as my best friend. I felt I deserved Derrick, not you. I learned a valuable lesson from that experience, and I'm not taking risks like that again. I love my husband and my daughter, and I'm not ready to go back to work. I love being here with Kamryn and taking care of my house. God has been good to me and has showered me with many blessings. The career is just not that important anymore. I choose my life. It's a shame that women have to choose, when men can have it all: career, wife, and family."

Mona folded her arms and crossed her legs. "Well, it sounds like you're speaking from the heart. There's nothing wrong with that."

"Yeah, I just have to figure out how I'm going to say it tomorrow in that meeting with all of the top execs at AND." Kailah's big brown eyes scanned the room as though she were a stranger in her own house.

Mona caressed Kailah's left arm. "You'll find a way. You always do. And you will do it with every ounce of tact and professionalism in you."

"Thank you, girl," Kailah said.

Chapter 21
Baby Mama Drama

Mona and Davis walked quickly on the deep blue carpet through the Tampa Airport to locate baggage claim. Few people were around, many of them sleeping in chairs and wooden benches. Davis thought it would be easier to catch a flight later in the evening and arrive close to midnight. Tired and cold from the flight, Mona wore a denim-blue jacket to try and stay warm.

"You feeling okay?" Davis inquired. "You haven't said a word since we left Chicago." He put his arm around Mona and squeezed her tight.

"Yes, I'm fine. Just got a lot on my mind."

"You seem deep in thought. Anything you want to talk about?"

"Not right now, but maybe later."

Mona enjoyed her trip to Chicago. She absolutely loved spending time with her adorable goddaughter, feeling that special bond and connection with a beautiful baby triggered something in her own spirit. Was it her biological clock screaming at her? Whatever it was, it ignited a yearning desire from within that seemed difficult to control.

Kailah's happiness was contagious, and Mona wanted it. The wonderful home, husband, and baby. Not sure whether or not Davis would be the person she could spend the rest of her life with, Mona decided it best to at least discuss her feelings with him. She needed to know how he felt and if their relationship had the potential to become something more. If not, Mona would have to decide if this relationship was worth any more of her time.

Davis and Mona collected their luggage and followed the crowd out to the parking garage. Davis loaded all of the pieces into the back of his SUV while Mona got in and waited. She dozed off and slept peacefully while Davis drove for almost an hour. He leaned over and tapped on her shoulder once he pulled up in front of his house and turned off the ignition.

"Mona, wake up." Davis tugged on her shoulder.

Mona opened her eyes slowly and stretched out her arms. "Already." Her eyes shifted left to right along the quiet, peaceful neighborhood while she took her bags and located her key to open the door to the house. Not even bothering to turn on the lights, she entered the code to silence the alarm on the keypad, found her way back to Davis' bedroom, and plopped down on the king-size bed, kicking her shoes off.

Minutes later, she heard Davis close the front door and set the alarm. She dozed off for a moment until she heard a woman's voice and recognized it as Doris' on the answering machine.

"So, you done took your ass off to Chicago with that bitch. I don't appreciate you taking off without letting me know about it!"

Davis skipped the message.

Mona sat straight up in the bed.

The second message played.

"I just want to know what's going on. You telling me you want to be with me, then you do something like this. Fucking me, and then turning right around and fucking that yella whore. And I know you fucking her. Just don't bring that shit back over here, talking 'bout how you love me. Nigga, go to hell with that bullshit!"

"Tell me it's not true, Davis."

"What? Doris is just tripping." Davis looked startled to see Mona standing there. "I told you she was going to act like that." Davis scratched his head and searched for his bags.

"Are you going to tell me the truth, or do I need to call Doris myself and ask her?" Mona walked over to Davis and pointed her finger at him.

Davis stared at her. "And ask her what?"

"Did you sleep with her? Did you tell her the two of you were getting back together?"

Davis turned Mona around, placing his hands on her shoulders. He directed her down the hall and back to his bedroom. "That's ridiculous. Mona, I'm tired. I drove all the way home after our flight, and I just want to go to sleep."

"You haven't answered my question. Now, we're not going to bed until you do just that. I want to know the truth." Mona folded her arms and twisted her lips.

Davis sighed. "The answer is yes," he said with his back facing her as he pulled his pajamas out of the drawer.

Mona tried to remain calm and mask her emotions. "When did this happen?"

"After our break up... when you were in Hawaii with your parents. I felt sorry for her... sorry for us... sorry for the kids. Doris convinced me into thinking maybe we should try to get back together and work things out. After it happened, I had my regrets. I don't love Doris. Probably never did."

"Did you tell her this?"

"Yes, but she never listens to me. Doris has her own way of looking at the world. It's either her way or the highway."

Davis was in a tough situation, having to deal with a woman who was the mother of his most beloved daughters. Doris wanted them back together again to be a family, and was using the kids to get her way. Was this a situation she wanted to enter into? Having to deal with Doris herself? It was too late to think about it now. Kailah had warned her about this. She loved Davis. There was no doubt about that. He was the one, and she would have to just deal with Doris, too. The mere thought of going toe to toe with Doris made her cringe.

"I'm sorry I got so upset with you earlier." Mona gestured with her hands. "It's just that when I ask you something, and

you avoid answering the question, it unnerves me."
"I'm trying to be protective of your feelings."
"You don't have to feel that way." Mona reached up to kiss Davis on the lips. "I know you love me. I know you would never do anything to hurt me. I love you."
"I love you. I'm really sorry for trying to lie to you. Well, I didn't actually—"
"Stop while you're ahead."
"Okay."

......

"It's good to see you, Mrs. Terrence."
"Nice to see you, Miriam. How is Bill?"
"He's great. He's been feeling much better since the surgery. How's the baby?"
"Growing everyday. Yes, I heard about your husband's sudden illness. I'm glad to know he's doing much better."
Miriam rested her elbows on her desktop. "Yes, he had a speedy recovery. I'll let Mr. Calbretti know you're here. And like I said earlier, it's really nice to see you." Miriam buzzed Mr. Calbretti. Kailah straightened her plaid, navy blue jacket. She already knew what to say, but she remained confused on how she would actually say it. She stood there admiring the view of tall high-rise buildings in downtown Chicago.
Seeing the same well dressed people at AND made her actually feel like an outsider. True, Kailah had made the decision to be a full-time mother and give up her career in the beginning. Being in love with her daughter, she couldn't imagine being separated for one second. As the months passed, though, Kailah began to miss her work. Having those feelings and desires to pursue her career, she felt as if she was a betrayer. Why couldn't she just be happy with what she had, which was a supportive husband, beautiful baby girl, and a nice

house? Resentment and bitterness began to reside in the place where she suppressed her longing desire to work. A part of her wanted to try and make this work just to feel whole and complete as a woman.

In her heart, she really wanted to be back and part of all the action. Of course, motherhood provided its own set of challenges. However, she still longed for the challenge of taking on a prestigious client, preparing for meetings, and making deadlines. She was a mother first, but was that all? Kailah had to explore this further.

"Mrs. Terrance, Mr. Calbretti will see you now."

"Thank you, Miriam." Kailah slowly turned and kicked one foot in front of the other. She strolled down the hallway in a very confident strut. Her long hair flowed from side to side with each graceful step.

Mr. Calbretti stood at the door and greeted her as she entered the large executive office with cherry wood paneling on the walls. All the top dogs were seated at the round conference table, including Atkins and Wallace.

Kailah shook Atkins' hand and spoke to everyone else in the room before taking her own seat in the middle. She felt as comfortable, poised, and confident as ever. This was where she had always wanted to be.

She thought about her life back in Gainesville, working at the Escapade and watching the women executives strolling through the mall in the evenings, dressed in classic tailored suits, with a cup of Barnie's coffee in one hand and a garment bag in the other. She would picture herself one day leaving the office, strutting down the halls telling everyone good night right before jumping into her BMW and whisking over to the mall to go shopping. Kailah made all of that come true when she took the chance at AND. Now being here, seated with these white men in the president's office, discussing her promotion was another dream coming to life.

......

"How did it go this afternoon?" Keith stood behind Kailah as she laid Kamryn in the crib. She lay sucking on her pacifier while she slept. It was amazing how she'd grown and almost doubled her size and weight in just five short months.

"It was interesting. Only thing I've been able to think about all day."

"Well, why didn't you call me?" Keith asked. "I told you I would clear my afternoon schedule if you needed me."

Kailah turned to face Keith, grabbing his hand and leading him out of the nursery so they wouldn't wake Kamryn. Keith shut the door halfway as Kailah walked down the hall to the bedroom that had been elaborately transformed into a home office, equipped with an executive-style desk with chair, two computers, a top-of-the-line laser printer, fax machine and copier, and a seating area with a couch and two chairs. When Keith entered a few minutes later, he found Kailah sitting at the desk with papers scattered all over the place.

"What's all this?" Keith asked.

Kailah sighed heavily. "This is the offer that AND says I won't be able to refuse."

Keith folded his arms, giving his full attention as Kailah explained the entire promotional package. Assuming her new position as Senior Consultant entitled her to lucrative stock options, a company car, and two weeks of additional vacation time. She also had the option of working at home for the next three months, while putting in at least twenty hours a week in the office to schedule and attend all meetings with the board and clients. Once returning, she would oversee the department and assume full responsibility of running it. Also, Taneisha would receive a raise and remain Kailah's executive assistant.

MIXED MESSAGES

"Oh, and did I mention my new salary?" She tossed her head back, flipping her hair off her shoulders.

"No, baby, what did they offer you?"

"A thirty-percent raise. I have forty-eight hours to think it over and give my final decision." Kailah continued to shuffle through all of the papers. "It's an offer that's hard to resist."

Keith leaned on the desk. "I agree with you. I mean, AND offered to meet all of your terms and then some. I don't know, baby. Maybe you should consider saying yes."

"What did you say?" Kailah's mouth fell open. "Did you say I should consider going back to work? I mean, I just want to make sure I heard you correctly."

Keith grinned. "Yes, baby. I know how much your career means to you."

Kailah squeezed Keith's hand while taking in a deep breath. "But, Keith, my family means more. I'm fully prepared to call Mr. Calbretti and turn down the offer."

"For what reason, Kailah? So you can stay home to be a mother to Kamryn and wish you were back at AND while changing dirty diapers all day? You are her mother no matter what you do. I have faith in you that you can handle the demands of a career and motherhood. And I'll help you to the best of my ability. Plus, Mama Anna promised to move up here and help out with the baby if you decided to go back to work. I'm sure I could find her a small apartment close by. Shit, I'll even buy her a car, too."

"No need. I'll loan her my Volkswagen while I'm cruising around in my new BMW," she kidded.

"That's the worse imitation of a British accent I've ever heard, Kailah."

They both laughed, then Keith kissed her softly on the lips.

"Keith, baby, I don't know what to say," she stood up from her chair and pulled him close to her, "except I love you."

Keith grabbed her hand and kissed it. "Well, I love you more, beautiful."

Chapter 22
You Have the Right to Remain Silent!
(One Year Later)

Mama, please pick up the phone.

"Praise the Lord."

"Mama, it's me."

"What's wrong with you, child?" Mama Anna asked. "You sound so upset."

"Mama, they got Keith. I don't know what I'm gonna do. They got Keith." Kailah cried uncontrollably. She paced back and forth with Kamryn in her arms.

"Girl, what is you talking about? Who has Keith?"

"The police...they picked them all up at Waltman. Everyone got arrested, even Demi. God, I don't even think she knew what was going on there. She has a husband and two teenage daughters at home—"

"Kailah, stop talking for a minute and listen to me. I don't know what kinda mess Keith's gotten himself into, but I'm sure he can find his way out of it. Everything's going to be fine. You hear me. Girl, don't you worry about a thing! God's gonna take care of you, just like always." Kamryn screamed uncontrollably. "You need to call your friend over to take care of Kamryn while you go up there to the jail and see about your husband."

Kailah sat down on the couch. Her mother always had a way of calming her. "Okay, Mama, I'll call Taneisha."

"I'll call back and check on you a little later on."

"Okay, Mama."

"All right, baby. I love you."

Kailah hung up and dialed Taneisha's number. Thirty minutes later, Taneisha rang the doorbell. As they embraced, Kailah tried her best to hold back the tears, but they just flowed like Niagara Falls down her face.

"It's going to be okay. Joe's at the house already. I can stay all night if you need me to."

Kailah nodded. "I may need you to do that. Thanks."

"Go take care of your business," Taneisha insisted as she rubbed Kailah's back for comfort. "Have you spoken with Keith's lawyer yet?"

"Yes, he's going to meet me at the jail. He says he can't do anything until first thing tomorrow morning."

Taneisha picked up Kamryn off the floor. "Well, get down there. I'm praying for you."

What little smile Kailah could muster up soon faded. "I appreciate everything—"

"Don't worry about it. Just get out of here." Taneisha pushed Kailah out the door and into the garage. Kailah climbed into her blue BMW and pulled out of the driveway.

Kailah drove slowly out of the Windermere Cove subdivision. She thought about how happy they were when they first moved here. That was almost two years ago. It was an exclusive gated community in the suburbs of Schaumburg with beautiful, extravagant homes and well-manicured lawns. Kailah felt so proud to live there, knowing where she came from. She went on many shopping sprees at the Woodfield Mall. Finally, she had made it. She had a wonderful husband, daughter, and a successful career. She really thought this was it. Kailah wanted nothing more from life than what she had.

But who was she kidding? *My husband is a drug dealer.* It was only a matter of time before everything would fall apart. Kailah felt so stupid for creating this mess for herself and her daughter, and for allowing Keith to continue feeding her false promises. Every month, it was the same old line: "I'm so close now. I promise, baby. Thirty more days, and I'm through."

A year had past and still the same old thing.

How could I have been so dumb?

MIXED MESSAGES

At three in the morning, Kailah arrived back home. She walked in the kitchen and put on a pot of coffee. Taneisha was asleep on the couch with the television still on. Kailah turned it off.

Taneisha slowly opened her eyes and frowned. "I was watching that."

"It looked like it was watching you."

Taneisha stretched out her arms and yawned. "Are you okay?"

Kailah's lips curled slowly into a smile. "Yeah, how's my baby?"

"Good. It took a while for me to get her settled down. You really had Kamryn frightened."

"I know. I better go check on her." Kailah turned. "Are you going to stay here for the night?"

"No," Taneisha said as she looked down at her watch. "I'm going to head on home. I'll call home from my cell and let Joe know I'm on my way."

"Okay. I won't be in the office at all tomorrow. I'll be at Keith's bail hearing. The judge set the time for ten in the morning, and you know I have to be there."

"I'll be sure to reschedule your meeting with Mr. Semibright. Call me and let me know how everything went. I'll come by after work and check on you and Kamryn."

"Thanks." Kailah hugged Taneisha once more.

She sat on the couch, drinking her coffee in a daze. Not more than twenty-four hours earlier, her life was completely normal. Now with all the latest events, it was no telling how long it would take before things would get better. After Keith's arrest, life would never be the same.

Twenty minutes later, as Kailah slept on the couch, she was awakened by the ringing of the telephone.

"Kailah, this is Dad."

"I'm sorry for not calling you back last night, but I was so tired. I wanted to get in a few hours of sleep before I had to go to court this morning." She slowly got up and dragged herself into the kitchen.

"That's quite all right, considering the circumstances. Juanita and I didn't sleep much either. We're torn up over this news. Our flight will arrive at O'Hare around four this afternoon. When we get there, we're all going to sit down as a family and discuss what the next plan of action will be."

Kailah closed her eyes shut in thankfulness. She was glad Keith's parents didn't cast blame, but instead showed love and support. "All right."

"Well, I know you have things to take care of this morning. I'll see you soon. Just know that we're behind you all the way. I appreciate all you've done for my son and granddaughter."

Kailah was now in the kitchen stirring warm oatmeal in a bowl for Kamryn. "Okay, Dad. I'll see you soon." She tested to see if it was too hot, and decided she had time to dress before feeding her.

Kailah darted upstairs to get showered and dressed before Kamryn woke up. After her shower, Kailah pulled out her deep plum two-piece pants suit to wear to Keith's bail hearing. Wearing her bathrobe and slippers, Kailah picked up Kamryn out of the crib and took her downstairs to eat her cooled bowl of oatmeal. Kamryn, now eighteen months old, played in the highchair and threw oatmeal all over the floor while Kailah drank a cup of coffee and read the newspaper.

It was no surprise that Keith's arrest, along with Andre and Seth, had made it to the front page of the newspaper. *How am I going to ever show my face at work?* The mere thought of AND suddenly made Kailah cringe. Going through a soon-to-be media circus made her want to crawl under a rock until it was all over. Hopefully, Mr. Calbretti would be understanding and believe that she could still handle her new responsibilities.

MIXED MESSAGES

Remaining focused on her job would be the distraction she needed to keep her mind off of this catastrophe. She breathed deeply. She was just putting the newspaper on the counter when the doorbell rang.

Kailah looked out the peephole and saw a man dressed in a dark suit. She adjusted her robe and opened the door.

"Are you Mrs. Terrence?"

"Yes, may I help you?" Two police officers stood behind the gentleman. She also caught a quick glimpse of several of her nosy neighbors standing outside on their lawns, too.

"Mrs. Terrence, I have a court-ordered search warrant to come inside and search your home for any evidence in our investigation leading to the arrest of your husband, Mr. Keith Terrence."

Kailah hung on the door. Maurice already told her to expect the search, but somehow it didn't seem real until that very moment. She slowly gave way to the door and allowed the officers to have access to her home. She ran into the kitchen and lifted Kamryn out of the highchair. Kamryn was laughing and making loud noises while offering one of the policemen her spoon of dried oatmeal.

"Come on, Ms. Kamryn. Let me get you upstairs and dressed before Theresa gets here to pick you up."

* * *

Kailah and Keith entered their home to find it completely ransacked. The kitchen cabinets were all left open with drawers taken completely apart. Papers were all over the floor in the family room. Keith charged upstairs to find it in worse shape than the first floor of the house.

He crept back downstairs and hugged Kailah. She was in tears. All of this was too much for her to handle.

"Baby, everything's going to be fine. Didn't you hear Maurice reviewing my case? They don't have enough evidence to take this to court. Most likely, the judge will dismiss the case."

"Yes, I heard him. He seems optimistic."

"He has every right to feel that way. We're going to beat this thing. Now you go upstairs and get some rest. I'll go pick up Mom and Dad from the airport. Theresa should be here any minute with Kamryn." He kissed her on the forehead and exited the house through the kitchen door leading to the garage.

Why is he so relaxed, while I'm feeling as though I'm losing my mind? This whole thing hasn't fazed him one bit.

To calm her nerves, Kailah ran a bubble bath. She finally decided she had the nerve to call Mona and tell her what had happened, knowing that Mona would be upset because she hadn't divulged Keith's secret in the first place. It was just too embarrassing to talk about with anyone, except Taneisha. Taneisha understood Kailah's situation, while Mona would've just tried to convince her to divorce Keith. Ready to do just that, Kailah had a change of heart when she learned of her pregnancy. Sanity turned to denial, then to pure insanity in her life.

Now what was she going to do? Prayer time would be doubled tonight. She would ask God for strength, courage, and wisdom to get through this. She'd heard the pastor preach on God providing a bridge over troubled waters and turning problems over to the Lord. Mama had always told her, too.

"The Lord never gives us more than we can handle," she mumbled to herself just before she dozed off in the tub. But just how bad would things get before they got better?

......

"I can hear the garage door opening now, Mona. I better go."

160

MIXED MESSAGES

"You need to check his ass. It's two o'clock in the damn morning! You know he's not out that long meeting with his attorney. If he walks in that house drunk again, put his ass on the couch. Don't put up with that shit, Kailah. You know you would tell me the same thing if Davis was trying to pull the same kind of stupid stunts."

Kailah placed her hand on her forehead. "I know. I'll call you tomorrow."

"Okay. Call me back tonight if you need me."

"I will."

Kailah put the phone back on the nightstand and grabbed her robe. She walked to the foot of the steps to meet Keith before he'd have a chance to start yelling loud enough that the neighbors could hear and wake up Kamryn. She could hear him slowly staggering in the house and opening the refrigerator. He must be getting a beer. *Damn him!* Suddenly, there was the sound of glass shattering on the floor.

"Keith, are you okay?" She peered down the stairs into the pitch-blackness. The only light came from the kitchen.

"Yeah, I…had…a…little…spill. I'm gonna clean it up, though, soon as I get up."

"What?" Kailah flew down the stairs. Keith was nowhere in sight. "Keith?"

"Yeah."

Kailah followed his voice and found him lying on the floor behind the island. She stood over him and placed her hands on her slender hips. *How long am I going to have to put up with this mess?*

Three months of worrying and waiting for his upcoming trial had taken its toll on him. Maurice advised Keith to turn over all evidence and testify against Andre and Seth.

The Defense Attorney's office promised to lessen the charges and hand over a shorter sentence. Why couldn't he just put his family first and follow his lawyer's advice? Keith wasn't being completely honest. Thinking back, he'd never been completely honest with her. What kind of a marriage was this? Not only had she'd married a lying drug dealer, but now he'd turned into a drunk. There were times when he really made it hard for her to love him.

After calling his name repeatedly, Kailah decided he wasn't going to wake up. So, she left his pitiful and sorry ass right there on the floor.

Chapter 23
Accept Your Fate

Mona stood in the kitchen pouring coffee into her mug when Davis grabbed her from behind to kiss her on the neck.

"Well, good morning to you," she said with a huge grin.

"Morning. Did you pour this cup of coffee for me?"

"Of course." Mona handed him the mug. Only three weeks had passed since she'd moved in with Davis. He'd asked her almost four months ago, but Mona didn't agree until she found a suitable buyer for the townhouse and a higher-paying job in Tampa. Today was her first day at Cohen-Meeke, a small law firm started by two women five years ago. Both women, Minda Cohen and Tara Meeke, were in their forties. No more male co-workers for Mona.

"You and Kailah were on the phone late last night." Davis sipped from his cup while he read the newspaper at the table.

"She's having a difficult time dealing with this. With Keith gone now, she has the responsibility of raising Kamryn all by herself. Single parenthood isn't easy."

"I know it. I have Doris to remind me every day." He frowned. "Well, at least Kailah's mother has moved up there to help out."

"Mama Anna has been a great help, especially since Kailah works so much. Sometimes, I can call her house as late as eight o'clock, and Mama Anna will tell me Kailah's still at work."

"Work can be the cure for depression. There's no sense in her moping around in that big house feeling sad about her husband's situation."

Mona squeezed her mug with both hands. "I know you're right. I'm just worried about her. Our lives have changed so much since college. Kailah has done her share of dirt, but life has dealt her a bad hand. She doesn't deserve this and neither does my goddaughter."

"Who said life was easy?" Davis leaned back in his chair and held up his hands. "Look at the situation with Doris and me. My daughters don't deserve to have two parents that hate each other, but that *is* the reality. Life is like a box of chocolates—"

"Yeah, yeah, yeah." Mona nodded. "I know."

Davis grabbed his jacket and laptop. "I have to go." He kissed Mona on the lips. "Good luck today."

"Thanks." Mona peered through the wooden blinds as Davis jumped into his Jeep Cherokee and drove off. Needing to relax for a moment before getting dressed for work, she sat on the couch with her feet propped up on a pillow. After minutes of indecision, she finally laid out her power red Chanel suit to wear on her first day.

......

Kailah sat on the toilet in the bathroom in total silence. *This just can't be.* She looked at the EPT stick once more. Three months had already come and gone. Still, no period. Please, God, let it be stress. Keith had been gone for two months now.

Two stripes. Pregnant. Now what?

Kailah turned on the shower and undressed while she waited for the water to get hot. She tested the water with her left hand and stepped in. How was she going to be able to raise a second child on her own, especially with a husband in prison? It was difficult enough raising Kamryn. Thank God Mama was there to help, because she didn't know what she would do without her. Her new position as Senior Consultant was a good move career wise, but it took up a lot of time. She had to oversee all contracts, as well as the clients she'd obtained on her own.

MIXED MESSAGES

How was she going to do this? When was she going to tell Keith? How was he going to take the news? Before Keith left for prison, he demanded a divorce. He'd almost insisted on it. He felt that five years in prison was a long sentence, and he couldn't be a father to Kamryn or a husband to Kailah while away. He felt it was best for her to go on with her life and eventually remarry.

"And who the hell are you, Keith? How can you just make decisions for me and tell me who to love and not to love?"

"Look at the shit I'm in right now! Everything I've put you through." Keith paced back and forth in their bedroom, waving divorce papers. "I want a divorce."

"No. I won't do it, Keith." Kailah folded her arms as she sat on the bed. "You can't make me do this." She began to cry.

Keith kneeled down beside her and grabbed her hands. "Listen to me. I'm looking out for your best interest and my daughter's. This is the right thing to do."

"No, it's not. I don't want to do this. I love you. I'll wait for you. It'll work out, Keith. Please don't do this."

Keith put his arms around Kailah. The life he built for his family was completely falling apart. His business was gone, and so was his freedom. Drinking had consumed his life up until Kailah had threatened to throw him out the house. He'd cleaned up his act then, asked God to forgive him, but he would have to pay for his sins. Keith and Seth had turned in the evidence needed to bring Andre down.

Turns out, the arrest was never about Keith and Seth to begin with. Apparently, Andre had been involved in criminal activities since he was a juvenile. His records were sealed back then, and James Andre Allen a.k.a. Andre Bowers went to college in D.C. From then on, Andre was involved in credit card and calling card scams to help pay for his education and other living expenses. Everyone believed his story of receiving a large inheritance from an insurance policy at eighteen after his parents were killed in a car accident when he was only fifteen. The truth was his parents were both locked up in prison, serving lengthy sentences.

The FBI knew that Keith and Seth didn't have knowledge of the other crimes, but they needed their help with the case. Keith's attorney had insisted on full immunity for his client to testify, but with the circumstances and the evidence on Keith, they would not accept his terms.

Kailah turned off the water and reached over for her towel. As she dried herself off, she felt nauseated. As she vomited with her face in the toilet, Mama Anna pushed the door open to the bathroom.

"Just as I'd suspected." The EPT stick sat on the sink. "Your body's trying to tell you to slow down. Why don't you stay home and get some rest, child? You've been up there at the office all night."

"Mama, I can't stay home. There's too much to do." She rinsed out her mouth with Listerine, grabbed a hand towel, and dried her face.

"Well, come on downstairs and eat some breakfast. You're not leaving this house without eating something. You're eating for two now. I fried ham and scrambled eggs. I got a big pot of grits warming on the stove, too."

"Okay, Mama. I'll be down in a few. Let me get dressed." Kailah leaned on the wall for balance. "Kamryn still sleeping?"

"I'm on my way to wake her up right now. I just wanted to check on you first."

"I'm fine."

"Don't look like it." Mama Anna put her hands on her hips as Kailah barely made it out of the bathroom.

Kailah joined Mama Anna and Kamryn downstairs in the kitchen. Kamryn was sitting at the table eating. Almost a two-year-old, she had grown into such a beautiful little girl. Her hair was thick and long. Mama Anna kept it in two big ponytails all the time. With skin a deep rich cocoa, she resembled Kailah and was a bit of a tomboy. Mama Anna would take her granddaughter to the park everyday and watch her run around with the boys and girls.

Kailah wished she could spend more time at home with Kamryn. Keith missed his daughter even more. Last Saturday's visit to the prison was very emotional. He held onto his baby girl and just wouldn't let go while she cried when Kailah told her it was time for them to leave and go home. Kailah had to drag her out kicking and screaming. Kamryn couldn't understand why Daddy couldn't come home with them. Kailah did her best to explain that it was her daddy's new home, and he would be living there for a while. Then he would be able to come home, but not for a long, long time.

Kailah sat across from Kamryn at the table. Mama Anna placed a plate in front of her. Kailah used her butter knife to spread butter on her toast. She had to admit having her mama there was nice. Mama Anna cooked, cleaned, and took excellent care of Kamryn. What a blessing!

"Thanks, Mama. I appreciate all you do."

"I'm just glad I can help you through this anyway I can." Mama Anna continued to sing an old gospel spiritual as she washed dishes. Kamryn sang along with her grandma. "His eyes are on the sparrow…"

Kailah finished eating and reached over to kiss her daughter as she put the plate in the sink. She gave her mama a big hug. "I love you, Mama. I'll be home early today. Don't cook, because I want to take you out to dinner."

"Okay. I'll be ready." Mama Anna started to laugh. "A night out on the town with my daughter. I can't wait."

......

"How was your first day?" Davis was standing at the door when Mona pulled up. He greeted her with a kiss on the forehead.

"Great! I have a good feeling about this job." Mona's eyes danced in circles. "I can't believe I'm practicing law again."

She plopped down on the couch and unbuttoned her jacket to expose her bra. Davis licked his lips hungrily as he eyed her large breasts hanging from the black lace bra.

"You look tired." He knelt down in front of her and helped her take off her jacket. "Let me help you with that."

"Thank you, baby." She laughed as Davis pretended to be so helpful. "What are you doing?"

"What?" he kidded. "I'm just trying to help you relax."

"Yeah, right."

"Okay. It's just that damn, baby, you look so good. I can't help myself."

"Is that right?"

"Yeah, that's right." Davis kissed Mona, then stood up and closed the blinds. Next, he pulled down his pants to reveal his huge erection. He undressed Mona and began to fondle her and suck on her breasts. She wrapped her legs tightly around his waist as he thrust in and out. He breathed heavily. Just as Mona was about to reach her climax, the phone rang. They both ignored it and kept going. Mona climbed on top while Davis sat up, cupping and squeezing each cheek as she went up and down.

"Oh God, I'm 'bout to come!" Davis yelled.

"Come on, baby."

Davis pushed Mona up higher as he reached his climax. He screamed one last time as he exploded inside of her like a volcanic eruption. Mona collapsed on top of him, breathing heavily.

The answering machine picked up on the fifth ring.

MIXED MESSAGES

"Daddy, *please* pick up the phone," Keisha said in her usual whiny voice.

Still breathing hard, Davis reached over for the receiver. "Hey. No, I just ran to the phone. I'm okay. What's going on?"

Mona lay still and listened. What had happened now?

"I'll be over there in twenty minutes. Don't worry about a thing." He hung up and put his hands on his head. "I swear I could just kill that bitch! I curse the day I ever met that woman."

Mona sat up. "What is it?"

"Doris kicked Keisha out of the house. Keisha walked in on Doris having sex with Craig last night. They got into a heated confrontation and Keisha called her mother a whore. I mean, what does she expect? Craig goes to high school with Keisha. It's just embarrassing for her to go to school every day and hear the guys sharing stories about her own mother. When Keisha got home today, Doris cursed her out and told her she had to go. I could hear that bitch screaming in the background."

"This doesn't make any sense."

"I know it doesn't. Well, I have to go." He grabbed his clothes and ran down the hallway to the bedroom.

Mona grabbed her stuff off the floor and followed him. "Okay. I'll put some clean sheets on the bed in the girls' room. How long do you think she'll be staying?"

"As long as it takes. I know this isn't going to be easy." He put his hands on Mona's shoulders and searched her eyes for honesty, as if he could see inside her. "Davis, don't worry about me. I knew what I was getting into the moment I agreed to move in with you. I can handle it. Really, I can."

"I just wanna make sure."

"I'm sure. Now," Mona looked at Davis seductively, "are you going to shower with me before you leave?"

"Of course."

Chapter 24
Girls Will Be Girls

Mona picked up the phone, then hung it up quickly. That girl was always on the phone or tying up the line on the computer. Mona went down the hall to use the phone in Davis' office. She was surprised to see Keisha with her bare feet propped up on the desk using the computer online and talking on the cordless phone all while sucking on a blow pop.

"Keisha," she said with an impatient tone.

"Hold on for a minute, Carrie." She put the phone on her shoulder and tossed her head to the side, ponytail plopping into her face. "Huh?"

"I need to make a phone call, but you're tying up both lines. Do you mind getting off for a few?"

"Yeah, in a minute." She went back to talking to her friend. Mona rested her arm on the door impatiently. "Carrie, I'm gonna have to call you back. My dad's girlfriend needs to use the phone. Why don't you just IM me online."

Keisha rose and pulled up her tight blue stonewashed jeans that barely hung around her hips, exposing her pierced belly button. Over the past two years, her height managed to spread the weight and she wasn't that chubby little girl anymore. All the make-up, glittered eye shadow, and bright-colored lipstick made her appear a lot older than she actually was. Her maturity, however, hadn't caught up with her looks. Her room and the bathroom always looked like a tornado had been through it.

Time after time, Mona tried to discipline Keisha and get her to take some responsibility around the house and respect a curfew with absolutely no support from Davis. Keisha was his little girl and could do no wrong. The whole situation, along with Keisha's mother from hell, was pulling them apart.

She was beginning to regret her decision to allow Keisha to move in. But who asked her anyway? It didn't seem like her

170

opinion mattered much in this house. She felt like a guest who was just visiting.

Keisha finally handed the phone over to Mona. She rolled her eyes and sucked her teeth.

Mona went into the bedroom to make her call. Ten minutes later, Mona popped her head back into Davis' office. "I'm off now. I just had to call my parents and confirm the date of their arrival. Also, I don't appreciate you getting an attitude with me when I ask you to get off the phone. I'm the adult and you're the child."

Keisha snatched the phone out of Mona's hand. "But this is my *dad's* house." She slammed the door in Mona's face. Mona almost opened the door to give Keisha a piece of her mind but quickly decided against it. She would let Davis handle it. After all, it was his daughter and his house. Mona went back to her room to finish watching the movie on *Lifetime*.

During the next commercial break, she decided to finish off the rest of the butter pecan ice cream. As she approached the end of the hallway, Mona realized Keisha was in the kitchen talking on the phone as usual.

"He doesn't have the money to help me pay for it. Damn jerk," Keisha said.

Mona stopped dead in her tracks. She stood behind the wall separating the living room and hall and listened intently.

"I already cleaned out my savings, but I only have two hundred dollars. I still need another hundred, or it's going to be too late. The clinic says the procedure is tripled when you go past the second trimester."

Oh, shit.

* * *

Davis walked in around ten o'clock that evening. He had gone with some of his male friends to hang out at the sport's bar and catch the Magic basketball game. Mona sat on the couch waiting for him.

"Why are sitting here in the dark?" Davis asked. He tossed his keys on the table and took off his brown leather jacket. "Where's Keisha?"

"She went out with Carrie to go see a movie."

"Oh."

"I need to talk to you about something I overheard today."

Davis sat down beside Mona, placing his jacket beside him. "What is it?"

"It's Keisha."

"That doesn't surprise me. What did she do this time? I've been meaning to talk to her, but—"

"Just listen to me, please, Davis. She's pregnant and been trying to come up with the money to have an abortion." Mona tried to hold Davis' hand, but he pulled away from her.

"What? Who told you that shit, Doris? I told you she was a liar."

"You know I don't talk to Doris. I overheard Keisha on the phone with Carrie."

"Tonight?" He stood up from the couch. His face was turning redder by the second. "She's only fifteen years old! What's she going to do with a baby?"

"The only thing she plans on doing with a baby is aborting it."

"When did this happen?"

"A few weeks ago, I think, because she said she was still in her first trimester."

"I wonder who the guy is." He paced back and forth. "Did she say who it was? Who was she trying to get the money from?"

"Uh…well…that's the other thing." Mona wasn't quite sure how to break the disturbing news.

"What other thing?" He stopped pacing. "Tell me!"

"Craig," she muttered.

MIXED MESSAGES

Outraged, Davis threw the table across the room. "I'm going to kill him." Seconds later, Davis stormed out the front door. Mona ran after him and tried to grab his arm, but once again, he pulled away.

"Davis, please, baby, don't do anything crazy." She was barefoot and following Davis out in the yard. When he opened the door to the truck, Mona stood in between.

"Move out the way. Damn it!" He pushed Mona to the side and turned on the ignition.

Quickly, Mona jumped in the back seat. Davis backed out and sped off. Mona sat back and prayed in silence. She hadn't prayed so hard since the time she was raped and waiting for help to arrive and save her.

Ten minutes later, Davis pulled up in front of Doris' house. He didn't turn off the truck or close the door. He knocked on the door and Doris opened it wearing a white silk robe. Mona stood in the front yard watching.

"What the hell are you doing here?" Doris asked.

"I want to talk to you about Keisha."

"Well, I got company, so you're going to have to leave."

Davis peeped in the door and pushed it open when he saw Craig sitting there on the couch watching television. "Oh, so you went and got my daughter pregnant, you son of a bitch!" He started punching him in the face.

Doris was yelling and trying to get Davis off of him. He slung Craig off of the couch and they crashed to the floor. Mona ran in as Davis continued beating the hell out of Craig. Tori stood in the living room crying as Mona ran over to comfort her. Doris grabbed the phone threatening to call the police.

Davis was still kicking Craig in the stomach when the police car pulled up. Two officers ran in and pulled them off of each other. Twenty minutes later, Davis was being escorted out in handcuffs.

Doris lit a cigarette and screamed, "Get yo' yella' ass out of my house, too, red bitch!"

Mona walked up to the officers to try to reason with them. She explained that she was a lawyer and demanded to know what they were going to do to him. The short and stout officer tried to calm Mona down. He told her they were taking him in for assault. An ambulance had arrived and the paramedics were treating Craig. His face was bloody and his lips were swollen. All the while, Doris tried to question him whether or not the accusations made by Davis were true.

When Craig finally admitted it, she went crazy, punching him in the face. Several officers had to restrain Doris.

She was yelling, "I'm gonna kill you, muthafucker!" at the top of her lungs as she cried uncontrollably.

Tori ran and put her arms around her mother.

Mona followed the police down to the precinct. While driving, she dialed the number to Mindy's house and asked her to meet her there.

Mindy arrived at the precinct a little over an hour later. By this time, it was two o'clock in the morning and Mona was exhausted. She bent over in her seat and massaged her temples. Davis had lost his mind and with good reason. Maybe she hadn't made the right decision by telling Davis. Maybe she should have waited and handled the situation herself. While Mindy was conversing with the officers, Mona called to check on Keisha.

"Hello," Keisha answered, sounding sleepy.

"Keisha, it's me. Did anyone call?"

"Yeah, Tori called and told me what happened. When I got home tonight, I found the house unlocked. I was worried. Where's my dad?"

Mona caught a glimpse of her somber face through the glass window and looked down at the floor. "He's in jail. He'll probably be home tomorrow."

Keisha cried through the phone. "It's all my fault. How did he find out? Why is this happening?"

"Keisha, calm down. I'll be there real soon. Try to settle down. This isn't your fault. Your dad's okay. Everything's going to be all right."

Keisha was still crying.

"Do you hear me?" Mona asked.

"Uh-huh."

"Okay." Mona hung up and talked to Mindy. If Mona could post bail, then Davis would be released in the morning. Mindy told her that nothing else could be done right now, and to go home and get some rest.

"I thank you for coming down here at a moment's notice," Mona said.

"I'm just doing my job. I assume you won't be in on Monday." Mindy pushed her auburn hair out of her face.

"Probably not. Thanks for being so understanding."

"No problem." Mindy held out her arms and gave Mona a big hug. She was so tall that Mona's head was practically buried in Mindy's pointy breasts.

The next morning, Keisha woke her up around nine o'clock. "Are we going to church today?" Keisha's face was red and swollen.

Mona sat up in bed. Keisha, being so young and naïve, had the face of an angel. This guy had eased his way into both mother's bed and daughter's bed, too.

"Yes, we can still go. Give me some time to get myself ready."

"I made you breakfast." Keisha tried to force a smile.

Mona smiled back at her and placed her hand on Keisha's face, stroking her cheek. "I'll be there in a few minutes."

Keisha closed the door as she left out from Mona's bedroom. Mona had never seen that look in Davis' eyes before. It frightened her, but at the same time, she had every ounce of empathy for him. It was the same look on her dad's face when he saw her in the hospital after the rape. At that moment, she knew she was in it for the long haul. Davis was the man for her.

Mona was surprised and stunned to see so much fire in him because of his endearing love for his children. Without a doubt, Davis would do anything for his girls, even if it meant going to jail. She admired that trait in him.

Mona dressed in her powdered blue two-piece skirt suit. The skirt was tea-length with a high split in the front. While curling her hair, she remembered she hadn't called Kailah to tell her what had happened after she told Davis about Keisha's pregnancy. Kailah had been the one to convince Mona that telling Davis was the right thing to do. *I'll call her as soon as I get back from church.*

After they ate breakfast, Davis walked in the door. Keisha hugged her daddy as she sobbed uncontrollably. Davis hugged her back.

Minutes later, Mona spoke. "We were on our way to service. Are you coming?"

Davis looked up. "Yeah, sure, just let me get dressed." He grabbed Mona by the arm and escorted her to their bedroom. "I messed up bad, didn't I?" he asked, holding her hands in his.

"You sure did." Mona tried not to get upset all over again.

"I'm going to make this up to you. I promise." He squeezed her hands tightly.

"I love you, Davis. Let's get married."

Davis smirked. "Huh?"

Mona smiled. "You heard me. Let's get married."

"You want to marry a criminal thug like me?" He pointed at his chest as he raised his eyebrows.

"Yeah, I didn't know you had any thug in you. It's so damn sexy."

"Is that right?"

"Yeah, that's right."

MIXED MESSAGES

Chapter 25
Relationships

"Okay, Mama. I'll be home real soon."

"How is Mama Anna doing?" Taneisha asked when Kailah hung up the phone.

"Better than ever. I think she loves taking care of Kamryn and the house. I know she's not crazy about trying to get around in a big city like Chicago. She knows how to drive, but she gets lost easily. Thank goodness, the ladies at the church will pretty much take her anywhere she needs to go."

Taneisha batted her chinky eyes. "Well, let me know if you need me to help out in anyway. You know I'm more than willing to leave during my lunch break and take her to run some of her errands."

Kailah could barely get Taneisha back from lunch in less than two hours. There's no way she was going to send her across town to run errands for Mama.

Taneisha continued to pick at her broken index fingernail. "I need to get out of here if I'm going to make my nail appointment. You know that little Asian girl with them messed-up teeth don't like to wait on nobody."

"I know." Kailah frowned. "I wanted you to go with me tomorrow at lunchtime. Now, I have to go all by myself."

"I can't wait 'til tomorrow with this nail looking like this." She held up her long red and white nails with disgust. Taneisha was very much into wearing the same colored outfits to match her nails each week. Today, she wore a short red skirt and multi-colored silk blouse. Her long, blonde ponytail hung over the chair almost down to her butt.

Kailah waved her hand in the air. "I'm gonna let you off the hook this time."

Taneisha smirked while rocking from side to side in the chair across from Kailah's desk.

MIXED MESSAGES

"Oh, I knew there was something I wanted to tell you." Taneisha got up and shut the door to Kailah's office. She tiptoed back over and sat on top of her desk. "Now, you have to promise me you ain't going to do nothing stupid."

Kailah nodded, even though she didn't mean it.

"There's been talk around here about you. Well, not about you, as much as it is about your home situation."

Kailah crossed her legs and folded her arms. "I'm listening."

Taneisha filled her in on all of the gossip stirred up at AND. Kailah's jaw dropped. Lynn was surely behind it all. Once Kailah returned to work and assumed Lynn's old position, Lynn's jealousy surfaced. Fortunately, they rarely saw each other, since Lynn worked in marketing on the fourteenth floor. After Keith's arrest and prison sentence, it became very difficult for Kailah to face her coworkers. Lynn took great satisfaction in Kailah's personal struggles. Just when things had settled down, here she was starting up more mess.

"Don't take this information and confront that bitch. You know that's what she wants."

"I know." Kailah shut down her computer and stood up. "I'm not going to stoop to her level."

"That's right. Plus, she's only going to deny it and play dumb like she didn't say it."

Kailah nodded. "Just like before."

Taneisha pointed her finger. "Right. Besides, she's not worth it anyway. I just wanted you to know what was being said. You know me. I'm gonna let you know what's being said and exactly who said it. Knowledge is power."

"I appreciate it, Taneisha. You're the only true friend I have here in Chicago."

"I feel the same way, girl. And I've lived here my whole life." Their friendship had grown over the past four years and the bond was stronger than ever, almost like sisters.

Kailah paced a few steps behind Taneisha to the elevator, pulling out her cell phone to answer it. "Keith, why are you calling me on my cell? Is everything okay?"

Taneisha pressed the first floor button on the elevator. They both stepped out when the door opened. As they passed the front desk, the security officer said good-bye and Kailah waved back.

She and Taneisha went their separate ways, and Kailah continued her conversation. Her heels clicked as she walked through the empty parking garage.

"It's not that late," Kailah said lightly.

"It *is* late. I expect you to be home before it gets dark. Baby, you know how much I worry about you."

Kailah's smile soon faded and her voice became stiff. "I know how to take care of myself."

"It's just not about self-defense. You're carrying my unborn child, and you need your rest."

Kailah nodded and made a left turn on State Street.

"Besides, I'm not there to run you out of the office anymore." Keith chuckled.

Kailah laughed. "Keith, even when you were here, you couldn't get me to come home early. What are you talking about?"

"So what are you trying to say, huh? You trying to say that you was running things?!"

Kailah paused. She knew where this conversation was heading, just like all the others. "I'm not trying to say that, Keith. And you know it. Don't start this."

"Don't start what? No, you're the one with your high ass stuck up on your shoulders."

Kailah massaged the back of her neck. "What? You sound ridiculous and just plain ignorant."

MIXED MESSAGES

"And you sound like a bitch. Funny how your own wife starts to treat you once a nigga is on lockdown and can't do anything about the situation."

"Oh, and how would you handle the situation if you weren't in prison, Keith?"

"You know."

Kailah pulled into the garage and listened to Keith selling out. She rested her head on the steering wheel. She was so sick of this. It was bad enough having to deal with it when he was coming home drunk every night. Now she had to endure the verbal abuse while he was in prison.

He continued. "And I know you fucking someone else, too. That's why you can't get home at a decent hour."

Kailah turned up her lips. *Here he goes again.* "And how do you know that? Did your little birdie tell you that, too?"

"I know because I married a freak, that's why. Always wanting me to fuck your ass every night. You can't be sitting over there not getting any. For all I know that probably ain't even my baby."

Kailah's mouth fell open. "Let me tell you one thing, Keith. You can listen to your mother or whoever else is putting those crazy thoughts in your head, but I don't have to listen to it. Don't call me until you're ready to apologize and talk like you have some sense."

She hung up.

......

"All the charges have been dropped," Mona cheered.

"Oh, that's so good to hear. I know you were worried. I've been praying for you."

"Well, it worked."

"Prayer changes things," Kailah said. She had certainly been through enough in her life to share a testimony.

"I know. So, enough about me. Are you feeling like you're going to give birth in a few days?"

"Oh yeah, I'm so exhausted. I tell you, I've gained so much more weight with this pregnancy than I did when I was carrying Kamryn." Kailah placed her free hand on her huge belly.

"The last time I saw you, you looked much bigger. Well, you should see Keisha. That girl has blown up." She laughed. "And I thought she was lazy before. That girl won't lift a finger to do anything around this house."

Kailah laughed. "Is Davis helping any?"

"Please. I'm cleaning up behind two. I'm looking for a cleaning lady to come by at least once a week. I work hard all day, and I'm way too tired to clean up behind them."

"I know that's right. There are not enough hours in the day. I don't know what I would do if Mama wasn't here to take care of things." Kailah took another sip of hot herbal tea.

"You know how much I love Mama Anna. Make sure you tell her I said hello."

"I will. How was your visit with your mom and dad last week?" Kailah asked.

"Pure torture. All Mother did was complain and make sarcastic remarks." Mona spoke in a mocking tone that resembled her mother's. "Why are you continuing to live in sin? Shacking up with this man while his wife calls over here all the time. And that girl should be ashamed of herself. Pregnant at fifteen."

Kailah scoffed. "Like Bea has room to talk about anyone."

"That's what I said. I just endured it." Mona said emphatically.

"Did you get a chance to have a heart-to-heart?"

"No, we never even sat down long enough to carry on a decent conversation," Mona responded. "I've come to the conclusion that she doesn't want to have that type of relationship with me. I give up. It doesn't even bother me anymore. I've accepted it. Now, I have to move on with my life with Davis. He's my family now."

Kissy noises sounded in the background, indicating that Davis must have been in the room. The suck-face noises were starting to bother Kailah, especially since she no longer had Keith around. Boy, did she miss him.

"Hey, how's the wedding plans going?" Kailah asked, changing the subject.

Mona sighed. "They're not going anywhere. Hopefully, once Keisha has her baby, there'll be time to think about it."

"Don't remind me." Kailah frowned as her thoughts turned to her own marriage and the awful phone conversation from the night before. Although she knew where the hostility and insecure feelings were coming from, Keith made it more and more difficult to keep peace. Throughout their marriage, Keith had always been sensitive, caring, and devoted. After the arrest, everything changed. The life she once knew was no more. Gone with the wind.

Now she was faced with the undaunted task of keeping the family together, delivering a baby all alone, and managing to hold onto her status at AND. All the time she spent at work deeply affected her relationship with Kamryn. With Kamryn being feisty with Kailah and clinging more to Mama, it made Kailah feel inadequate as a mother. How would she handle the demands of her son's needs when she already felt like a failure? It became impossible. She continually prayed for strength and courage to handle these trying times and still maintain a positive attitude.

Many people helped. Mama was one of them, of course. Then the ladies at the church volunteered to take Mama to her doctor appointments, grocery shop, baby sit, and even cook dinners at the house. Keith had been a member and large monetary contributor of Calvary Assembly for quite some time. In her husband's absence, Kailah continued to attend the women's ministry meetings and received encouragement and advice from other church members whose spouses were incarcerated also.

Kailah thanked God for her very blessed life.

"Why do you say it like that?" Mona asked incredulously.

"More problems. He's tripping."

"Again?"

"Yes." Kailah put her brush down and looked at herself in the mirror. She was already dressed for bed in her extra large pajamas. "He's gotten worse. Last night, he accused me of sleeping around."

"He's said that before."

"Well, this time he went so far as to say that the baby probably wasn't his."

Mona gasped. "Oh, now he's lost his mind."

Kailah twirled her fingers though her hair. "Tell me about it."

"You know you don't have to put up with that."

"I know. I just feel bad for him," Kailah defended. "His life has changed so much. It's not easy for him."

"And he's not making it easy for you. Your life has changed, too. Keith has brought all of this on himself, and now you and your daughter have to suffer. It's unfortunate. I say cut your ties. He doesn't deserve you."

Kailah cocked her head back. "What do you know about being married and remaining faithful?"

Mona didn't respond.

"Right. Only what I tell you. You don't know anything about what I'm going through. I'm not going to divorce my husband, and that's that. In the future, please take this bit of advice and keep comments like that to yourself." Kailah waved her hand in the air, even though no one was looking. "I already know how you feel about relationships. As soon as a person doesn't give you what you need or you find out they're not perfect, you drop them like a bad habit." Kailah switched the cordless phone to the opposite ear.

"That's not fair," Mona blurted.

"Maybe it's not. But, it's the truth. I call it as I see it."

Mona cleared her throat. "Sounds like you have permission to speak your mind, but I have to keep my comments to myself."

"No, but once you've made your point, simply drop it. Okay?" Kailah corrected.

"Okay, I can do that. I'm sorry."

Kailah slowly sat down on her bed and leaned back on her propped up pillows. "I accept. Look, Mona, I don't mean to be so sensitive, but you—"

"You're pregnant. I can't wait until somebody has some babies around here! I get major attitude from Keisha all day, and then attitude from you."

Kailah started to laugh.

"When I get ready to have a baby, I'm going to make sure to return the favor," Mona said.

"I know you will." Kailah looked over at the clock and realized the late hour. "I better get some rest before I have to get up every hour on the hour to pee."

"Yeah, you do that. I love you, girl."

"I love you, too. Don't wait so long to call me next time either." Kailah sat up to brace herself for another kick in the stomach. The baby she was carrying must have been performing cartwheels. And like clockwork, it always happened as soon as she wanted to get some sleep. It felt like God's way of letting her know that her days of peaceful sleep were numbered.

"I won't. I promise. Call me as soon as you feel the first contraction. I don't care if it's a false alarm."

"And likewise, let me know when Keisha goes in."

"Okay."

......

Keith greeted Kailah and rubbed her stomach as she entered the visitor's room. She was holding onto Kamryn's tiny little hand. They embraced, then he picked up Kamryn and spun her around while her legs dangled in mid-air.

"I missed you. Give your daddy a big one."

Kamryn gave her daddy a big, wet kiss on the cheek. Keith's eyes lit up as he savored it.

"I didn't think you would come today." He sat down at the long rectangular table shared by another visiting family.

"I almost didn't," Kailah snapped. She sat down across from her husband with Kamryn on her lap. "However, I knew you would be full of apologies, and I wanted to get them in person."

Keith chuckled. "Well, I am. I'm so sorry, baby." He rested his hand on her leg. "It's just that sometimes these wild thoughts start running through my head, and when I call and you're not at home, I just—"

Kailah threw her hand up in the air. "I know. I understand, but I can't continue on like this. *We* can't continue on like this. It has to stop." Kailah stared into his deep brown eyes and sucked in a deep breath. "I advise you seek counseling while you're here, like I am. Make the most out of your situation. Pastor Jenkins told me that he's willing to drive up here on Sunday afternoons and pray with you. I think you should take advantage of it."

"Yeah, I should." He watched his three-year-old drawing and coloring a picture of a butterfly. "What's this?"

"A picture." She held it up for him to see.

"I love it, Pumpkin."

"When you coming home?" Kamryn pulled on her ponytail.

MIXED MESSAGES

Keith smiled. Tears welled up in his brown eyes. "Not for a long, long time. But, I promise to call you every night just like I always do. Is that okay?"

"Okay"

Kailah and Keith laughed.

Chapter 26
Labor and Delivery

Mona paced back and forth while Davis stared blankly out the window. Thirteen hours had passed. Tori sat in a chair next to Keisha's hospital bed, listening to Destiny's Child on her Walkman. Her head had been bopping back and forth nonstop.

Doris burst back in the room dressed in a short red dress with fishnet stockings, resembling a stripper getting ready to perform a raunchy strip tease. She sat on the other side of the bed and held Keisha's hand. Keisha felt much better now that she'd been given an epidural. She sat up in bed while Tori fed her small ice chips.

Mona was at work when Keisha called to tell her she was in labor. Tori, who had been staying at the house since Keisha was eight months, drove her to the emergency room. By the time Mona arrived, Davis and Doris were engaged in an argument in the hall outside of Keisha's room. Mona didn't even want to know what the drama was all about. She walked right past them and entered to find Keisha screaming in horror. Keisha managed to force a smile and asked Mona to coach her through the breathing. Thirty minutes later, Davis came back in the room without Doris.

They sat in complete silence for over an hour.

The nurse entered the room to see if Keisha's labor had progressed. "It looks like you're complete and ready to start pushing," the nurse said, smiling at Keisha.

Keisha clinched the sheet with her nails. "Push?"

Doris smirked. "If you can spread your legs like a woman, then you need to take the pain like you're a woman."

"Doris, what the hell are you talking about?" Davis asked with a tight-lipped grimace. "Like you know the first thing about being a woman."

"Muthafucker, don't start no more shit in here." Doris walked up and pointed her finger in his face.

Davis pushed her hand away. "I know you better get out of my face."

Keisha started to cry. Tori brushed her hand across Keisha's cheek.

"If you two can't lower your voices and stop shouting, I'm going to have to ask you to leave," the nurse interjected.

"Why don't you guys just shut up!" Tori screamed. "I'm sick of you guys always arguing. I thought that shit was supposed to end once you two got divorced." Tori put both hands to her head. "Don't you see this is how my little sister got in this situation in the first place? God!" Tori stormed out of the room. Davis glared at Doris, then ran after Tori.

Doris stood with her mouth wide open. She turned in Mona's direction. "What you looking at, bitch? This shit is all your fault anyway. If you hadn't come in the picture, Davis and I would still be together."

Mona knew that couldn't be any further from the truth. Davis had told her how Doris made his life a living hell from the first day of their marriage. Doris was always accusing him of sleeping with other women, embarrassing him in front of his friends, and kicking him out of the bedroom every time she got pissed about something he had absolutely nothing to do with. Needless to say, they only had sex when she was in the mood, and that wasn't very often. Not to mention it wasn't that good to begin with.

Mona traipsed over to Doris and stared directly in her face. This time, the nurse looked on.

"I don't appreciate you calling me a bitch every time it suits you." Mona took a step closer into Doris' clown-painted face, towering at least two inches taller than she. Doris backed off scared that in any second Mona was going to drag her ass all over the floor.

"Secondly," Mona cocked her head and jabbed the air with her finger, "you know damn well your divorce was final two years before I met Davis." She curled her finger. "You need to just get it through your sick head that Davis doesn't want you anymore. Never did. Never will—"

"I just—"

"I'm talking. You listen. I suggest you keep your comments to yourself, show some self-respect, and pay attention to your daughter. She needs you right now."

"Mama, please, stop this," Keisha pleaded. "I need you."

Mona stepped back while Doris straightened up her clothes and her platinum-blonde wig.

Mona left to find Davis in the hall by the elevator trying to console Tori. He held his finger up to her chin, forcing her to look at him while he talked. Mona waited for the conversation to end. A few minutes later, Tori gave her dad a hug and went back into the room.

"Hey," Mona said.

"Hey."

"Look, I don't think I should be here. I'm going home."

Davis grabbed her hand. "You don't have to—"

"Yes, I do. I do, however, want you to call me when the baby is born."

"Fine, I'll call." Davis frowned while he ran his hand through his wavy, curly hair as he watched the elevator door shut.

Later on that night, Mona awoke from her sleep and answered the phone on the third ring.

"Hey, honey. I wanted to let you know Brianne Denise Simpson was born less than fifteen minutes ago."

"Oh." Mona could hear Davis sniffling. She knew he must have cried during the delivery. "How's Keisha?"

"Exhausted. Emotional. We all are."

"I'm sure," she said. "When will you be home?"

"First thing in the morning," Davis responded. "I'm going to sleep here."

"Okay. Tell Keisha I'll be there when I get off from work tomorrow."

"I'll tell her. Oh…and…Mona?"

"Yes, Davis." She placed her hand on her warm forehead.

"I'm really sorry for acting like such an ass."

Mona sighed. "Your apologies belong to your daughters, not me."

"Done already. I owe you one, too. You've been so supportive through all of this." He breathed heavily into the receiver. "I know it's been hard, and you haven't complained one bit about it. I want you to know how much I appreciate you."

Mona closed her eyes for a moment to savor the words. She needed to hear that. Leaving the hospital, she thought about ending the relationship for good. All of this craziness wasn't worth it. Davis wasn't her husband. Not yet anyway. And Keisha wasn't her daughter. Why would anyone want to walk into a messed-up situation like this one? Never in a million years had she thought she would.

Her thoughts went back to her phone conversation with Kailah. She replayed it over and over in her head: *"As soon as a person doesn't give you what you need or you find out they're not perfect, you drop them like a bad habit."*

Kailah was right. Sometimes, she felt like Kailah knew her better than she knew herself.

Muster up the strength. You can do this. You love this man. He means everything to you.

......

Kailah continued to rock back and forth in the rocking chair, nursing her newborn son. Hunter Blake Terrence had been delivered by Cesarean section just one week ago, weighing eight pounds two ounces. Now at 3 a.m., she hadn't slept a wink. Hunter had kept her up all night with his crying and constant every hour-on-the-hour irregular feedings.

Finally, he closed his eyes and puckered his little lips. Afraid to move and wake him, Kailah continued to rock in the chair. She dozed off to sleep with her son in her arms.

Around six o'clock, Mama Anna tapped Kailah on the shoulder. "Let me put Hunter down in the crib. You go get yourself some rest in your own bed."

"Okay, Mama." Kailah ran her fingers through her kinky, wild hair. She couldn't remember the last time she combed it. Slowly, Kailah dragged herself down the hall to her bedroom and climbed into bed. Just as she was nodding off, the phone rang.

"Yeah," Kailah said barely above a whisper.

"Yeah?" Mona asked. "Guess you've been up all night again."

"Uh-huh." Kailah snuggled under the covers.

"Keisha gave birth last night to Brianne Denise Simpson."

"Well, congratulations. What do I call you now? Step-grandmother?"

"Ha! Ha! Funny."

"I thought you would like that one," Kailah said.

"Well, I won't keep you. I just wanted to tell you the good news. Call me back later."

"Sure thing. Bye."

......

"How long do you plan on giving me the silent treatment?" Davis asked.

"Who said I was doing that?"

192

MIXED MESSAGES

"You haven't said more than three words since I picked you up at your office."

"Not true."

Davis pushed the shopping cart in Wal-Mart while Mona stuffed a car seat in an already fully loaded cart. They were picking up a few more items before they drove over to the hospital to pick up Keisha and the baby.

"And besides, this is neither the time nor the place to discuss what happened yesterday at the hospital."

"Fine." Davis groaned and crossed him arms.

In line at the register, Mona watched the lady in front of them trying to control her infant son while her daughter, a small toddler, cried uncontrollably.

Is this what I have to look forward to?

After they loaded up the bags in the back of the SUV, Davis said, "We need to talk about this."

Mona took in a deep breath and exhaled slowly. "I'm getting a little tired of the fighting between you and Doris. Tori was absolutely right. You two act like children when you're together in the same room. I think it's time for you to agree to disagree and let it go."

Davis hugged the steering wheel. "How can you say that I'm acting like a child? You know all of the terrible things that Doris has done to me."

"Oh really?" Mona twisted her lips. "Well, you're no victim. You've done some pretty rotten things, too. Sleeping with her and lying to her. Don't get me started."

"Okay. But—"

"But nothing, Davis. I'm not asking you to do this. I'm telling you, or—"

"Or what? Are you going to leave me?" Davis hung his head down low.

Mona almost burst into tears at Davis' vulnerability. It almost broke her heart. She reached over and softly brushed her hand along his cheek.

"Or...you're going to lose your daughters. I'm not going anywhere."

He turned and smiled. "You mean that?"

"Yes. I'm in this for the long haul. I love you. You're the man for me."

Davis pulled Mona close to him, kissed her, and ran his fingers through her silky auburn-red hair.

"Now that this baby madness is over, we can move forward with our wedding plans. Make things official," Davis said.

Chapter 27
An Offer You Can't Refuse

Mona entered her home with a stack of bills in hand. She opened and studied each one carefully. Massaging her temples, she reflected on a long day in the mediation session of Palmer vs. Palmer divorce case. Her client, Mrs. Palmer, was becoming more demanding. After such a challenging day, Mona needed a bubble bath to calm her nerves before dinner with Davis. He had promised Mona dinner at her favorite restaurant, and she had been looking forward to it since Sunday. She planned to work on the case at home this weekend. No way would she show up unprepared like she had done earlier that day. It was a wonder the partners didn't fire her on the spot. Mona rested her head on her folded arms on the counter and exhaled.

Mona's head popped up as loud screams emitted from Keisha's room. She burst in to discover Brianne standing up in the crib, screaming at the top of her lungs, while Keisha slept in her canopy bed. Mona picked up the baby and tried waking Keisha.

"Keisha, Keisha." Mona tapped on her shoulder. "I know you hear this baby in here crying." She shoved Keisha once more harder.

Keisha rolled over rubbing her eyes. "What?"

"Get your behind up and take care of this baby." Mona placed Brianne on Keisha's chest. "I can't believe you've been sleeping while this baby was crying like that. And when was the last time you changed her diaper?"

Keisha turned up her nose. "I changed her already. She must have diarrhea or something. I'm getting tired of changing her."

Mona put her hands on her hips. "Well, I'm getting tired of having to tell you that you need to change this baby more than once a day. This is ridiculous. I mean, what have you been doing all day?" Mona picked up dirty clothes off the floor and tossed them in the laundry basket. "You're supposed to straighten up around here while we're at work all day. That sink is full of dishes and dirty baby bottles."

"I'm going to clean up as soon as I get some sleep around here. This baby kept me up crying all day. Shoot."

"She's teething, Keisha. What do you expect?"

Keisha carried her daughter over to the changing table. She sighed. "All out of diapers."

Mona swung around, tossing her hair off her shoulders. "Excuse me?"

Keisha rolled her eyes and cocked her head back. "I said, ain't no more diapers."

Mona took in a deep breath and exhaled slowly. "You mean to tell me that we bought you a car for transportation, and you couldn't get up off your lazy behind to go to the store and buy some pampers."

"I would've bought some diapers, but I don't have any gas in my car. Besides, all my money is gone," Keisha muttered barely above a whisper.

Mona came closer and held her hand to her ear. "Come again. I didn't hear you very clearly." She trembled with rage.

"I'm broke!" Keisha yelled, throwing her hands up in the air. Brianne started crying again while she lay on the changing table with her bare bottom showing. "I don't have anymore money. It's gone, okay? Are you happy?"

Davis entered. "What the hell is that smell?" He pinched his nose.

"Your granddaughter. That's what smells. Apparently, Keisha ran out of money and couldn't buy diapers, clean up this house, or even her room for that matter." Mona folded her arms and kicked her leg forward.

"Is this true, Keisha?" Davis looked puzzled.

Keisha nodded. "Yes, but I…"

MIXED MESSAGES

"You were what? I can't believe you spent the four hundred dollars I gave you Friday!" Davis paced in the room. "I don't understand this. This is so irresponsible. I mean, what do you expect? Do you expect Mona to take care of your baby and me to take care of your finances? This is going to change. And it's going to change right now!" He threw up his hands and stormed out.

Mona followed behind him. "Davis, where are you going?"

He sighed. "To get diapers."

Half an hour later, Davis came back home with a case of Huggies Supreme and Similac formula. Mona lay asleep on the couch while Brianne sat in the playpen shaking her rattle and giggling.

"Thank you, Daddy," Keisha said as she grabbed a diaper out of the pack. She removed the shirt that covered Brianne's bottom and changed her. "I promise next time…"

"There isn't going to be a next time, Keisha." Davis raised his eyebrows.

He tapped Mona on the shoulder.

Mona opened her eyes slowly and sat straight up.

"Let's go," he said.

"Go where?"

"I promised you dinner. We can still make it in time if we leave right now."

"Good, 'cause I'm hungry." Keisha rubbed her belly.

"Then I suggest you cook a meal," Davis snapped back.

* * *

An hour later, Mona and Davis were sitting on a wooden bench in the front entrance of Leverock's Seafood Restaurant, waiting for a seat. Dim lights cascaded over the ceiling in the room with stone-like flooring. Crowded with couples, both young and old showed the popularity of the restaurant. Mona absolutely loved the food and the nice intimate dining with the huge open view of the Gulf of Mexico.

Mona sat quietly as Davis stroked his fingers through her auburn-red curly hair. What a stressful day she'd had. She patiently sat through a longer-than-expected mediation session, representing a bitter spouse wanting to take her husband "to the cleaners." The hostess came out and led them to the small round table in the center of the dining area.

"Thank you, Davis." Mona smiled as Davis pulled out her chair.

They placed their dinner and drink orders, and then Mona started talking about her awful day at work. She also brought up her frustration with Keisha. The last thing she needed was to come home and deal with more drama from Keisha. It seemed like the situation had worsened and she didn't see how it could get any better. Drastic changes would have to be made where Keisha was concerned.

"Well, what are we going to do?"

Mona twiddled her thumbs. "I don't know. What do you want to do?"

"I was hoping you could tell me. I mean, you're always getting on my case about Keisha. I'm a little surprised you don't have an answer." Davis chuckled.

"Well, that's just it. We wouldn't have this problem if you would have dealt with these issues back then."

Davis cleared his throat. "Are you saying this is somehow my fault?" He buttered a biscuit and took a bite.

"Davis, I'm not saying that at all. You're a wonderful, supportive father. I just think you tend to be naïve when it comes to Keisha. No matter how much I try to bring Keisha's behavior to your attention, you choose not to do anything about it." Mona took a sip of iced-tea with lemon.

The waitress placed their plates in front of them and left.

MIXED MESSAGES

"I really don't think you're being reasonable about this. Keisha has only lived with us—"

"For almost two years. You can't continue to blame Keisha's behavior on her mother. Davis, I give you credit for stepping up to the plate and providing structure and a stable environment in Keisha's life." She continued. "However, you have failed to establish set rules in your own house. Keisha has been allowed to come and go as she pleases. I don't know how you thought she would somehow be responsible once she had a baby. Discipline is taught, then learned." She ate a forkful of shrimp and pasta.

Davis shuffled in his seat. "Okay."

"Okay?" Mona said as her voice went up an octave. "Is that all you have to say?"

Davis slammed his fist on the table. As he looked around at the patrons whose attention he had drawn, he whispered through clenched teeth, "You're right. I'm not perfect. There I said it." He wiped his face with his napkin. "Now, what do you suggest we do to fix the problem?" he asked, his voice returning to normal.

"Davis, I'm not saying this to hurt you or make you upset."

"Then what do you call it? Huh? I'm really getting sick of your snotty attitude."

Mona gasped, placing her hand on her forehead. "Oh, I can see where this is headed. This conversation is over. Let's just finish our dinner and get out of here."

How is it that she managed to cause an argument with everyone she loved today? Mona had to stop, rewind, and play back the events that had taken place earlier that day. Bottom line, she was wrong. Patience is a virtue. After some consideration, she figured she could have handled the situation with Keisha and Davis better than what she had. If only she hadn't had the worst day of her life at work, then she wouldn't have lost her cool at home.

* * *

Mona parked her Lexus in the driveway. As she turned off the ignition, she looked at Davis. "I think I owe you an apology. I needed to vent, but not take out my frustrations on you."

Davis reached for Mona's hand and squeezed it tightly. "Don't worry about it. I just wish you would've taken one second to ask me how my day went."

Mona slowly shook her head back and forth. "I never realized...that I was being so inconsiderate of your feelings, baby." She extended her arm and rubbed his wavy hair. "I'm sorry."

"I'm sorry, too. I don't think you have a snotty attitude." Davis smiled.

Mona raised her thin eyebrows. "Yes, you do."

"Well, I love you no matter what. I want you in my life forever." Davis reached in his pocket and handed Mona a small, red velvet box.

Mona slapped him on the head. "I can't believe you." She laughed as she opened the box to reveal a two-karat diamond platinum ring. "Aaahh, Davis, it's beautiful."

Davis slid the ring on Mona's finger. "This evening didn't go as planned, just like our life. What I do know is that I want to plan my life with you."

Mona kissed Davis. "Me, too."

......

Kailah stood in front of the boardroom reviewing her proposal in great detail. An hour had passed as she attempted for the final time to get Okoyo Enterprises to go along with her latest revised contract she was sure would make both parties quite pleased. This multi-million dollar deal guaranteed another promotion for Kailah, maybe even partnership.

MIXED MESSAGES

Confidently poised and careful not to stumble over one word, Kailah made eye contact with all in attendance and answered each question with research and data as support. She delivered a flawless PowerPoint presentation, thanks to Taneisha's hard work of staying three hours late to add the finishing touches. At home, Kailah stayed up all night in her study reviewing every last detail and making last-minute changes as needed. No time for sleep. Once this meeting ended, Kailah planned to drive straight home and hit the hay. With Kailah fueled on pure adrenaline and wrapped up in her presentation, it felt like Finals Week at UF.

"You delivered a nice presentation, Kailah," a voice from behind spoke.

Kailah turned around and noticed a tall, caramel-colored brother standing behind her dressed in a mint-green suit. His soft dreadlocks were pulled back in a ponytail

"Allow me to introduce myself. I'm Corey Sanders. I'm heading up the marketing department on the fourteenth floor." He held out his hand.

"Right." Kailah shook his hand. Her eyes were fixed on his hazel green eyes. The only other person she knew with beautiful eyes like those was Mona. She cleared her throat. "Where are you from…uh…what did you say your name was again?"

"It's Corey." He ran his fingers across his goatee as he flashed a toothy smile.

"Oh yes. Of course." Kailah felt a nervous twisting in her stomach. "Nice meeting you."

"Same here." Corey waved, then left.

She waited until everyone cleared the boardroom, before packing up.

Taneisha peeked in. "Hey, Boss Lady. You need some help?"

"Do you have to ask? Get in here." Kailah waved her hand.

"I saw Mr. Calbretti beaming from ear to ear with those Japanese men. So, how did it go?"

Kailah straightened her navy suit jacket. "We did it!" She tossed her arms straight up.

Taneisha wrapped her arms around Kailah. "I knew you would win them over today. You're gonna make partner. I just know it."

"Thank you for all of your hard work. I couldn't have done it without you. You're the best, girl." Kailah closed her eyes to hold back the tears.

Kailah discussed the details of the meeting as they finished clearing the room. With a box full of handbooks in tow, Mr. Calbretti stepped out of his office as Kailah passed. "Kailah, can I see you for a moment," he said as he summoned with his hand.

"Sure." Kailah handed the box to Gladys, straightened her jacket, and entered.

Mr. Calbretti sat down and buzzed Gladys. "Please send for Bill."

A few minutes later, Mr. Gleichman entered and shook hands with Kailah. "You did an excellent job in there today, Kailah. You looked like a real pro. I'm awful proud of ya."

"Thank you." Kailah smiled and slid back in her seat, crossing her legs.

Mr. Calbretti cleared his throat. "We're not going to keep you. I wanted to run a few things by you and get some feedback."

Kailah nodded. "Okay."

"We, at AND, are most impressed with your solid performance here. Your record is impeccable," Mr. Calbretti said emphatically. He leaned forward and handed her a black folder. "Go ahead. Take a look at that."

Kailah opened it and quickly scanned through the folder.

"We're very pleased to offer you an opportunity we know you can't refuse."

MIXED MESSAGES

"This states that AND's new offices will open in the DC area and will be overseen by…" Kailah caught her breath.

"By you, Kailah. You will head up our new consulting offices as Vice President," Mr. Gleichman added.

Kailah put her hands over her mouth. As she felt pure excitement about the new offer, her thoughts drifted to Keith. How could she accept a new position halfway around the country while her husband remained in prison? This was her chance to climb the ladder of success that she single-handedly created with blood, sweat, and tears, and now she couldn't possibly take it. *Damn him.* Her thoughts rapidly raced as she listened to Mr. Calbretti provide the specifics. She would have to put her house on the market, and convince Mama into moving with her. Of course, the kids would be closer to their grandparents, Juanita and Blake, who lived in Virginia. However, that might be too close for comfort. Sure, she and Juanita were civil towards one another, but now they would have to be more than that.

As Kailah struggled to carry the heavy box back to her office, she tried to figure out how to turn her dream offer down. Asking for forty-eight hours to think it over, in her heart she knew that it wouldn't be right to put her own selfish needs before her family's.

"I thought you would be gone by now." Taneisha met Kailah at her desk. "I just came back from lunch."

Kailah glanced at her watch. "Taneisha, it's two o'clock."

"Yeah, and?" Taneisha squinted.

"You left at noon."

Taneisha laughed. "Girl, you're going to find this so funny." She playfully nudged Kailah. "See, I was on my way out, and then I stopped by Jill's desk and we just got to talking. Then she decided to hang out with me, and then when we got to the restaurant there was this long line and we—"

"Forget it." Kailah folded her arms. "You're going to have to do better than this. These two and three-hour lunch breaks have to end, Taneisha. I mean it." She looked down at her feet to avoid eye contact.

Taneisha sucked her teeth. "What's your problem? You've never said anything about it before."

"I'm saying it now."

"Hold up, Kailah." Taneisha held up her hand. "I stayed here until ten o'clock last night helping you with your little presentation. Now that ought to count for something." She put her hands on her slender hips.

Kailah's eyes swept the room. "We need to discuss this in my office." Taneisha followed and closed the door.

"Taneisha, you need to stop taking long breaks without my permission." Kailah slid back in her leather chair. "Getting paid overtime more than compensates for the extra hours you've put in this week. Don't get me wrong. I appreciate everything you do around here. We just need to make sure no one is taking advantage of the other here."

"I agree," Taneisha said. "But, something else has you in a funky mood. Now, what is it?"

Kailah suppressed a grin. "You think you know me so well."

Taneisha crossed her legs as she sat back in her seat. "That's because I do. Come on, spill the beans, Kailah."

"All right." Kailah took a sip from her water bottle. "You know Calbretti called me into his office."

"Right. He offered you a promotion, didn't he?" Taneisha stood.

"How did you know?"

Taneisha ran over and jumped on Kailah. Her little petite legs were dangling wildly mid-air. "I just knew it. Congratulations!" She leaned on Kailah's desk. "So, give me the juicy details. Oh, and I'm going to get another raise, right?"

"Not unless you want to move to DC," Kailah replied.

Taneisha raised her eyebrows and squinted. "Come again?"

"AND is opening up new offices in DC, and they're offering me a VP position to relocate and head it up." Kailah shrugged.

"Oh my God, Kailah, you must be so excited. This is exactly what you wanted."

Kailah nodded. "It is, but it's too bad I can't take it." She rested her chin on her hand.

Taneisha leaned forward in her chair. "What! And why the hell not? I don't understand."

Kailah tossed her head, flinging her long hair off her shoulders. "I can't leave Keith."

"Who said anything about leaving Keith?" Taneisha asked. "He's locked up."

"I know that." Kailah shifted her eyes. "If I took on such a huge responsibility as VP, then I wouldn't have time to visit every weekend. Not to mention the distance." She took another sip of water.

"Before you say no, I think you should talk to Keith about it. I really don't think he would want you to put your career on hold. I know he wouldn't."

Kailah put her head on her desk. "Why does life have to be so hard?"

Taneisha rubbed Kailah's head. "It's not. You're making it difficult. You know what you want to do. Talk to Keith. He's your biggest supporter."

Kailah nodded. "True."

"When do you have to make a decision?" Taneisha asked.

"Monday. I have the weekend to think about it." Kailah planned to see Keith tomorrow. They were getting along so well, she didn't want to say or do something to ruin it.

After their long talk, Kailah decided to head home early and gave Taneisha the rest of the day off as soon as she returned a few calls. As she was singing to "Rapture" by Anita Baker, she made a sharp turn onto Jackson Street, remembering she promised to bring home dinner from Army & Lou's soul food restaurant. Many deals and contracts were negotiated and signed at the upscale restaurant with the best fried chicken and ribs on the south side of the Loop.

Kailah pressed the speed dial button on her cell phone and quickly placed an order for ribs, chicken, greens, and baked beans. Since it was only four o'clock, it would be hot and ready by the time she arrived. She found a parking space a few stores down on Roosevelt Street. Just as she hoped, the take-out order was on the counter when she got inside.

As soon as she walked in the house with mail in one hand and dinner from Army & Lou's in the other, Kamryn came charging towards her, nearly knocking her down.

"Mommy, Mommy, I'm so glad you're home." Kamryn grabbed Kailah's knees.

Kailah placed the items on the counter and stroked her daughter's hair. "I'm glad to be home." She knelt down to gaze in Kamryn's beautiful dark brown eyes. "Did you have fun today?"

Kamryn nodded. "Uuuh-huh. Nana took us to the park."

"Really?" Kailah smiled. "Anything else special happen today?"

"Yep. Then we got ice cream, but I didn't eat all mine, so Nana put it in the 'frigerator for me to eat after dinner, and Hunter got it all over his clothes, and then Nana had to clean—

"Kamryn, are you going to let your mama have a seat first before you tell her everything?" Mama Anna interrupted with her hands on her hips, standing in the space between the family room and kitchen.

Kamryn put her hands to her mouth and giggled.

MIXED MESSAGES

"Now, you're going to miss the rest of Barney if you don't get in here," Mama Anna said.

"Go ahead, Kamryn. I'll be there in a minute."

"Okay." Kamryn kissed her mother's hand and took off running back into the family room.

Kailah sat on the stool and thumbed through the stack of credit card bills while Mama Anna poured two glasses of grape Kool-Aid.

Kailah took a sip. "Thanks, Mama." She massaged her temples as she thought about her most recent dilemma.

"Well, are you going to tell me about it, or do I have to guess?" Mama Anna asked as her lips curled slowly into a smile.

"No, you don't, Mama." Kailah sat straight up and squeezed her fingers around the glass. "AND offered me a promotion to be Vice President today."

Mama Anna's eyes widened, revealing her crow's feet. "Praise the Lord." She raised both hands up. "Kailah, this is such good news. Why are you just sitting there like you ain't grateful?"

"I'm grateful, Mama. I didn't tell you everything." Kailah took another sip of Kool-Aid.

"What else is there?"

"I would have to move to Washington, DC. That's where they're setting up the new offices."

Mama Anna nodded, then paused for a moment.

"I see. So, what did you tell them, Kailah?"

"I asked them to give me forty-eight hours to think it over." Kailah cleared her throat. "I don't know what to do. I mean I want to take it. It's what I've worked so hard for. I'm not sure if I want to move, though, and what about Keith? I don't think this is the right time."

"Opportunities never present themselves at what we feel is the right time. As far as what direction to take, I think you should discuss it with Keith tomorrow. Tonight, you need to seek the Lord for his guidance and counsel. He will direct you on the right path." Mama Anna took both of Kailah's hands in hers. "Remember, not your will, but His will be done."

Kailah shook her head while a single tear rolled down her cheek. "You're right, Mama."

"Mommy, you gonna miss the best part!" Kamryn yelled from the other room.

Kailah and Mama Anna burst into laughter.

"If that little girl isn't just like her mother," Mama Anna said.

"I know." Kailah wiped her face, exhaled slowly, and entered the family room where her daughter was seated on the floor, surrounded by dolls, in front of the big screen television. Hunter was napping on his stomach in the playpen.

After the show ended, they ate several helpings of dinner. That night, Kailah found some scriptures from Psalms in the Bible to read and pray over. One in particular was Psalms 46:1: "God is our refuge and strength, a very present help in trouble."

After praying, she felt at peace. The next morning, she would talk to Keith and reach a decision.

Chapter 28
A Change Is Gonna Come

On the way to visit her husband in prison, Kailah ran different scenarios through her head of how to discuss the possible promotion. Taking the kids while she talked about important decisions would cause too much of a distraction, so she left them at home with Mama Anna.

For a while, Kailah had a tough time getting Kamryn to calm down and follow rules. Kailah realized her daughter's behavior was a matter of "acting out" her frustration with not having her father around. It didn't help that her mother worked long hours as well. Mama Anna pleaded with her to come home at a decent hour and spend quality time with Kamryn. Kailah thought her daughter needed a good spanking, but begrudgingly followed her mother's advice. Immediately, Kamryn's behavior improved, and she now agreed to wear dresses and carry matching purses to church on Sundays.

Guilty of spending way too much money, Kailah enjoyed working a half-day earlier that week to take her daughter along on a shopping trip to the Woodfield Mall. Now learning to walk on his own, Hunter was a handful. Kailah's weight remained at one hundred-thirty having to chase Hunter around all day.

If Kailah made the move to DC, she would have to find a nanny to take care of her children. Mama Anna told her last night she would be moving back home next year. She missed her husband, church, house, and other grandchildren. Although deeply hurt by the news, Kailah understood, surprised her mother stayed as long as she had to help out. All of her career success could be credited to Mama. She would surely miss her presence.

Sitting in the crowded room of families there to see the inmates with gray tables and uncomfortable chairs made it difficult for Kailah to relax. Her stomach felt airy and jumpy, refusing to settle down. The door to the right opened and Keith appeared wearing a tan prison uniform with his hair freshly braided back. The wide tooth smile let Kailah know he was delighted to see her, despite the fact that Kamryn and Hunter weren't there.

The couple embraced for what seemed like an eternity before Keith finally let go to run his rugged fingers through Kailah's jet-black long hair.

"I miss the smell of your beautiful hair." Keith inhaled once more and took a seat next to his wife.

Kailah smiled coyly. "Is that all you miss?" she asked, placing her hands on her hips.

"Of course not." Keith gently grabbed her hand and pulled her down. Kailah slid closer as he rubbed her back. As an officer walked by, Keith removed his hand and placed it by his side.

Kailah sucked her teeth and rolled her eyes. "I guess we're not supposed to get close, huh?"

Keith waved his hand in the air. "Kailah, why you tripping? You know the rules in this place."

"I know. I know." Kailah scratched her head. "It just gets to me sometime. Sorry."

"Well, we may not have to deal with it much longer," Keith responded.

"What do you mean?" Kailah's voice went up an octave as she sat up straighter in her chair.

Keith looked around as if he was about to reveal plans to destroy the world. He lowered his voice as he spoke. "Maurice says my parole hearing will be coming up in February. He seems to think I have a good shot."

Kailah covered her mouth with both hands.

"I know. You're speechless, right?" Keith asked.

MIXED MESSAGES

Kailah took a deep breath. "Keith, this is the best news. I mean…you actually might be coming home in eight months…and then you can be—"

"Wait…wait…wait. Kailah slow down." Keith caressed her hands. "Don't get excited yet. I mean, this is just my first parole hearing. Most of the time, the first one is denied. This is a long shot, but I believe it's going to work out in my favor."

"Keith, I believe God is going to work it out in your favor," Kailah said.

Keith nodded. "There's something else. Now don't get mad, but…"

"But what?" Her voice suddenly became stiff.

Keith squeezed Kailah's hand as she prepared to hear bad news. "I already told my dad about the parole hearing, and he has offered me a job at J & B Industrials."

Kailah crossed her arms and leaned back. "How do you feel about that? I mean, working for your dad's company and all."

Keith chuckled and shook his head. "It's wild, Kailah. I spent my entire adult life trying to escape working for my father, trying to pave my own way in the world. And look where that got me. In prison locked up." Keith made a tight fist. "I'm tired of running. I need to concentrate on getting the hell out of here and take care of my responsibilities. If that means picking up the family and moving to Virginia, then Kailah, I really need you to support me on this."

Move. She almost forgot. Kailah grabbed his hand. "Keith, I can't believe this! Oh my God! I was so excited to hear your news that I almost forgot to tell you my good news."

Keith squinted. "Go ahead. Tell me."

"Keith, you're not going to believe this. This was the reason why I came to see you without the kids." Kailah patted Keith on his shoulder. "AND offered me a promotion as the new VP, but it's in DC. So, if I want the position, I have to move next year. And here I was thinking that you were going to say no. Now you're telling me that it's all right." Kailah delivered a wet kiss on Keith's sexy lips. In an instant, they were passionately tonguing one another down. The guard walked over and tapped Keith on the shoulder.

"All right, man." Keith raised his hand and wiped the juices from his mouth with his free hand. "Just chill. This is my wife here."

"I don't care who it is. If I have to come over here again, I'm sending you back to the hole."

"You won't have to." Keith cleared his throat as his eyes lingered on Kailah. "So, if I heard you correctly, you just said that AND is offering you a promotion if you move to DC?"

"Yes. Keith, don't you see? This is God. We're going to be together. Just wait and see."

"It certainly seems like it. More surprising things have happened," Keith said while he tapped his fingers on the table.

"True. Okay, I'll be praying even though I know what the outcome is. I'm claiming this in the name of Jesus Christ." Kailah held her hands up.

Keith playfully poked her in the side. "Not to change the subject, but why didn't you bring my babies with you? You know how much I miss seeing them."

"I know. I'm sorry. I really wanted to talk this over with very little distractions. Believe me, Kamryn was hot with me this morning." Kailah scratched her head. "I promise to bring them next week."

"Okay."

They talked over the details of Kailah's promotion until the end of the visit. The feelings of sadness resurfaced as Keith left the room. Every step out of the correctional facility weighed as heavy as a ton. Like always, Kailah cried on the way home. But this time was not tears of pain. Instead, the tears were praise for serving such an awesome God. Miraculously, He was putting her family back together.

Two hours later, Kailah drove into the garage of her home. Mama Anna poked her head out the door and waved. She had called her mom as soon as she turned on Roselle to let her know she was almost home. That's when Mama Anna told her she wanted to take the kids to the park for a picnic. Kailah went inside and grabbed the cooler and basket by the door to place in the trunk of Keith's Lincoln Navigator.

Kailah shuttered nervously at the thought of driving her husband's SUV. She barely drove it because it always made her realize how much she missed him. Mama Anna came out holding Kamryn and Hunter's hands. Breaking free, Hunter quickly ran towards the driveway.

Kailah reached down, scooping him up. "Where do you think you're going?" she asked as she tickled him in the stomach. Hunter cracked up laughing. Kamryn ran over and grabbed Kailah by the leg. "Mommy, Mommy, tickle me, too!" Kailah growled like a monster and tickled both of them as their laughs grew louder and louder.

Arriving at the park, Kamryn took off for the kiddies' playground. Kailah walked Hunter over while carrying the cooler, and Mama Anna held the basket on her arm. Kailah watched her kids playing as she helped her mom set up the wooden table under the covered pavilion. Mama Anna prepared turkey and cheese sandwiches for her and Kailah, peanut butter and jelly for the kids, and potato salad.

"It sure is a nice day for a picnic," Kailah said, looking up at the clear blue sky. The sun had finally decided to rear its head after a week of strong winds and rain.

Mama Anna nodded as she poured Sprite in her plastic cup. "You're right, Kailah. Feels like Florida without the humidity. I must admit, I do miss the hot weather."

Kailah massaged her mom's shoulder. "I know you do. We're going to miss you when you go back."

Mama Anna gently touched her daughter's hand. "Yeah, but you'll manage without me. You're strong, Kailah. Everything's going to be fine."

"Yes, it will." Kailah smiled while taking a quick glance over at the play area to check on her little ones. She reached in the bag of sour cream and onion chips and munched on a handful. "I didn't get a chance to tell you how everything went today. Keith had better news to share than I did."

"Oh, really?" Mama Anna sat down on the wooden bench.

"Mama, Keith's parole hearing is coming up in February. His lawyer thinks he may have a good shot."

"Shut your mouth," Mama Anna said as she clasped her hands together. "Kailah, see what I told you. You just need a little faith. God will surely make a way out of no way."

Kailah unwrapped the Saran from around a turkey sandwich and took a bite. "Yes, He will."

"I need to tell everybody in the women's group to add this to our list of prayers. And honey, Keith will be home in no time," Mama Anna said.

Kailah nodded.

* * *

As soon as she got home, Kailah checked her Caller ID and answering machine, hoping that Keith may have called. No such luck. Realizing that Mona had left two messages in the past hour, Kailah decided to call her back.

Mona picked up on the third ring.

"What's up, girl?" Kailah asked. "Is there a sense of urgency?"

"Uhh, yes, there is. I wanted to know how the visit with Keith went today."

MIXED MESSAGES

"It went fine," Kailah stated, talking while she helped Mama Anna unpack and clean up in the kitchen.

"So, what did Keith say about your promotion?" Mona asked.

"And how did you know about my promotion?" Kailah responded with a slight smile. "I haven't talked to you since Thursday."

"Mama Anna, of course."

"You know what," Kailah shook her head, "I'm not even going to go there. Anyway, he took the news very well."

"I knew he would. Keith knows how important your career is at AND."

"I guess so. Well, to my surprise, I learned that Keith has a parole hearing coming up in February." Kailah walked in the family room where Kamryn and Hunter were playing and watching a Barney video. "Or did you hear that, too?"

"No, I didn't. I can't believe his parole hearing is here already. But, you do know the statistics."

"That more times it's denied than approved. Keith told me." Kailah stared out the sliding glass doors, admiring the view of her backyard. "Regardless, I'm hopeful. And guess what else?"

"What?" Mona asked.

"Keith has decided to go work for his dad's company when he gets out."

Mona was speechless. "Kailah...I don't know what to say. I hope your family is reunited soon. I've been so worried about you trying to handle everything on your own. I know that Mama Anna is helping out. Still, I admire you. I hope I'm half the mother you are."

"You're too kind. But, thank you," Kailah responded. Exhausted from a long day, she plopped down on the brown leather couch and kicked off her sandals. "First, we got to get you married. How are the plans going?"

Mona sighed. "Not good. I need your help. Considering you're a pro at planning weddings, you should come down and lend me a hand," she said.

"Well, I wouldn't say I was a pro. Still, I'll help you."

"When are you coming?" Mona asked anxiously.

"Dang, let me get back to you on that. I know Mama wants to go home and check on things in Micanopy. Maybe then the kids and I can sneak away for a few days to see you."

"I would love that! I miss my godchildren. I know they're getting so big," Mona said. "Kamryn's going to be four years old soon."

Kailah laughed. "I know it. You should see how tall she is now. And swears she knows everything with her grown self. She thinks Hunter is her son."

Mona giggled. "Just like her mama."

Kailah stuck her tongue out. "Now, you know you wrong for that. I'm gonna let that one slide." She sat back and crossed her legs. "Anyway, I got to get these kids in the tub. They got all stinky at the park today. I'll call you tomorrow."

"All right, then. Love ya, girl."

"Love you, too," Kailah said as she kissed into the phone.

......

Mona looked down at her watch. *What?* It was only nine o'clock. She'd only been in her office for three hours, but it felt like she'd been there all day. She leaned forward on her desktop and twiddled her thumbs. *Focus.* Staring over the paperwork for minor glitches or mistakes strained her eyes. Before she went back into that mediation representing Mrs. Palmer, she vowed to review her notes carefully, making sure every "T" was crossed and every "I" dotted.

After dealing with more Baby Mama Drama with Doris, Mona couldn't get to work fast enough this morning. Any escape would do, even if it meant coming in to work early. Mona had a trick for Ms. Keisha. This was the last time she would lie on Mona and get away with it. Everyone agreed, including Doris, that if it happened again, Keisha would find herself out on the street without her daughter.

Mona's stomach rumbled like a volcano about to erupt. Holding her stomach, she went to the lounge area to grab a snack. Her coworkers, Debbie and Paige, stood at the water cooler gossiping as usual.

"Good morning, ladies," Mona said as she put in her money to purchase a strawberry Nutri-Grain bar from the vending machine.

"Glad to see we're not the only ones burning the midnight oil," Paige pointed out. She took another sip of coffee.

"More like the early morning oil." Mona poured coffee in her mug. "I'm scheduled for court at one o'clock today. Representing Mrs. Palmer has been rough."

"So we heard," Debbie said. She sat down at the table, crossing her legs.

Mona shook two bags of sugar and emptied them in her coffee. While stirring, she took a seat across from Debbie and Paige. "I'll bet everyone at the firm has heard about the Palmer drama." She raised her eyebrows. "I'm hoping we can reach a decision today. Mrs. Palmer seems a little more cooperative now. I think even she's worn down by the drawn out divorce proceedings."

Paige munched on her last piece of pastry. "Mona, how are the wedding plans going?"

Mona smiled. "I'm glad you changed the subject. Everything's going great. My matron of honor is coming down to help me out."

"Oh good. I just got my invitation to the engagement party in the mail, so I'm very excited," Paige said as she squeezed her shoulders.

Mona sat up straighter in her chair. "Well, you didn't send the reply card."

"You haven't given me enough time, Mona. Didn't I say that I just got it?"

"Well, Debbie sent her reply card back two weeks ago," Mona replied.

Paige shot a stupefied look at Debbie.

Debbie squirmed in her chair. "What are you looking at me for? I can't help it if I'm not lazy like you." Debbie rolled her eyes.

"I'm not lazy. I just...well... I, uh—"

"Whatever, Paige, save the excuses." Mona hugged Paige tightly. "I love you anyway."

Just then, Mona's assistant, Wendy, entered the break room. "Excuse me, Ms. Richards. I have your dad on the line, and he says it's important."

Mona took another slurp of coffee. "I better go get that. I'll talk to you later."

"Good luck today with Mrs. Palmer," Paige said as she turned around.

"Thanks. I need it." Mona sprinted in her black two-inch heels back to her small office.

Wendy looked up from her desk. "Your father's on line two."

"Thanks," Mona responded with a slight smile. "Hello, Daddy."

"Hey, baby."

"What's up? Wendy said your call was urgent," Mona said. She swiveled her leather chair around to face the window.

Charles cleared his throat. "It's your mother."

Mona sat straight up. "What's wrong with Mother?"

"Well, she had a car accident. Don't worry, she's fine. She only suffered a few bumps and bruises, and no one else was involved"

MIXED MESSAGES

Mona grabbed her chest. "Daddy, I don't understand. How could this happen?"

"I know damn well how it could happen." Charles sharply raised his husky voice. "It's your mother's drinking. That's the problem. The officer on the scene said her blood alcohol level was above the legal limit. She was arrested. Luckily, I got in touch with Larry. He had her released in a couple of hours."

"Daddy, I just can't believe this is happening," Mona said. She gently massaged her neck and lowered her head.

"Believe it. We both know Bea has a serious problem. Now, it's gotten to the point where we're going to have to do something about it," Charles responded.

"Yes, we do. Daddy, I'll call you back this evening. I have to appear in court today. I'm going to have Wendy arrange a flight out first thing tomorrow." Mona scribbled notes on her pad. "Are you sure Mother's okay?"

"Oh, she's good. Bea doesn't understand what all the fuss is about. I'm telling you if she doesn't get her act together, I'm going to take more drastic measures." Charles breathed heavily into the receiver.

Mona sighed. "Don't go packing your bags, Daddy. She needs you right now. We're going to convince her to enter rehab. Just wait. Okay?"

"Anything you say."

"Thanks, Daddy. I love you," Mona said. "I'll call you tonight."

Mona hung up, stretched out her arms, and exhaled slowly. This was too much. As if she didn't have enough going on already with the stress from planning a wedding to take place in less than four months, dealing with Keisha at home while trying to help take care of Brianne, and not to mention work. Juggling this crazy life left very little time to relax and do anything for herself. She guessed the lack of sex resulted in her feelings of pure frustration and her inability to concentrate at work.

Well, she had to do something about that, especially considering the fact that she would probably be in LA for a few days. Mona glanced at her watch. Just enough time to get to court. On the way, she would stop by Victoria's Secret at the Westshore Plaza to pick up something special for her man. Hurriedly, she stuffed her notes in her briefcase, put on her brown suit jacket, and made a mad dash out of her office.

After court, Mona headed straight for home. On I-275, she dialed her office number.

"Mona Richards' office. This is Wendy."

"Hi, Wendy. It's me," Mona said. She adjusted her headset. "I'm leaving the courthouse now. Since I'm not coming back, I need you to give me the flight information."

"Yes. Hold on one sec." Wendy paused. "Here it is. Your flight number is 942. Departure is 8:00 and arrival is 10:30."

Mona jotted with her right hand on her note pad. "Thank you so much, Wendy. Which airline?"

"Oh yeah. United Airlines." Wendy giggled. "I guess that's important. First class."

"You're remarkable. I'll be back first thing Monday morning. Please forward all calls to my cell. It's definitely a working trip," Mona added. "That is unless Mr. Angelo calls. Send his calls to my voice mail." She switched into the far right lane as she neared Exit 40 on Dale Mabry.

Wendy laughed. "Is there anything else you want me to do?"

Mona's green eyes swept across her dust-filled dashboard. She needed to take her Lexus in for detailing. "That's all I can think of right now. Don't work too hard."

* * *

The next day, Mona's plane arrived at LAX exactly at 10:30 Pacific Time. Her father greeted her at the baggage claim area downstairs. Charles hugged his daughter for what seemed an eternity before letting go.

"Look at you. You're beautiful," Charles said. "Have you lost weight?"

Goosebumps rose on Mona's arms. "No, Daddy, I've gained twenty pounds."

Charles took a step back while still gripping Mona's shoulders tightly. "It must've gone in all the right places." He squeezed her once more.

"Maybe." Mona squirmed to free herself. "Daddy, I can't breathe."

"I'm sorry, baby." Charles let go and picked up the bags beside Mona. "It's so good to see you. I sure missed you."

"I missed you, too." Mona casually strolled behind him adjusting the strap on her leather Coach bag. "Where's Mother?"

"She's at the house." Charles waited for the pedestrian light to turn green. "When I told her you were coming today, she perked right up, started talking about wedding plans." When the light turned green, they crossed the street to enter the parking garage. "I wanted to tell Bea she wasn't going to be alive to attend her own daughter's wedding if she continued on with this drinking."

"I'm sure it must've been hard for you." Mona placed her sunglasses atop her head as they walked through the dark parking garage to her dad's ivory Cadillac Escalade.

"Oh, let me get that," Charles said as he took her arm bag and tossed it in the back. He slammed the door shut.

Charles paid the toll at the garage exit and headed to their home in Westwood. They drove on the circular brick driveway in front of their pink, Spanish-styled mansion. Mona noticed more palm trees had been added. The front lawn transformed into lavish gardens entrancing gorgeous arrays of flowers. The flowerbeds had been enlarged since the last time she'd seen them. A beautiful arrangement of bright, bold colors definitely reflected her mother's direction and Abner's handiwork. She waved to Abner, dressed in denim overalls, as he assaulted large shrubs with a hedge trimmer.

"I'll take care of the bags, Mona. You go in and find your mother," Charles said. Abner wiped his face with a rag and came over to help Charles with the bag.

Greta greeted Mona at the door with a huge embrace. She told Mona her mother was waiting for her in the sitting room. Mona straightened up her white tee underneath her oversized red cotton shirt and stonewashed jeans. She jogged up the plush carpeted stairs to the second level of the house. Being out of shape, Mona stopped at the top of the steps to catch her breath.

Bea stuck her head out. "I thought you were your father with all that heavy breathing." She walked out wearing a silk leopard print top with black stretch pants and a cigarette in her hand. "Now, aren't you going to give your mother a proper greeting?"

"Of course." Mona smiled. She gently wrapped her arms around her mother's neck, trying to avoid getting burned by the cigarette. "Hello, Mother. How are you?"

"Fabulous, darling." Bea flung her shoulder-length, flip-style wig off her shoulders and took another puff. "Don't I look it?"

Mona's hazel green eyes scanned her mother from head to toe. *Damn.* She had to admit her mother was wearing those tight pants very nicely with her slim but shapely figure. "Yes, you do. Humph, I need to eat what you're eating."

Bea twirled her daughter around, raising her brown penciled eyebrows. "I'll say that again. I know this ain't my daughter with this big old behind." She smacked Mona's butt.

Mona gasped. "Mother!"

Bea cocked her head back. "What? I'm only telling you the truth. And the truth is you need to go on a diet before your wedding." Bea took another puff and then blew cigarette smoke in Mona's face. Mona coughed loudly. Bea ignored her daughter and continued. "At this rate, you won't fit in your dress. And there's simply no more room to adjust it."

"Mother, can we please change the subject," Mona said through clenched teeth.

Bea curled her lips and waved her hand in the air. "Oh, girl, you're taking this way too seriously." Bea grabbed her daughter's hand. "Let's go take a walk so you can calm your nerves. Come see what I've added to the gardens."

"All right." Mona followed.

Her dad was right when he told her Bea was acting like nothing had happened. She seemed her same old bossy, criticizing self as usual. Of course, that didn't mean anything either. Being an alcoholic most of her adult life, Bea often acted normal even after she downed vodka and gin like glasses of water. Mona wondered how a woman could drink hard liquor without it burning her throat. Bea drank like an old pro. It reminded her of the students at the college parties at UF. Mona refused to drink, let along hang around with anyone who drank. She always believed alcoholism was genetic, and she wasn't taking any chances.

Mona pretended to be interested in Bea's rambling on and on about the geraniums and hollyhocks she planted herself evoking more vibrant colors in the garden. Bea even added an herbal and vegetable garden. Somehow, Mona had a tough time picturing her mother planting and potting in high heels and gloves while managing to balance a cigarette in her hand.

At the same time, she waited for the perfect opportunity to engage in a serious conversation. The last time her mother visited her in Tampa, Mona was unable to sit her down long enough to have a real heart-to-heart. She felt sorry for her mother, because she had no idea the wonderful person her daughter had become. Didn't she care that she was now a woman or practicing law again? Didn't she care that in less than four months she, too, would be a married woman? Where was the motherly advice about marriage and the talk about having grandchildren? She felt completely disconnected from her mother. Bea was like a stranger, and she had no idea how things ended up this way.

She struggled to think of when this could have happened...when their relationship changed. Then she remembered. It suddenly came crashing in on her like a ton of heavy weights. It must have come about during her last visit in Miami when Bea spent some time with Lois, who suffered an emotional breakdown after her divorce from Darren Thomas. That had to be it. Somehow, her mother must have felt a heavy burden having to nurse her daughter and best friend at the same time. Why didn't she take one moment to think about her mother's feelings? Mona had been so insensitive to her, accusing Bea of loving her best friend more than her. *Damn. Somehow, this breakdown must be my fault.*

"Mother, let's sit down for a minute," Mona suggested as she sat on the white bench. Enough of the pretending, Mona had to get this off her chest. "You know the reason why I'm here, don't you?"

Bea straightened her wig. "What in heavens are you talking about?" She pointed to her chest. "I know you're not listening to that nonsense Charles is talking about." She lit another cigarette and puffed a cloud of smoke.

Mona closed her eyes as she made a tight fist. "It's not nonsense, Mother. And you know it." She relaxed her hand and faced her mother. "Daddy's concerned about you, and so am I. You can't continue on like this. You need help."

Bea fidgeted nervously and straightened her blouse. "I thought you were going to at least wait until you had settled in before you started in on me like this."

MIXED MESSAGES

Mona folded her arms and looked down at her Nike sneakers. "No time like the present. And besides, me and Daddy are taking you to the rehabilitation center first thing tomorrow morning."

Bea stood and squinted. "You'll do no such thing. I'm your mother, young lady! You seem to have forgotten. I take no orders." Her jaw tightened as she rolled her eyes.

"We're only doing this for your own good. You need to—"

"I'm not subjecting myself to be ridiculed by anyone. Never!" Bea put her hand to her ears. She huffed and quickly stormed back in the house.

Whoa. She handled that one well. Mona grabbed her shoulders, hugging herself, as she cried. She felt like her life was falling apart one piece at a time. Four months from now, she would be a blushing bride marrying the man she loved more than life itself. *Damnit, I'm supposed to be happy. Not going through this shit!*

* * *

At dinner, Mona barely touched her plate. The beef topped with wine sauce, sided with wild rice and mushrooms smelled absolutely divine. Her eyes drifted around the dining room redecorated with carved-wood furnishings to match the chairs stained with the color of desert sand to set the mood. An iron chandelier with heavy parchment shades added a whimsical touch, along with a brilliant abstract painting by Scott Hill on the opposite wall. Her mother had certainly done a great job.

Charles cut a slice of beef with a knife and took a bite. "This is a delicious meal Greta prepared tonight."

"Well, Greta went through extra pains for Mona's visit," Bea added as she gulped down her third glass of wine. She raised her eyebrows as she swallowed. "What's everybody looking at? I can't have wine with my meal?" she scoffed.

225

"I'm sick of the way you're taking this situation so lightly." Charles' eyes were still fixed on his wife. He was agitated.

"Oh and how is that?" Bea sat straight up in her chair.

"Like you're too busy trying to save your own precious little reputation than trying to help yourself. Have you forgotten about your accident already? You could have died. We're worried to death about you." Charles took a sip of wine. "You act like you don't give a damn about your daughter or me."

Bea stomped her fist on the table. "How dare you say such a thing?"

Charles waved his big hand in the air. "How dare I? I'm not the one laughing and talking with the very same people that are gossiping about you behind your back!"

Bea gasped.

Charles continued. "I have sat back and watched how you've drank yourself into a stupor and taken your little pills over the years, and I can't keep quiet anymore." He stood up and punched his fists in the air. "Sometimes, woman…"

"What, Charles? Say it."

"Sometimes, you make me sick." He walked out the room and yelled, "I'm going out!"

Bea ran out of the room after him. Mona followed in pursuit.

"Now you wait just a minute." Bea boldly stepped in front of Charles with her chest stuck out. "You're not going anywhere until you let me say what I have to say."

"Woman, you're talking foolish. Get out of my way!"

Bea stood her ground, even though Charles was at least five inches taller, along with a two hundred and fifty pound frame. She pointed her finger in his face. "I don't have a problem, and I'm not going to some damn rehab!"

"Do you hear what you're *saying*?" Charles pushed Bea out of the way and shot out of the door like lightning.

MIXED MESSAGES

Mona tried to grab her mother, but she snatched away from her tight grip.

Bea sprinted behind Charles' SUV. "Charles, we're not finished! You get back here and finish this like a man!"

Charles sped off.

Bea burst into tears holding her chest as she began to hyperventilate. Mona put her arms around her mother as she sobbed endlessly.

Chapter 29
Field of Dreams

Kailah drove on I-75 South to Tampa with Kamryn and Hunter in their car seats sleeping peacefully in the back of the rental mini-van. She smiled as she watched Hunter sucking on his pacifier like a warm bottle of milk. Glancing at the clock, she realized she had one hour left of driving to go. *Good, it won't be dark for another four hours.*

She scolded herself for not going to the bathroom before she left. Mama Anna had reminded her, but Kailah was too busy gathering all the kids' bags and traveling toys to remember. After finishing a Big Gulp, she squirmed in her seat trying to keep her bladder under control. She thought about waking up the children to stop at the next convenience store to pee. Then again, she would never get Kamryn back to sleep. That girl would talk Kailah to death if she were awake. Kailah felt like pulling her hair out on the plane ride to Gainesville from the thousand questions Kamryn asked. One question always led to another question.

Once more, she tried to sneak in another peak to check on her kids. Kamryn's full lips resembled her mother's. That girl was definitely going to break some hearts. She was such a gorgeous little girl. Pride and love encircled Kailah's heart when she looked at her children. It was hard to believe those cute babies came from her, even though she didn't deserve either one of them.

Yes, these three grueling years without her husband had certainly tested her faith. Courage and strength resonated within her, and she never would have known she had such an abundance of it had she not gone through this trial. No, she certainly wouldn't know this.

Ten years from now, Tanya Tucker couldn't have told her to stand by her man in prison! She would've slapped the taste out of Tanya Tucker's mouth. She mumbled the scripture just above a whisper, "I can do *all* things through Christ who strengthens me." There is nothing a woman wouldn't do to keep her family together. Keith was her life partner, and she would help him through this ordeal until he was ready to help himself. She loved and trusted her man so much that she would literally follow him to the far end of the earth and back.

Kailah rubbed her eyes. She looked at the next sign. Sixty more miles. Yeah, she could make it. It felt so good to be back in Florida where the green grass and beautiful trees hugged the edges of the interstate, inviting her to come in. Simple beauty and wonders made her feel close to God, admiring what He created. Somehow, she just didn't get the same feeling when she looked at the dirt, concrete, and tall high-rise buildings in Chicago. That was man's work.

Kailah pressed the scan button on the radio, tuning in to 105.5 just in time to hear "Man Enough" by Toni Braxton. She loved that song. It reminded her of all the sorry, no-good men she wasted her time with in the past. *He wasn't man enough for me.* She snapped her fingers and rhythmically rocked her head from left to right.

Kailah spotted the Busch billboard and made the next exit off of I-275. She cruised along Howard Avenue on the newly paved road. The rows of small houses looked similar, but had well cared for lawns. An older woman planted flowers in her small garden while her husband poured mulch around a large oak tree. Hard to believe Mona lived in a working middle-class area, considering five years ago she would have balked at the notion. A lot had certainly changed. No one had to tell her that Mona loved Davis, because if she could move from South Beach to live here, that more than proved her love and commitment to her relationship.

It showed Mona's growth as a human being as well, because Kailah saw her as a very shallow and spoiled person back in college. Sometimes when Kailah talked to her on the phone, she had to check her Caller ID box to make sure she knew who was on the opposite end. Mona talked, walked, and loved differently. Her view of the world reflected values and morals instead of materialism. She really enjoyed spending time with Mona than she did in the past.

When Kailah pulled up in front of Davis and Mona's red brick home, Mona opened the metal screen door holding Brianne on her hip.

Kailah hugged the door and yelled, "Well, don't you look motherly!"

Mona tossed her free hand in the air. "Awww, shut up."

Davis came over to help Kailah with her bags. Kamryn woke up and waved her hands in a wild frenzy until Kailah undid the strap of her booster seat. She climbed over her younger brother to clutch her arms around her mother's legs.

"Pick me up, Mommy," Kamryn whined.

"Kamryn, I'm not picking you up. You're a big girl. Now help me with your brother's diaper bag." Kailah placed the strap on Kamryn's shoulder. "There you go. Remember, you're Mommy's little helper." She kissed her daughter on the forehead. Kamryn smiled proudly.

Still peacefully sleeping in his car seat, Kailah picked up her one-year-old, being careful not to wake him. Davis opened the back of the Toyota Sienna and carried the luggage to the house.

"How long do you plan on staying?" Mona asked.

Kailah raised her eyebrows. "What are you trying to say? I have too many bags." Kailah put her arm around Mona. "You know I have to pack for two children now."

Mona hugged back, twisting her thin lips. "I know you don't expect me to believe those bags aren't yours."

"Well…uh…you…well, okay, they're mine." Kailah held up her free arm as if swearing herself in.

"Anyway," Mona grinned, "I'm glad you're here." Brianne laughed and threw her head back. Mona leaned over to steady her.

"Is she walking yet?" Kailah asked.

"Not by herself." Mona put Brianne down on the concrete driveway and held her two tiny hands. "I still have to hold onto her, but she's getting there."

"She's a pretty little thang," Kailah said admiringly.

Kamryn walked over to Brianne and stared in her face. "Hi, are you a baby?" she asked. Kamryn looked up at her mother. "Mommy, why can't she walk?"

Kailah sighed. "Because she hasn't learned yet."

"Isn't she one year old like Hunter?"

"She's a little younger than your brother." Kailah wiped the sweat from her forehead and then proceeded to guide Kamryn to the house. "You never know, sweetie. Brianne might start walking on her own while we're here."

"Yeah. I want somebody to play with, Mommy."

She opened the screen door for Kamryn. "I know you do."

Kailah followed Mona to the back of the house. She walked into the guest bedroom and her eyes swept the cluttered mess of a room.

"I know. This room is an even smaller space since the last time you visited." Mona pointed to the corner of baby toys. "As you can see, we've grown out of this house. Remember, Davis lived here by himself, except when the girls came to visit." Mona scratched her head. "After we get married, we're buying a larger home over in Brandon. We've already signed a contract with a real estate agent."

"Uh-huh." Kailah put Hunter on the bed and then plopped down beside him. "Sounds like a plan." Kailah rubbed her son in the middle of his back.

Keisha's door from her room swung open blasting 50 Cent's new CD loudly, causing the picture in the hallway to rattle.

Mona cleared her throat. "Aren't you going to speak?"

Keisha turned around, smiling coyly. "Hey, Ms. Kailah." She fumbled with her keys.

"Hi, Keisha," Kailah replied. She frowned at Mona.

"Going somewhere?" Mona asked with her eyes fixed disapprovingly on Keisha.

"Yeah, I'm going over to my mother's to see Tori." Keisha responded. "I want to know how her first week went at UF."

Mona shook her head. "Make sure you and your sister are here for dinner. And are you taking Brianne with you?"

"Of course." Keisha rolled her eyes as she uttered those words. "Where is *my* daughter anyway?"

"In the living room with your dad," Mona said sharply.

Without so much as a good-bye, Keisha eagerly strolled down the hall. A few minutes later, the front door slammed shut.

Mona turned off the music in Keisha's room. When she returned, Kailah tossed her hands in the air. "Okay, what was that?"

Mona looked at her strangely. "What was what?"

Kailah snapped her fingers. "What's up with the major attitude from your step-daughter?"

Mona leaned on the dresser. "Girl, that's nothing." She swallowed hard. "I don't know who she thinks she's fooling either. She might be going over to her mother's house, but she's not staying. She'll be there long enough to drop Brianne off before she hits the streets."

"Doing what?" Kailah asked.

Mona put her hands on her hips and looked up at the ceiling. "God only knows."

MIXED MESSAGES

Kailah puckered her lips and shifted a strand of red curly hair from Mona's eyes. "I'm sorry. Things will get better." She grabbed Mona's hand. "You remember what it was like when you were a teenager."

Mona cocked her head back. "I wasn't that bad."

Kailah sucked her teeth. "Maybe I need to ask Bea about that."

Mona pretended to slap Kailah upside the head. "Now see, I thought we weren't going to talk about my mother."

Kailah held her hands to her mouth. "Oops, my bad."

They both held each other and laughed.

Kailah took a deep breath. "Okay, okay. Let's change the subject." The aroma of garlic drifted over to her from the kitchen. "What's for dinner?"

"Davis is cooking shrimp and chicken in a white garlic sauce. It's so good. He prepares the sauce and meat over angel hair pasta." Mona rubbed her stomach. "You're going to just die when you taste it."

Kailah patted Mona's stomach. "Davis must be throwing down over here. Girl, you have put on some weight."

Mona nodded. "Don't remind me."

"Well, if Davis doesn't mind, then don't worry about it."

"No, Davis doesn't mind. You should see his first wife." Mona looked at herself in the mirror. She turned sideways. "Still, I want to lose the weight. I'm going to start the Atkins Diet real soon."

"Be careful with completely eliminating carbs from your diet." Kailah adjusted her ponytail. "I saw on 20/20 where it can lower your energy levels. And you're always complaining about being tired all the time."

"I know," Mona said. "I don't have time to go to the gym three times a week like you. I have to do what works for me." Mona held up her hands. "Don't worry, I've done my research."

Kailah sat back down on the bed. "That's good." She looked over at Hunter on the bed and rubbed his back.

"I'm surprised he didn't wake up from all the noise we're making in here," Mona said.

"Child, Hunter sleeps hard. An earthquake could hit this house, and he wouldn't flinch one muscle. Now, Kamryn, on the other hand, if you breathe, she's awake."

Kailah's eyes scanned down the hall. "Speaking of Kamryn, it's awfully quiet in this house. I wonder what she's up to."

Kailah entered the living room and saw Kamryn in the kitchen with Davis.

"Mommy, Mommy, come see what I'm doing!" Kamryn yelled. She carefully stirred the sauce in the mixing bowl. "I'm helping Uncle Davis cook."

Kailah folded her arms and tugged at her ear. What a sight! How she wished Keith was here at this very moment. She felt a strong pain in her chest. She missed Keith so much. It hurt like hell. Mona came up behind her.

"What's wrong?" Mona asked as she tightened Kailah's loose ponytail.

"Everything." Kailah's sorrowful eyes cast downward. "I'm kind of tired. I think I'm going to go lay down for a bit," Kailah said as she traipsed back to the room, closing the door behind her.

As Kailah nodded off to sleep, she dreamed she lay in a meadow filled with purple, pink, and white flowers surrounding her. A dark shadowy figure approached her as she sat up with her back perfectly arched. Her long hair blew in the violent wind while the sun blocked her view of the image. As the figure came closer, she recognized him. The strong, muscular man stood in front of her dressed in white linen shorts and a matching shirt. He revealed a huge dimpled smile and lay on top of Kailah. She pulled off his shirt and slid down his shorts. Keith undid the spaghetti straps of her yellow slip dress and pulled it over her head. Neither one of them wore underwear. The couple froze in place. Keith kissed his wife and his tongue slightly parted her lips. He guided himself inside of her. Kailah wrapped her arms on his broad muscled shoulders and her legs around him as she gyrated up and down.

Her eyes cast upward at her husband. His intense gaze fixed on her as he continued to pulsate through her body like electricity. A drop of sweat rolled off his face onto hers. He licked the sweat off her face and swirled his tongue in her ear. She jerked from left to right as her body tingled. As she neared her orgasm, she squeezed her legs tighter and arched her back. Kailah squinted as the bright sun shone in her eyes. *Oh... oh... I'm coming!*

"Mommy. Mommy."

Kailah felt someone tapping on her shoulder. She slowly opened her eyes. Hunter was sitting up in the bed.

"What is it, baby?"

"Eat. Eat," Hunter babbled.

"All right, honey. Mommy's going to get you something." Kailah stood up to straighten her dress. *Whew! That dream seemed so real.* A few seconds more and her panties would have been soaking wet. She ran her hand through her untamed hair, grabbed a wide-tooth comb out of her bag, and took a few strokes.

This parole had to go through, because she wasn't so sure if she would be able to hold it together much longer. Last week, Corey Sanders from the marketing department brushed up on her from behind as she used the copier. Of course, he immediately apologized, but Corey was well known around the building as a bona fide player. Taneisha told her that Corey had many talents, and even though he had a girlfriend, a brotha like him knew how to be quiet with his indiscretions. If he continued to make frequent visits on her floor, she just might be tempted to—

The rapid taps at the door broke her concentration. Mona softly knocked a few more times to announce it was time to eat. Good thing, because Kailah had allowed her mind to wonder, knowing full well that possessing those impure thoughts was indeed a sin. Kailah caught a glimpse of herself in the mirror. *Get a grip, girl. You can't be perfect all time, especially under these extreme circumstances.*

A few seconds later, Kailah came out holding Hunter on her hip. Tori and Keisha were fixing their plates in the kitchen, while Davis, Mona, and Kamryn were already seated at the large rectangular whitewashed wood table in the open dining area.

"Hey, Mommy," Kamryn said.

"Hey, yourself," Kailah responded. She patted her daughter on the head. "Do you have enough food on your plate?"

Kamryn nodded. "Yes. I helped cook dinner, Mommy."

"I know, honey. That's great." Kailah put Hunter down on the tiled floor. He ran for the kitchen and hugged on a cabinet door just before falling down. Tori reached down and picked him up. As she bent down, her denim hip huggers revealed a wavy designed tattoo on her back. She kissed him and started making playful baby noises. Kailah wondered if Davis had seen the tattoo. Probably not.

"Tori, can you hold him while I fix a plate?" Kailah asked as she washed her hands at the kitchen sink.

"Sure." Tori sat on the floor and fed Hunter some pasta noodles.

"Thanks." Kailah helped herself, then sat at the table to eat. She quietly whispered grace and then tore into the delicious meal, remembering she hadn't eaten since breakfast at Mama Anna's.

Kailah buttered a piece of garlic bread. "This is really good, Davis. I didn't know you could cook."

MIXED MESSAGES

Davis' eyes lit up as he wiped his mouth with a paper napkin. "Thanks, Kailah. Well, you know. I try to do a little something around here." He chuckled.

"I see." Kailah took another bite of shrimp.

"Actually, Davis does most of the cooking. Keisha helps out, too, sometimes." Mona swallowed a mouthful of pasta.

Keisha sucked her teeth.

Kailah cut her eyes at Keisha, then turned to Tori. "Do you like it at UF?"

Tori nodded, trying to swallow. "Yeah, it's great."

"What dorm are you staying in?" Kailah asked.

"Fletcher Hall," Tori said as she clapped her hands together. "Oh my God, I have this roommate and her name is Hilary. She's so wild and crazy. She goes to a lot of parties and gets pissy drunk. Those guys are turning her out already." Tori chewed on a piece of shrimp, then continued. "But, my other roommate, Shauna, is cool. We hang out together since we don't know anyone. She's from Melbourne."

"Australia?" Davis asked.

"No. Melbourne, Florida." Tori laughed.

Davis nodded. "Oh yeah, right." He buttered another slice of garlic bread.

"Well, you know, Mona and I used to run things out there." Kailah pumped her fists in the air.

"Back in the day," Keisha mumbled under her breath.

"I'm thinking about joining a sorority, too." "Oh yeah?" Mona jumped in. "Well, you should at least wait until your sophomore year to make a decision. But, I would love for you to become a Delta."

"Me, too," Tori said. "Maybe you can give me some pointers."

Kailah and Mona looked up at each other and smiled.

"We'll hook you up," Kailah said as she patted her chest. "Break you off a little somethin' somethin'."

Everybody laughed. Keisha smirked.

"That line is so old," Keisha mumbled once more.

Davis sat up in his chair. "Now, that's enough from you, young lady."

Keisha's mouth hung wide open. "What? I didn't even say nothing."

"Keisha, just eat your dinner," Mona said curtly.

"No, I will not." Keisha scowled. She poked out her narrow lips and folded her arms like a baby.

"Oh, here we go again," Davis said through clenched teeth. He took a sip of iced tea.

"Davis, we have company. Let's not cause a scene," Mona said, trying to coax Davis. "You want me to pour you another glass of tea?"

"Yes." Davis handed his glass to Mona.

Kailah quickly scanned the room. Keisha sat there refusing to finish dinner with her arms folded. Davis pretended to be fixated on his meal, not looking up from his plate. Mona scurried around anxiously. Kamryn made a huge mess, with more pasta on the table than on her plate. Hunter was doing the same thing on the tile floor.

Keisha threw her napkin on the table and walked outside. Tori quickly ran after her. Kailah fidgeted in her seat. She searched Mona with her eyes asking what she should do next.

Mona shook her head back to do nothing.

Kailah decided to change the subject. "Well, it looks like the Williams girls are going to play each other for the championship again."

Davis looked up. "Yeah, isn't that something?"

......

On Sunday, Kailah attended church services with Davis and Mona. Keisha decided to ride in the same car as Tori. She still had an attitude at breakfast and seemed to get angrier by the minute, partly because everyone except Tori ignored her whining and balking. Tori tended to her younger sister's needs like she was Keisha's mother. Kailah felt sorry for Mona as she watched her struggle to care for Brianne. Davis nonchalantly pretended not to notice. This situation was jacked up!

Kailah's face lit up when Keisha announced she wanted to ride with her sister. At least she would have some peace and quiet on the way to church. No such luck. Hunter's teething made him irritable and Kamryn wouldn't stop talking. At church, Hunter kept trying to leap down from Kailah's lap. Several times, she had to run to catch him just before he made it to the altar while Pastor Jenkins preached the sermon.

After church services ended, the two families went to an early dinner. Kailah overindulged at the all-you-can-eat-buffet at Quincy's Steakhouse. She rubbed her stomach as she sat back in the green plastic chair on the patio.

"My stomach feels like it's going to burst." Kailah closed her eyes for a moment.

"It should." Mona laughed. "You ate enough for an entire football team." Mona bounced Hunter on her lap and kissed his chubby cheeks.

Kailah groaned. "I think I need to take something."

"I can get you some Mylanta," Mona said. "Will that do?"

"Yeah, that's fine." Kailah rubbed her stomach again.

Mona put Hunter on the patio to play with his toys while she disappeared inside.

"Here you go." Mona reappeared with a green bottle and spoon.

"Thanks, girl." Kailah swallowed two spoonfuls of Mylanta. "This tastes awful."

"Really?" Mona asked as she stretched her arms wide. "I actually like the taste."

Kailah rolled her eyes. "You would."

"What's that supposed to mean?" Mona frowned.

"It probably tastes better than Bea's cooking," Kailah joked, bursting into laughter.

Mona playfully jabbed Kailah on the shoulder. "Stop talking about my mother. Even though, you're probably right."

"See!" Kailah yelled. "I know I'm right." She became silent for a moment and massaged her wounded shoulder. "Seriously, how's your mother doing?"

Mona took a sip of wine. "Much better. Daddy says she'll be home from rehab in ten days."

Kailah clasped her hands together. "That's good news. I'm glad." She gently stroked Mona's arm. "God is going to work everything out. You're going to have the perfect wedding day. And you'll be the most beautiful bride."

Mona's eyes looked upward to the evening sky. "Well, I hope so."

Kailah smacked a mosquito biting her on the leg. "We better go in. The bugs are attacking." She picked up Hunter and carried him back in the house, taking a seat on the couch in the living room.

"Do you want some more wine, Kailah?" Mona asked as she refilled her glass.

"Sure." Kailah held up her glass.

"So, what did Keith say about the parole hearing?" Mona asked.

"He didn't say anything last night. He just wanted to talk to the kids." Kailah scratched her head. "When I last spoke with Maurice, he told me that all the necessary forms had been filed. He really feels that Keith has a good shot."

"What do you believe?" Mona asked. She placed the glass in front of Kailah and sat down.

"I believe in God. I believe that He knows what's best for me and my family." Kailah shrugged. "I know Keith is coming home real soon."

"I admire the way you've pulled yourself and your family through this entire ordeal." Mona crossed her legs. "You have a lot of strength and courage."

Kailah nodded. "I'm barely holding it all together. God has carried me. I tell you, I almost suffered a breakdown twice."

Mona munched on a handful of cheese crackers. "You sure could have fooled me."

"Well, I'm so fortunate to be surrounded with great people who keep me on my feet. Like, Mama. She has really helped me out with Hunter and Kamryn. I don't know what I would've done without her. Taneisha pulled it all together for me at AND. Then you..." Kailah stretched her left arm along the top of the couch and faced Mona. "You're the sister I never had. I love you."

"The feeling is mutual."

"Well, I better get the kids off to bed. Kamryn can't wait to see Mickey Mouse tomorrow." Kailah smirked. "Hunter will probably be terrified."

Mona chuckled. "Yep, I bet Brianne is going to scream, too. I'm gonna go check on Davis." Mona stood up and stretched. "The game's almost over. I guess I'll catch the last quarter."

"All right, Mona." Kailah hugged her best friend. "I'll see you in the morning." She carried Hunter on her hip and knocked on Keisha's door, opening it slowly. "Kamryn, time to go to sleep."

Kamryn whined. "I'm not sleepy."

"You will be after you take your warm bath. Now, let's go." Kailah raised her voice. She knew being direct with her daughter was the only method that worked.

Kamryn followed her mother to the guest bedroom.

Kailah yawned. "Good night."

"Good night," Mona said as she entered her bedroom.

Chapter 30
Indiscretion

Listening to Sean Paul's CD on her Walkman kept her motivated as she pumped her arms. Kailah lowered the speed as she stopped jogging to power walk for her last ten minutes on the treadmill. Having put in an hour of weight training, another thirty minutes of cardio on the bicycle, and thirty on the treadmill, her sweaty body ached all over. The punishment did her body some good since she hadn't worked out in two weeks. She would take one day to rest the muscles she worked out that day, and then come back Wednesday for her kickboxing class.

Exercising not only allowed Kailah to keep her slim and physically toned figure, but it was also the perfect stress reliever. Lately, her workload had doubled in preparation for her new position as VP, Mama Anna was preparing to go back home, Mona stressed her everyday about the wedding, and Keith's parole hearing was coming up next month. Not to mention the fact that she wanted Hunter potty trained before Mama Anna left. She didn't remember it being as hard when she trained Kamryn.

Coming to the gym gave her time to escape her problems, pray, and focus on the task at hand. It was a way for her to spend a few hours with herself and not have to think about clients, husband, friends, or even her kids. Even though she loved her family, she needed that break to help maintain some level of sanity in her life.

Dr. Phil always said taking time for yourself makes you a better mother. She taped his shows regularly and watched them uninterrupted at night after she put the kids to sleep. First, she'd watch Dr. Phil, followed by Oprah in less than two hours because she would fast forward through the commercials. What she really needed to buy was the TiVo that everybody talked about at work. She made a mental note to take a trip to Circuit City that coming weekend.

When she finished, she wrapped her towel around her neck and headed to the locker room to take a shower.

"I didn't know you came to this gym." Kailah turned around to see who was speaking to her.

Corey Sanders stood there in a Detroit Pistons jersey and black athletic shorts. She assumed he came out of the adjacent men's locker room and just so happened to spot her face out of the hundred other beautiful women there. *What a strange coincidence!* What made it more of a coincidence is that she'd been running into him more often at AND, even though he worked on the fourteenth floor as head of the marketing department with Lynn.

"Yeah, my husband and I have been coming here for years." She dried her face with a towel. She wanted to make sure he remembered she had a husband. Since Lynn made it her personal business to tell everyone at AND about her husband's prison sentence, she was sure Corey knew.

"Really?" He smiled a toothy grin.

Kailah gazed intently at Corey's muscular build. A little thin for her taste, his legs and arms were ripped very nicely, though. The large imprint in his shorts showed he was well endowed. *Oh God, I'm eyeing the man's penis.*

Kailah looked away quickly. "So, uhh…well, it was nice to see you." As she turned to walk away, she closed her eyes and exhaled. If her complexion were a few shades lighter he would have noticed her blushing.

Corey cleared his throat. "Nice to see you, too."

Kailah showered and dressed in a pink sweat suit. She waved goodbye to the girl at the desk and exited the gym. There standing in front of her BMW was Corey. *This guy doesn't give up.*

MIXED MESSAGES

He shifted his dreads nervously and smiled as she approached. "Hey, you wanna grab a bite to eat?"

"No, I'm in a hurry. I have to get home." Kailah eased past him and opened her door. "Maybe some other time." Corey held the door open wider for her as she tossed her gym bag in.

He raised his eyebrows as he undressed her with his hazel green eyes. "I'm gonna hold you to that."

Kailah swallowed hard. "You do that."

As Kailah backed out of her parking space, Corey waved goodbye. *What is he trying to prove? He couldn't possibly think he has a chance in hell with me.* Yes, he did make her heart flutter and skip a beat in passing at work. Kailah wondered if an attraction of some sort actually existed. *Naw!* She had a fine husband, and this young boy didn't even compare. She believed these feelings only existed because he was the only guy that showed her any attention. It felt good to have a man be attracted and respond in a respectful, but also sexual nature.

When she first started working at AND, she received the stares and compliments on a regular basis. Once she married, got older, and reached a higher status, the men didn't take notice anymore. Of course, she never expected them to. But she would be lying if she said she didn't miss it. Instead, she observed the young female interns and trainees receiving the attention she found herself now desperately craving. Kailah knew Corey had an agenda, and against her best wishes she continued to flirt back with him anyway.

Kailah shook her head in disgust as she clutched the steering wheel with both hands. Her inappropriate behavior had to stop. She rested her left arm on the window as she waited for the traffic light to change. Keith would be home soon, and she needed to hold on a little while longer. She tried hard to fight back the tears as her eyes welled up. *You can't do this. You have two children depending on you to keep this marriage together. Don't blow it!*

* * *

The next day at work, Kailah noticeably turned her head opposite of Corey and strolled past confidently. She knew she looked damn good dressed in the mahogany suit she purchased while in Florida.

Twenty minutes later, Corey stuck his head in Kailah's office. "Got a minute?"

Kailah turned away from the computer and leaned back in her leather chair. *Tell him you're busy.* "Sure, I have a minute." She straightened the sleeves to her wide-collared shirt and crossed her legs.

Corey unfastened his taupe suit jacket and took a seat. "How are you doing?" He seductively licked his lips.

Kailah clasped her hands together. "Good."

"Glad to hear it. Oh, and congratulations on your promotion to VP." Corey grinned. "I know I'm a little late."

"Thanks," Kailah said, forcing a smile. "Better late than never," she kidded. She leaned over on her glass desktop. "Look, I don't mean to be rude, but I have a lot of work to do."

His eyes lingered for a moment.

There he goes undressing me with his eyes again.

Suddenly, he threw his hands in the air. "Me, too." He rose and turned to leave. "I just wanted to remind you of our date."

Kailah smiled coyly. "Excuse me?"

"Remember, you said I could take you to lunch sometime. I was just thinking that—"

"That today was a good day," Kailah chimed in.

"Yes," Corey affirmed. He held her eyes as he leaned with his arms on the back of the chair. "Can I meet you downstairs at noon then?"

MIXED MESSAGES

Kailah placed her hand under her chin as she thought it over. No, she didn't want to risk being seen by coworkers. She bit down on her French-manicured nail. It's not like she had anything to hide. She'd gone to lunch with other male coworkers and clients before. That wasn't unusual. But then again, Corey was a known playboy.

"Why don't I meet you at Gold Coast's instead?" Kailah finally responded.

Corey flashed his toothy grin. "All right. Don't be late." She leaned to the left to see him walk down the hall to the elevators.

"I won't." Kailah went back to preparing her report on the computer. It had to be finished in a couple of hours, and she needed to type like a maniac to make the deadline. As she glanced down at her watch, she hadn't realized how much time had passed. Her little lunch date with Corey would have to be canceled. *What a shame!*

"Taneisha."

Taneisha stuck her head in the door. "Yes, Boss Lady."

"Can you call Corey Sanders and let him know I can't make it to lunch today."

Taneisha wrote on her small notepad. "Are you going to reschedule?" She twisted her lips.

"No, I'm not," Kailah said coolly. She knew exactly what Taneisha meant by that question.

Taneisha stuck out her tongue. "Good, 'cause you don't need to go anywhere with that slimy jerk anyway."

Kailah cocked her head back. *Dang!* Deciding it was best not to respond, she went back to working on her report. "As soon as I print this out, I need you to call the courier for me."

"I'll take care of it right now. Anything else before I head out to lunch?"

"Nope. Nothing else."

Taneisha returned to her desk.

For lunch, Kailah grabbed a snack from the vending machine and went back to reviewing reports for the rest of the afternoon. After a long meeting with all of the department heads, she called her mother to let her know she was on her way home. As Kailah was about to step onto the elevator, she saw Corey standing inside laughing with another male coworker. He stopped laughing and locked eyes with Kailah. She cringed and quickly looked down in her leather bag pretending to be searching for something important.

"Go ahead. I need to get something from my office." Kailah stepped back, letting the doors shut in front of her. She wiped her forehead. She managed to dodge that bullet.

"Hey, wait up!" a voice cried out. She pretended not to hear anything, hoping it wasn't who she thought it was, and dug in her heels to get back to her office.

"Kailah."

Corey walked in her office and bent over still trying to catch his breath.

Kailah put her hands on her hips. "What do you want?" Kailah's voice was impatient.

She lingered in her office shuffling through papers on her desk, hoping he would get the message and leave. Instead, he moved so close to her she could feel his warm breath on her face.

Boldly, Corey came behind her and squeezed her ass firmly. "I want you," he whispered. His warm breath danced circles in her ear.

"Excuse me?" Kailah's voice snapped. She wanted to turn around and slap the taste out of his mouth for disrespecting her in that way.

While her mind told her one thing, her body remained perfectly frozen in place. An electric pulse shot through her body like a lightening bolt as he lightly kissed her on the nape of her neck. As if she was on automatic pilot, Kailah tossed her head back, flinging her hair off her shoulders. Corey cupped her breasts. Kailah pushed Corey away as hard as she could, causing him to stumble backward.

"I don't know what you think of me, but…" Kailah tucked in her shirt, "this can't happen. I need to go home."

Corey shook his head as he went to close the door, locking it.

This was her chance to get rid of him. To her surprise, she remained perfectly still. *What the hell is wrong with you? Move. Do something.*

He removed his jacket, tossing it on a chair as he made his way back to Kailah who stood nervously behind her desk.

She held up her hands. "Look, I know—"

"Now where was I?" He turned Kailah around and forcefully kissed her while he lifted her skirt and shifted his body closer. Feeling his hardness between her legs, she opened her eyes and watched as he removed his shirt to reveal his six-pack. Without any hesitation, Kailah began licking his chest.

"Uhhmm." Corey bit his lip. "That feels so good."

Kailah needed a release so damn bad. Corey was just the one to make it happen.

She worked her hands down and massaged his penis. Just as she figured, he was well endowed. He unbuttoned her blouse and stroked her breasts. Kailah tightly grabbed his dreadlocks as he sucked on her right nipple. Then he lifted her up on her glass desktop, pulled down her purple g-string, and wriggled his fingers in her hairy wet pussy.

"Somebody's been waiting for Big Daddy," he whispered. "You want this big dick, don't you?"

Kailah's eyes cast downward as she nodded.

"I know you do." He continued to work his fingers inside her as he sucked on her breasts wildly.

"Yeeeess." Her voice was breathy. Kailah's eyes swept the room. She couldn't believe she'd just said that.

Corey shook his head. "No, not yet."

Kailah sat up. "Huh?"

Corey grabbed her head and pushed it down. His forcefulness turned her on even more. How she loved a challenge!

"Suck it, bitch."

Oh, so now I'm his bitch. Kailah smiled wickedly. She knelt down and licked and sucked on his manhood. He thrust his penis in and out of her mouth harder and harder. Kailah almost gagged on it, but she wasn't going to let him get the best of her. She sucked the tip harder and licked his balls.

"Oh shit. Oh shit." He grabbed her shoulders and threw his head back as he shot his warm manly juices all over himself. A few drops landed on her, so Kailah wiped her face with his shirt. No sense in ruining her three-hundred dollar Bill Blass shirt.

They both stopped to breathe heavily for a few moments.

"Whoa!" Corey said and laughed. "I know you didn't think we were finished." He ran his hands through Kailah's long hair. Then pulled Kailah up and turned her around. He pulled her skirt up over her bare ass and plunged into her from behind, thrusting violently.

"Oowww." Kailah felt her lips rip wide open.

"I love me some tight pussy." Corey slapped her on the ass. He opened his legs wider and pulled her thighs up higher, leaving Kailah's legs dangling wildly mid-air. She knocked papers off her desk as she gripped the edge firmly for support.

"Oh my God!" Kailah squealed as she squeezed her eyes shut. She felt her insides burst.

Moments later, Corey pumped faster and harder than ever. He groaned with satisfaction.

"Oh shit!" He parted Kailah's thighs and pulled her closer.

As Kailah felt his warm semen enter her, she suddenly realized he wasn't wearing a condom. He landed on her back and his cold sweat made her jerk. He continued to breathe heavily in her ear. Kailah turned her head and rubbed her sweaty forehead.

Corey collapsed in her chair and sighed. "Damn." His chest rose and fell as he took in deep breaths of air. He shook his head from left to right. "That was good."

Kailah rose from her desk where she was laid like a piece of raw meat and stood in front of him.

"Oh yeah? Well, I was just getting started."

She watched Corey's penis stiffen again and rise at full attention as she climbed on top. She opened her legs and came fully down on his member. She slowly rode on his shaft like she was a cowgirl bucking a horse. Corey grabbed Kailah's hips and buried his head in the back of the chair.

He licked his lips. "Ooohh, this so damn good."

Kailah would have to call home as soon as she finished. This was going to be a late night at the office after all. She hoped her mother didn't mind that her daughter had to get her much-needed freak on.

* * *

The next morning, Kailah sat quietly in the same office where she had gotten her brains fucked out the night before. Staring out the window, she swayed her chair from left to right, admiring the beautiful sunrise. She ran her hand through her hair. In her mind, she replayed last night's sexual encounter over and over again. A tingling feeling overpowered her in between her legs where she had allowed another man to enter without question. She crossed her legs to calm the feeling. How could she do it? What the hell was wrong with her? Old habits and sexual tendencies die hard. And just when she thought she buried that sucka, poof, here it came again.

Repenting for her adulterous sin wouldn't be easy because Kailah had no shame or guilt for what she'd done. In fact, she felt relieved if anything else, like a heavy weight of burden had been lifted from her shoulders. She took another sip of coffee and placed the mug back down.

Before leaving last night, she and Corey agreed it would never happen again. Kailah knew how much he loved his girlfriend, so she knew that he wouldn't risk his relationship by telling someone. She could trust him.

After three years of celibacy, Kailah had given into a moment of weakness. She loved her husband and wanted to be the perfect wife. But she wasn't perfect. No one was. A single tear rolled down her cheek. As she wiped it away, Kailah asked God for forgiveness, and then she forgave herself. One day she would find a way to tell Keith about this.

Kailah straightened her blue silk blouse and rolled her chair over to her desk. Tossing her head and flinging her hair back off her shoulders, she picked up a pen and began to revise the presentation laid out before her.

......

Kailah danced in the mirror wearing only a slip. She sang along with Gerald Levert's song playing on the radio. "And it's funny you should call today…"

When she heard the phone ring, she dodged out of the bathroom to answer it.

"Hello."

"Hi, Kailah. I tried calling you at your office, but Taneisha told me you weren't coming in until this afternoon."

"Maurice, I wanted to wait for your call first." Kailah felt a twisting in the pit of her stomach. "So, how did the parole hearing go?"

Maurice sighed. Kailah closed her eyes and prepared for the bad news.

"Keith's parole was approved. He'll be home in April."

MIXED MESSAGES

"What!" Kailah screamed at the top of her lungs. Mama Anna came bursting through the door. "You really mean it? My husband's coming home?" Kailah grabbed the back of her head and cried. Mama Anna put her arms around her.

Kailah tried to listen as Maurice stated the conditions of Keith's parole. No matter how hard she tried to remain calm, her hands continued to shake rapidly. As soon as she hung up, she fell into her mother's arms.

"Mama." She spoke just above a whisper. Her eyes were filled with tears of joy. "We're going to be a family again." She rested her head on her mother's shoulder and sobbed like a child. She would always remember this day for the rest of her life.

Taking the rest of the day off, Kailah spent the last three hours calling everyone she could think of to share the good news. First, she called Juanita and Blake. Then, Taneisha to let her know she wouldn't be in, and now she was dialing Mona's number on her cell phone from her car. Mama Anna sent her to the store to pick up a few items for their family celebration dinner.

Mona's voicemail picked up. *She must be out to lunch.* Kailah decided to leave a message telling Mona to call her back on the cell.

Kailah pulled up in front of Kroger's. Her cell phone rang just as she was about to open the door. *That was fast.* She didn't expect Mona to call her back so quickly.

"Hey." Kailah smiled.

"I guess you didn't make it in today."

"Well, I decided to stay home." Her smile soon faded. "I'm at the store right now. Can I call you back?"

"Yeah. Oh, and Kailah?"

"Uh-huh."

"I already heard the news about Keith. So, if you were wondering how to break the news, don't. I'm happy for you," he said in a lowered voice. "Really."

"Thank you." Kailah zipped up her leather jacket. "Corey, I promise I'll call you back."

He was silent for a moment. "All right."

Kailah pressed the off button on her cell. She massaged her temples, attempting to avoid an impending migraine. At the same moment that her life was coming together, another part was slowly falling apart. Vowing never to become involved with Corey again, she broke that promise every time she agreed to meet him privately at an undisclosed location.

He knew and understood her in a way that no one had, not even her husband. On a deeper level, Kailah made a connection with him that wouldn't be easy to just throw away and pretend never happened.

Kailah fought with the strong winds to open the door to her BMW. Then she wrapped her crème-colored scarf around her face for warmth. She squinted as she struggled to get inside the safe haven away from the February cold. She purchased the items she needed and then headed home. Still, no call from Mona.

She dialed Corey's direct line to his office. He answered on the first ring.

"Corey Sanders speaking," he answered with full enthusiasm.

"Hi," Kailah said.

"Oh, hey, wait just a minute."

Kailah adjusted the dial on her radio as she waited. She hoped he wouldn't be long, because she was only two blocks away from her house. "I'm back. How are you doing?"

Kailah bit her lip. "I'm fine. I need to talk to you. You think you can get away?"

MIXED MESSAGES

"Yeah, I think I can pencil you in," Corey said. "Just let me know when and where."

"Okay. Our usual spot. Room 522 at eight o'clock." Kailah pressed the button to open the garage door.

"Eight it is. See you then."

After dinner, Kailah made up an excuse to leave the house. She asked Taneisha to be her alibi if Mama Anna called looking for her.

Kailah checked in at the Hyatt South of the Loop and left the other key at the desk. The executive suite had served as her romantic nest with her lover for close to a month now. She kicked her shoes off and grabbed the remote. Stopping on a rerun of Fresh Prince, Kailah lay across the bed.

Click. Corey entered the room looking fabulous in a charcoal gray Armani two-button suit. Playfully, he jumped on top of Kailah and nuzzled his head in her chest.

"Oouch!" Kailah frowned. "That hurts. Boy, get off of me!"

Corey put his index finger to his mouth. "Shhh, be quiet. You trying to get us kicked out or something." He kissed her on the neck, inhaling her fragrance of Donna Karan perfume. "Baby, you smell so nice. What's that you're wearing?"

Kailah sucked her teeth. "You should know. You bought it."

"I did. I bought you that." Corey raised his bushy eyebrows. "Smelling this fragrance on your perfect body is like breathing for the first time." He leaned forward and sucked on her neck, working his way southward.

He sure didn't waste any time. Kailah put both arms around his neck and ran her fingers through his dreadlocks. Corey undid her jeans and struggled to pull them down.

"Wait, wait!" Kailah squealed. "Let me help you with that." She stood up and peeled out of her snug jeans.

Adjusting her head on the pillows stacked behind her, she closed her eyes as she braced for Corey's tongue slowly working its way down to her vagina.

"Mmmmm." She twisted her lips.

He grabbed her thighs and squeezed them over his shoulders as he gave her extreme oral pleasure.

"Yes, baby. Ooohh, stay right there." Kailah moaned and lifted her head, rotating her hips up and down in a rhythm that matched his.

Kailah's body contracted then pulsated as she reached her climactic level. Corey licked his lips as he sat up on his knees. He undressed, revealing a huge erection. Kailah removed her blouse and bra as he put on a condom.

Corey entered her strong and fierce like a crashing wave in the ocean. He rested his head on her neck as he slowly made love to her. Kailah moved in the opposite direction to meet every stroke. Tears rolled down her cheeks and spilled onto his shoulder. They both knew this would be the very last time.

Kailah adjusted her tired eyes to the blinding light coming from beneath the bathroom door. She scanned the dark room and checked the time. One o'clock. Sitting straight up in bed, she grabbed the sheet to cover her nude body. Corey opened the door, bearing in more light. Kailah held up her arm and turned away.

"You okay?" Corey asked.

"Yes. I didn't realize it was so late." She grabbed the receiver and dialed. "I'm going to have Taneisha call and cover for me."

Corey scratched the back of his neck, still standing naked in the doorway. "When you finish, you wanna join me in the shower?"

Kailah leaned back on the headboard as she waited for someone to answer. Knowing Taneisha would be pissed off at her for calling so late, she nervously ran her fingers through her hair. "Yes, I'll be right there."

......

"Uh-huh. You know I gots beef with you this morning," Taneisha said. She casually strolled into Kailah's office, waving her hand in the air and closing the door behind her. "Now, you interrupted my lovemaking with my *husband* to call your mother and lie to her, just so you could spend the night with your lover friend."

Kailah rolled her eyes. "I—"

"No." Taneisha swirled her curly sky-blue fingernail in Kailah's face. "I'm not finished yet. I hope this was the last time I have to cover for you, Ms. Boss Lady. 'Cause I'm through. Now, I done sat back and watched this fucked up shit take place, excuse my language, but no more. I'm through."

Kailah clapped her hands together. "My heart aches. But don't worry, Taneisha. It's over. I ended it last night."

Taneisha smirked. "I've heard that before."

Kailah decided not to respond. Instead, she sighed. "And you can take the rest of the day off for your trouble. I'll manage on my own today."

Taneisha's smile revealed her gold tooth. She turned to walk away, then stopped in her tracks. "Treat me and Joe to dinner at Red Lobster and it's a deal."

"Fine," Kailah said through clenched teeth.

"Good. I'll drop Tyree and Shyla off at your place, say around six?" Not waiting on an answer, Taneisha pimped her way out like she had negotiated a multi-million dollar deal. Kailah shook her head and laughed, then went back to work.

* * *

When Kailah entered her home that evening, Mama Anna stood in the kitchen talking on the phone.

Kailah tossed the mail on the counter and slipped off her heels.

"Keith. Keith. Kailah just walked in the door." Mama Anna handed Kailah the cordless.

"Hey, sweetie." She tried to sound cheerful even though she was worn out.

"Tired, huh?"

"Yes. Long day at work," Kailah responded, hoping he wouldn't ask her about her whereabouts the night before.

"So, where were you when I called yesterday?"

Too late.

"Oh, I was out with Taneisha. We hung out for a little bit," Kailah said coolly.

"Really?" Keith's voice was flat.

"Yes, really," Kailah snapped. "What, you don't believe me?"

Keith chuckled. "No."

Oh God. Kailah held the phone away from her ear and tried not to remain calm. *Don't panic.* What would she say now? She grabbed her shoes and tiptoed upstairs to her bedroom.

"You still there?" Keith asked.

"Yeah." Kailah sat on her bed. Her feet traced a pattern in the carpet.

"Kailah, you don't have to lie to me. You don't even have to tell me if you don't want to. I already have some idea what's going on. I'm not a fool."

Kailah was speechless. Caught and trapped. She shook her head in pure angst trying to think of what to say next.

"Your silence tells me that I'm right." Keith sighed. "I can't believe this shit. You wait until I'm about to come home to go out and fuck another nigga!" he screamed.

Silence.

MIXED MESSAGES

"You know what?" Keith's voice lowered. "You don't have to say shit to me. Kailah, when I get out of here, I'm going to start a new life. That's right, without yo' no good ass."

Kailah could hear Keith sobbing through the receiver. She felt a yank in her stomach and a knot in her throat. If only she could go back and erase time. She would change everything if she had it to do all over again. There were no words she could say to ease her husband's gut wrenching pain of betrayal. She recognized it, knowing it all too well from the last time when she inflicted this kind of pain on her best friend.

"I'm sorry, Keith."

"Yeah, you're sorry all right. And I want a divorce."

Chapter 31
An Ounce of Integrity

"Kailah. Kailah." Taneisha snatched the covers off the bed. Kailah lay perfectly still.

Taneisha placed her hands on her hips. "Girl, you're going to have to get out of this bed." She turned to look back at Mama Anna who stood watchful by the door.

"I told you. I tried the same thing yesterday, and it didn't work." Mama Anna shook her head. "This child done slap lost her mind."

Taneisha sat next to Kailah and rubbed her wild uncombed hair. She whispered in her ear, "It's going to be all right." She waved at Mama Anna. "You can go back downstairs. It's okay."

Mama Anna hesitated for a moment and then left.

Taneisha rubbed Kailah's back. "Now you know Keith's just tripping. He's not going to divorce you."

Kailah's glossy eyes welled up with tears as she lay on her side with her hand supporting her head. As she replayed the conversation in her head, she began to cry.

Taneisha wrapped her arm around Kailah. "That's right. Let it all out. It's gonna be okay. I promise."

After an hour of coaxing, Taneisha finally convinced Kailah to take a shower. Letting the warm water cascade down cleansed both her soul and body. She prayed all night that God would somehow get her out of this mess she'd created for herself. Strangely, no matter how screwed up her life was, just knowing that God loved her anyway gave a huge feeling of relief. While she stood there, she completely surrendered her life to Him, because only He could sort this out and make it right.

It wasn't a question of whether she trusted God, but whether she trusted herself to make the correct choices from this point on. Living life as a Christian differed from her life before she knew Christ, because now she knew accountability of sin. The good news meant she could repent and pray for deliverance. Being a strong Christian woman mattered, because she knew the legacy she would pass on to her children. It was important for Kailah to be the best role model for her son and daughter. One parent had already failed them. No way could she do the same thing, too.

As Kailah opened the glass door and stepped out of the marble-tiled shower, she overheard her mother and Taneisha whispering in her bedroom. She knew her mother now knew that her suspicions were right all along. Noticing the dryness of her skin as she looked at her reflection in the mirror, Kailah took out a bottle of moisturizer.

Several times, Mama Anna asked her about her relationship with Corey. Kailah either avoided the question or asked her mother to stay out of her business. Her life would be better had she chosen to take heed to her mother's advice. Mama Anna was a smart God-fearing woman. Never once had she steered Kailah wrong. No. Kailah's mistakes were a result of her own stupidity.

Slowly, she massaged her legs with cucumber melon lotion, then slipped on her robe and opened the bathroom door.

Taneisha shot her a worried look. "You look much better," Taneisha said.

"And I smell better, too," Kailah added.

Kailah dropped her eyes to the floor. "Don't try and change the subject. I know you and Mama were in here talking about me."

Taneisha sat up straighter on the edge of the bed. "Of course, we were. You got everybody 'round here worried about you."

"Well, in case you hadn't noticed, Taneisha, I'm fine." Kailah raised her voice.

"Right. That's just what I was about to say," Taneisha said anxiously. She held her hands up. "Now, Kailah, I know you don't want to hear this. But, girl, you need to get it together. You haven't come this far to just give up and throw your marriage away."

Kailah shrugged. "It's no use. Keith told me the other night he wanted a divorce. Say what you want, but I know my husband. He's serious about this. He wants nothing to do with me."

Taneisha waved her hands in a wild frenzy. "So you just gon' let the man you love just walk away? Oh, I don't think so. Your mother is right, Kailah." Taneisha grabbed Kailah's hand. "Yes, you messed up. However, Keith messed up, too. Might I remind you, this wouldn't even be an issue if Keith hadn't lied to you and ended up in prison in the first place." Taneisha gestured with her free hand. "You've managed to save a house, marriage, and family all on your own. Keith hasn't done a thing. Shoot, he's lucky to have you."

Kailah nodded and turned up her thick lips. "Taneisha, you're right. I'm a strong black woman."

"Ain't nothing for you to do but go see Keith tomorrow and talk this thing out," Taneisha stated. "And if Keith wants to go through with this divorce, then you're going to have to accept it and move on. You got too much going for you to just let everything fall apart."

"Taneisha, what are you saying? You sound like you want me to leave Keith." Kailah looked at her strangely. "I love him. I love him." She began to cry.

Taneisha put her arms around Kailah and rubbed her head as she painfully wept. "I would never tell you to get a divorce. You know me better than that. Marriage is sacred."

"It is sacred. And I didn't respect my marriage. Now, I have to face the consequences." Kailah buried her face in her hands, inhaling deeply. "You're right about one thing. I need to go see Keith tomorrow."

* * *

The next morning, Kailah folded her arms as she sat waiting for Keith to walk through the metal door. *Why is he taking so long? Maybe he is refusing the visit.* Nervously Kailah drummed her nails along the table as her eyes drifted around the room. The other families appeared to be so happy. Another prisoner playfully tickled his young son. The little boy looked to be the same age as Hunter. It pained her to think her son would never get a chance to live in the same house with his father.

The door creaked open and Keith appeared, standing tall with his broad shoulders, his dark complexion, and strong facial features that resembled those of an African king. He raised his eyebrows as he searched the room for his visitor. Kailah waved to get his attention.

Kailah kept her hands to her side as he approached the table. Keith held her eyes as he came closer. Kailah cast her eyes downward and scratched the back of her neck.

Keith grabbed her hand and hugged his wife.

"Hey, baby."

She held her breath as he squeezed her tightly.

"I'm surprised you showed up today." Keith straightened his pants leg before he sat down in front of her.

"I surprised myself."

Keith slowly curled his lips into a smile. Shaking his head, he grabbed her hand. "Man, it's been rough these past couple of days."

"Yeah," Kailah responded with a slight smile, "it hasn't been easy for me either."

"I know. I feel bad about that." Keith stared up at the ceiling and squeezed Kailah's hand tighter. "Just forget what I said to you on the phone. I mean…about the divorce. I was so angry."

Kailah bit her lip. "I understand. You have every right to be angry with me. Keith, I was wrong for—"

Keith held his fingers to her lips. "Stop. Stop. Baby, don't sit here and apologize to me for anything. You don't owe me one. It's all right."

Kailah buried her head in Keith's thick chest.

He rubbed his hands through her long, silky hair. "Really, you don't. I forgive you."

She cocked her head back in pure disbelief. "Huh?"

"Is it over between you and this nigga?" Keith searched her eyes for the truth.

Kailah scratched her head and looked away. "Yeah."

"Are you sure?"

"Yes, I'm positive. I'm not seeing him anymore," Kailah answered.

Keith sighed. "I'm relieved. Man, you just don't know. I was sure you were going to tell me you were leaving me."

Kailah did a double-take, holding her chest. "Me leave you? Never. I love you, Keith. You gave me a chance to divorce you, and I absolutely refused to do so. I don't know what I would do if you weren't in my life."

"Me neither. You stood beside me through all of this. Most of these guys in here have lost their families while being locked up." Keith took a deep breath before he proceeded. "I admire you for holding it down. Kailah, you paid the bills, gave birth to my wonderful son, and managed to keep me in check the whole time. I have no right to judge you. In fact, I'm surprised you didn't do it sooner."

Kailah was speechless. Three days ago, this man called her everything but a child of God. And now here he was telling her how much he admired her. She wanted to pinch herself, because she had to be dreaming. This was not happening.

Keith adjusted his position. "Well, enough about that. Did you bring me some pictures?"

Kailah laughed. "I forgot all about these pictures." She slid the manila envelope over to him. "I figured if you didn't want to see me, I could at least share some happier moments."

"Let me see this." Keith held up a picture of Kamryn standing next to the Christmas tree. He grinned. "She's beautiful like her mother."

Chapter 32
Here Comes the Bride

"How am I going to get your make-up on your beautiful face when you won't stop crying?"

"I can't help it. I'm so nervous," Mona said.

Rona leaned back. "Nervous of what? Hell, you've practically been my cousin's wife for the past two years. You're living with him, doing the cooking and cleaning, and taking care of his granddaughter."

"So true," Kailah chimed in. She sat right next to Mona trying to help her remain calm. She was the matron of honor and her hair was pinned up in a French twist to accentuate the long, sleeveless lavender gown with a high split in the back.

Rona and Tori's bridesmaids' dresses were similar, but flared a little more at the bottom. Keisha helped Tori slide on her matching long gloves that came up to her elbows. She wore her hair up in a bun. Mona's third bridesmaid was her twenty-two-year-old cousin Dana from LA.

Mona's bedroom at her parent's house grew more crowded by the minute. Relatives and friends stopped in to get a glimpse of the bride before she walked down the aisle. Finally, Bea asked everyone except Kailah to leave so she could help her place the veil on Mona's head full of dangling curls.

After some maneuvering, shifting, and pinning of curls, they were done. Bea stepped back to admire her daughter. Mona's silk gown was simply cut and hung off her shoulders with a beaded bodice. Two slips had to be worn just to fill in the lower half of the dress. The train was six feet in length.

"I've never seen you more stunning than you are right now," Bea said. A single tear rolled down her face. "I'm so proud to be your mother."

Mona tried to fan the tears away, but she couldn't. "Thank you, Mother."

They held each other.

Kailah grabbed more Kleenex out of the box and blew her nose loudly. Mona and Bea laughed.

"I can't help it. I get emotional at weddings," Kailah said in between blows. She looked in the mirror to fix her makeup and applied more powder. She stood sideways to admire her slim figure. "Still fine."

Mona grinned. "Conceit doesn't suit you."

"After you've had two babies, let's see how good you look."

Bea kidded. "Let's just get her married first. Then we'll worry about my grandbabies."

They all laughed once more.

"I better get out there and find Charles." Bea adjusted her skirt and checked herself in the mirror. "I'm sure he has probably fallen apart by now. You know, I don't think he slept a wink last night."

After a few more hugs and kisses, Bea left the room.

Kailah held the door. "Finally, I have you all to myself." Kailah knelt down in front of Mona and grabbed her hands. "This is a blessed day, and I'm truly grateful to be here to share this day with you." She took in a deep breath then proceeded. "We've been friends for ten long years, and we're closer than ever. I haven't thought of you as a friend for a long time. I think of you as my sistah."

Mona was crying again. "I think of you as a sistah, too. Our bond is so much stronger. I love you."

"I love you, too. I wish you and Davis so much happiness. After everything you've been through, you deserve it." Kailah kissed her and then wiped away the plum-colored lipstick print she left on Mona's cheek.

"You know I wish the same for you. Keith is coming home in two weeks, and I know the best is yet to come."

Kailah smiled. "Thank you."

After having served more than half of his prison sentence, Keith would return soon. Kailah gladly accepted her new promotion as Vice President at AND with the opportunity to open a new office in the DC area. Mama Anna had decided that the cold winters were too much for her to handle. Therefore, Kailah would help her mother move back to Florida in a couple of days. Kamryn was going to be thrilled to have her dad back home, but sad her grandmother was leaving.

How would Kailah handle living in the same city as Juanita? While her in-laws lived in Alexandria, she'd figured the elegant home she purchased in Arlington would provide the distance needed to avoid any surprise visits.

Taneisha helped her to see everything would work out for the best, and to look at the positive side of things. It would be great for Kamryn and Hunter to be able to spend time with their nana. Whatever the future held, Kailah knew it was indeed bright, considering everything she'd been through. And she'd made it. With God's help.

Eight years had passed since Kailah and Mona walked across that stage at their graduation. They were so naïve back then, full of motivation and enthusiasm to conquer the world. Life had already thrown both of them some hard blows. Still, they managed to survive it all. Mona, no longer as shallow as Kailah, was ruthless. Turning in their boxing gloves and making the decision to forgive and let go of the past for love and happiness wasn't an easy exchange for either of them. In the end, they were both better for it. Stronger than they ever imagined they would be. Sistahs.

"Okay, okay. We got to cheer up. It's your wedding day." Kailah handed Mona another Kleenex.

"All right." Mona held up the compact mirror as she patted around her eyes.

Kailah stood in front of Mona and held her hands out. "Now, let me help you out of this chair."

MIXED MESSAGES

The wedding ceremony took place on the lawn of Charles and Bea's home. One hundred guests attended, including Lois Clarke with her new young beau. Charles escorted Mona down the aisle to Luther Vandross' "Here and Now" played by a live band. She held her bouquet of long-stemmed, fresh white lilies. Kailah cried when Mona and Davis lovingly stated their wedding vows. They looked each other in the eyes with such admiration.

The reception was held under huge white tents on the lawn, with the band playing jazz music and a full buffet and bar. By this time, the newlywed couple had reappeared and Mona wore a long fitted gown with a high split on the side. The wedding cake was three-tiered with fresh lavender and white flowers on top. Davis' brother, Gene, was the best man and gave the toast.

Two hours later, the reception ended and all of the guests stood in front of the house throwing rice at the newlyweds as they ran towards the limousine. The children ran behind the limousine to wave goodbye as it slowly pulled away, headed for their cruise to the Caribbean.

......

Kailah propped her arms on her lap and rested her head on them. Bumping into Corey and Lynn in the hallway made her want to dive into her skin and hide. *What a coward!* Instead of simply playing it cool, she reacted nervously. In her head, she envisioned the puzzled look on Lynn's face while witnessing the awkward encounter. Kailah wondered if Lynn would put two and two together. If anyone caught wind of what had happened, it could potentially ruin Kailah's career. With all the animosity existing between her and Lynn, Kailah knew she would eagerly jump at the chance. News of an affair with two top executives at AND would spread like wildfire on a hot summer month.

Kailah stared up at the ceiling and took a deep breath. No, this could not happen.

She jumped when she heard tapping on the door.

"Kailah, you in there?"

"Yes, Taneisha, I'm here."

"Good, I've been looking for you. You okay?"

"I'm fine. I can't use the bathroom?" Kailah asked sarcastically. She flushed the toilet and swung open the red stall door while zipping her pants.

"Yes, you can use the bathroom. You know what I'm talking about." Taneisha applied brown lipstick on her thin lips. "Judging by your reaction to you-know-who in the hallway, I had to ask."

"I know…I know." Kailah turned to face Taneisha as she washed her hands. "Do you think she noticed?"

Taneisha smirked. "That dumb ass ain't that smart. Of course, your boy didn't help with all that staring. Girl, he was eyeing you like he wanted to sop you up with a biscuit."

"Really," Kailah said flatly. "I didn't notice."

"You didn't notice because you had that stupefied look on your face and then took off for the bathroom."

Kailah shook her head as she dried her hands with a stack of paper towels. "I hope you covered for me."

"You know I did. Like Tony Soprano would say, forget about it!" Taneisha rubbed her growling stomach. "A sistah is huuungry."

Kailah finger combed her hair. "Me, too. They're having Fish Friday at Soul Queen Restaurant. You wanna go there?"

Taneisha snapped her fingers and cocked her head to the left. "Oooh, you ain't said nothing but a thang. You know I love me some fish."

"Who's driving?"

MIXED MESSAGES

Taneisha sprayed perfume on her wrist, then rubbed both wrists together. "Well, I drove the last time." Kailah grabbed Taneisha's wrist and inhaled. "Mmmm, that smells nice."

Taneisha sucked her teeth. "I know. It's Romance from Ralph Lauren."

"I'll have to get me some of that," Kailah said. "So, you're driving, right?" she asked as she exited the ladies' room.

Taneisha followed. "Yeah, I'll drive."

As soon as Taneisha started her Toyota Camry, "Love at First Sight" by Mary J. Blige blared from the speakers. "That's my jam." Taneisha rhythmically rocked her head left to right to the beat of the music. "Could it be love…" Taneisha pumped her fist in the air as she peeled out of the parking garage like she was in the car-chasing scene in the Matrix Reloaded. Kailah gripped the handle on the door as Taneisha popped a quick turn onto the next street.

Taneisha pulled onto the corner of 90th and Stony Island Avenue ten minutes faster than it would've taken Kailah to drive there. Walking down the assembly line, Kailah heaped a pile of fried catfish, grits, and greens on her plate from the buffet. She sat across from Taneisha who was dropping hot sauce on her fish until it was completely smothered.

Kailah said grace and proceeded to get her grub on.

Taneisha licked her long red fingernails. "Uumphh. This is so good. I'm glad you thought of this place. We haven't been here in months."

"I'm trying to hit the best spots before the move." Kailah ate a forkful of fish mixed with grits.

Taneisha frowned and leaned forward. "Don't remind me. I'm going to miss you like crazy when you're gone. It's hard to believe in just three weeks you'll be outta here for good."

"I know. The moving counselor is stopping by today to take inventory of the items in the house." Kailah took a sip of water.

"Really. You need me to watch the kids for you?" Taneisha asked.

Kailah shook her head. "No, it's okay. I appreciate you asking, though." Kailah scratched her ear with her pinky finger. "I may have to take you up on your offer tomorrow." Three days had gone by and Kailah missed her mother's presence throughout the house already.

Taneisha rose from the booth. "Excuse me while I go for seconds."

Kailah twisted her lips. "You make me sick."

Taneisha snapped her fingers and rolled her neck. "Don't hate, appreciate."

Kailah couldn't stand the fact that Taneisha could eat three or four plates of food and still wear a size three. Her petite figure resembled Jada Pinkett Smith's, and men and women groveled all over her. Joe was one lucky man, considering he'd managed to let his football athletic-shaped body turn to jiggling body fat. It's not like Taneisha wasn't trying to get him to exercise, but the only exercising Joe did was walk to the kitchen for more food or beer.

As Taneisha sashayed her way back to their booth, wearing a red mini skirt and black blouse, three men at a table whistled. Taneisha flirtatiously smiled and slid in the booth.

"Uh-huh."

"What?" Taneisha asked innocently.

"I saw you." Kailah laughed. "You were twisting so hard I thought your little hips were going to snap right off."

Taneisha burst out laughing and fell backward. "You need to stop. I can't help being fine, darling." She batted her chinky eyes.

"I wouldn't know." Kailah wiped her mouth with her napkin.

"Yeah, right." Taneisha took a sip of iced tea. "You know you look good."

MIXED MESSAGES

"But I have to bust my butt at the gym to keep this figure," Kailah stated. "And only eat one plate of soul food."

"That's just genetics. You know how sexy my mama is and how plump Mama Anna is." Taneisha leaned forward and bit her tongue.

"All right, now. Don't be talking about my mother. Or I might just have to cut ya'." Kailah sliced her hand in the air.

They both burst into laughter.

Taneisha doubled over and wiped her face. "Ooohh, you need to stop making fun of my family."

"Then you better stop talking about my mama." Kailah's voice went up an octave.

Taneisha's smile soon disappeared as she fidgeted in her seat. "What if we talk about Corey instead?"

"You just had to slide that in." Kailah teased her by refusing to make eye contact. "What about him?"

"Well, you haven't talked about him. I know you must miss him."

Kailah placed her fork on the table and raised her head. "Yeah." Her voice was stiff. She looked away from the table.

"It must be hard seeing him at work and not being able to talk to him," Taneisha said.

Kailah had a puzzled look on her face. "Like you really care. All you did was dog me about our relationship the whole time." She went back to eating her fish.

"That's because I didn't want to see you get hurt. I mean, I thought Corey was trying to play you." Taneisha cleared her throat, then continued. "Then when I saw how much he really cared for you, I knew this whole thing was going to blow up in your face. And it did."

"Is this about to turn into an I-told-you-so speech?" Kailah asked incredulously.

"No, it's not." Taneisha grabbed Kailah's hand. "You know I'm happy things played out the way they did. Your husband will be home next week. I mean, your life is good. Still, I know you're hurting."

"It shows, huh?" Kailah bit her bottom lip.

Taneisha tossed her head to the side. "No, it doesn't show. Hell, you look better than ever. We've worked together for eight years now. I know how you work and how you think."

Kailah raised her finger. "True."

"I just want you to know that I'm here if you need someone to talk to." Taneisha pushed her plate forward. "Now, if you don't mind, I'm going to help myself to some peach cobbler. You want some?"

"Yeah, hook a sistah up." Kailah smiled.

Kailah drummed her nails along the table and looked up at the red and yellow chandelier lighting above her. She didn't want to divulge her true feelings to Taneisha. Even though she knew she could trust her not to tell anyone, Taneisha could sometimes be judgmental when it came to matters of the heart. Now, when it came down to buying stolen or bootleg merchandise, Taneisha could see no wrong.

Internally, Kailah was torn apart. Sure, she masked it at work when she had to project a professional image. With the kids, it basically was the same thing. Kailah never wanted her children to see her in a miserable and depressed state, but at night, she cried herself to sleep.

Emotionally, she allowed Corey to get under her skin and get close to her. Bottom line, she loved him and it had absolutely nothing to do with the sex...even though that was good, too. But that wasn't it. In the past, she had been able to distance emotion from sex without a problem.

To be frank, if Keith had been honest with her about his dirty business dealings up front, she would have never dated him, let alone marry him and have his children. Corey had been honest from day one, and deep down inside, she knew that man could possibly be her soul mate and not Keith. Unfortunately, she couldn't afford the luxury of tearing her family apart to pursue another relationship. Her children didn't deserve that. She loved Keith, and she was willing to spend the rest of her life with him. With only one tiny regret. To her, it was a very small price to pay for her children's well being.

"Here you go." Taneisha placed a hot plate of peach cobbler in front of her.

"Thank you." Kailah rubbed her hands together. "I hope it tastes as good as it looks," she said as she eyed the cobbler with the thick golden layer of crust on top.

"Me, too," Taneisha said. "Well, don't just look at it. Dig in, girl."

Chapter 33
Homecoming

"Daddy! Daddy!" Kamryn and Hunter ran towards their father as soon as he strolled from the back entrance of the correctional facility escorted by Maurice. With a huge grin on his face, he scooped up his kids and affectionately kissed them. Juanita squeezed Kailah's hand tightly as she held her chest with the other hand. She had been crying nonstop since she'd arrived that morning. Blake tried to console his wife, but Juanita was on a roll and showed no sign of abating until her only son was freed from prison.

Blake grabbed his son's shoulders so hard Keith almost stumbled forward. He caught himself and tried to remain composed as Juanita wrapped her arms his neck. *Poor Keith.* With the children jumping up and down and his parents clawing away, it looked like an angry mob was attacking him. Kailah covered her mouth as she chuckled.

His eyes swept the room, and as he caught sight of his wife standing there alone, it was as if time suddenly stood still. Kailah shifted her legs nervously as she noticed her husband's intense gaze as he pushed everyone aside to get next to her. Keith's dimpled smile grew wider as he opened his arms and lifted Kailah off the floor. Suddenly, her stomach felt light and airy as she kissed his wrinkled forehead.

"God, I can't believe you're in my arms," Keith said. "Man, I hope I'm not dreaming."

Kailah straightened her skirt as Keith put her back down. "No, you're not dreaming. It's real, baby." She kissed him on the lips.

Keith turned around and gave the prison a final once over. "Let's get out of here. I don't want to ever see this place again for the rest of my life."

MIXED MESSAGES

"That's right, son." Blake slapped his son on the back and pinched his shoulder.

Keith picked up Hunter and grabbed Kailah's hand as she grabbed Kamryn's hand. As a family, they exited the building with Juanita and Blake following closely behind.

After enjoying a delicious dinner at Hong Min, Keith's favorite Chinese restaurant, the family headed back home. Keith happily volunteered to give Kamryn and Hunter a bath, so Kailah joined her in-laws for coffee in the family room. One of Keith's jazz CD's was playing on the DVD player.

"Thank you, Juanita," Kailah said when her mother-in-law handed her the coffee mug. She tried to cool it with her breath.

"And I added lots of sugar and cream. Just the way you like it," Juanita explained as she sat down on the leather couch next to her husband. She pinched her lips as she seemed quite pleased with her self.

Blake patted his wife on the leg while looking over at Kailah. "We're really proud of the way you've kept this family together. I can't wait to get you guys over to DC."

Juanita grabbed her chest and grinned from ear to ear. "I can't wait either. I'm going to spend so much time with my grandchildren."

Don't remind me. Kailah crossed her legs and nodded. "Yes, we're definitely looking forward to it."

Blake laughed. "You just don't know how long I've been trying to get Keith to come and help me out down at J & B. But, he's stubborn. Never would agree."

"Just like his father," Juanita chimed in.

"It's a shame my son had to go all the way to prison to finally see the light. I always knew those guys who called him into that so-called partnership were up to no good." Blake sat up and gestured with his free hand. His glass of brandy almost toppled over. "God has a way of breaking a man down like that to make him do what's right."

Kailah's eyes widened. She hoped her in-laws didn't see the expression on her face. She adjusted the Lazy-Boy as she tried to gain her composure. She couldn't believe it. Here Keith's father had the nerve to say that her husband's prison sentence was the Lord's way of bringing him back home. Now it all made sense. Keith fought like hell to make his business succeed in order to prove he could make it on his own without his father's help. It pained Kailah to know how much Keith was sacrificing to finally submit to his father's selfish wishes.

Kailah scratched her head. She hoped they were making the right decision to relocate to DC. At first, she believed this was God's work, but now she wasn't so sure. She had her doubts.

Keith startled her when he rested his hand on her shoulder.

"Oh, I didn't hear you coming," Kailah said.

"Are you all right?" Blake asked. "You seem like you're deep in thought."

Kailah smiled. "Yes. I guess I'm a little tired."

"I'll bet you're tired. Probably can't wait to climb in the bed with your husband," Blake kidded as he finished his drink.

Kailah's jaw tightened. Keith's grip on her shoulder grew stronger.

Juanita laughed sheepishly. "Blake, you're embarrassing Kailah." She patted him on the leg. "Be quiet, honey."

"What? I'm only telling the truth. Hell, the woman's gone a long time without her husband. That ought to count for something." Blake sat up and stood straight up. Standing handsomely tall at six feet five inches, he was an older version of Keith.

He slapped Keith on the back. "You need to take that beautiful lady upstairs and treat her real nice." He smiled a wicked grin. "If you know what I mean." His laughter roared as he walked up the stairs. "Have a good night," he sang as he disappeared.

MIXED MESSAGES

Juanita stood up. "Don't mind him. You know how your father gets when he's had too much to drink. Good night." She kissed her son on the cheek and headed upstairs.

"Good night."

Keith wiped his tired eyes. "I hope you didn't pay any attention to my father."

"No, of course not," Kailah said coolly. She hoped she sounded convincing. Plopping on the couch next to Keith, she rubbed her hand down his arm.

"Come here," Keith calmly whispered. He pulled Kailah inside the fold of his arm as he lay back on the couch. "I love you, baby."

Kailah rested her head on his chest. Slowly, she turned around to face him. "I love you, too."

Kailah's tongue slightly parted her lips as she French kissed him. She climbed on top of him, lifting her skirt. Keith rested his hands firmly on her behind. Kailah felt her husband's penis poke her underneath.

Keith growled. "I couldn't wait for this," Keith said. His eyes lingered over her hungrily.

Kailah smiled coyly. "Me neither."

Once they were in the bedroom, Keith turned the radio dial to 91.5. Jazz music filled the air to create a romantic ambiance. Kailah undressed and slipped under the covers. Keith stripped out of his clothing to reveal a large erection. He pulled the covers back and grabbed Kailah's legs. As he fondled her clitoris, she rolled her neck from side to side.

"Ooohh," Kailah hummed.

Keith softly kissed her lobe and stroked her breasts. Kailah's body tingled as Keith ran his tongue in circles around her nipples.

She purred.

Then he eased his way back down to her vagina and stroked it fiercely with his tongue. Kailah squeezed her eyes shut and arched her back. Without so much as a warning, Keith parted her thighs and rammed his dick inside, not wasting any time.

Keith plunged deeper and faster. She never imagined it would feel this way. Keith's dick was hard like a brick as it bruised her walls. His lovemaking had been gentler in the past. Forceful, but slow.

He panted. Then he growled.

Keith looked her squarely in the eyes. "Oh, baby. Damn. Baby." His back stiffened. Then he let out a loud wail, collapsing on top of her and breathing in her ear.

Kailah turned her head and twisted her lips. *That was it! What just happened here?* Even if she wanted to fake an orgasm, time never allowed it.

Keith wrapped his arms around her and whispered in her ear. "I love you." Within a matter of seconds, Keith was sound asleep.

Kailah blinked. What had she done? Clearly, this was not the man she'd married. For three years she romantically fantasized and dreamed this? Disappointment couldn't even scratch the surface for what she felt at that very moment.

Had it always been this way? Women at work often joked about their husbands being one-minute men. She couldn't relate. Perhaps she was so in love with Keith that she made him out to be larger than life, when in fact he was just like every other average man.

No. They had experienced hot and sizzling nights together. Keith used to put it down and Kailah was left more than satisfied. Or was she?

* * *

The next morning, Kailah awoke to the smell of fried bacon from the kitchen. She hadn't inhaled the aroma of breakfast since Mama Anna had left. She pulled the pillow over her face as an attempt to shield the sunlight from her eyes. After shifting her position several times, she sat straight up, noticing the left side of the bed was empty. Slowly, she willed herself downstairs.

She adjusted her robe as she entered the kitchen. Juanita and Blake sat out on the patio enjoying breakfast and talking. With the high chair pulled up to the table, Juanita fed Hunter some scrambled eggs. In the kitchen, Kamryn kneeled on a stool stirring in a bowl. Keith stood behind her.

"Mommy! Mommy! I'm teaching Daddy how to make pancakes!" Kamryn yelled with her mouth covered with bacon grease.

Keith shrugged helplessly. "It was her idea. You want something to eat?"

Kailah shook her head as she yawned. As she adjusted herself on the stool, she poured herself a glass of orange juice. Keith placed a plate of bacon, eggs, and two pancakes in front of her. Then he poured syrup on her pancakes.

"Thanks, Keith."

Keith brushed his hand across her cheek. "You're welcome."

He held her eyes as he took a sip of orange juice. "Did you sleep well last night?"

Kailah cringed. "Very well," she lied.

Keith stretched his arms along the island. "It was the best feeling to sleep in my own bed next to my gorgeous wife." His rough hands caressed hers.

Kailah pulled away and chewed off a piece of bacon.

Keith looked at her strangely.

"Daddy, I'm finished," Kamryn sang.

"Okay." Keith went over to help her place the pancake on the plate. Kamryn carried her plate out on the patio to join her grandparents and brother.

Keith and Kailah ate quietly at the island.

"Do you want to tell me what's bothering you?" Keith asked, stuffing a forkful of eggs in his mouth as he awaited her answer.

"Nothing." Kailah didn't bother to look up. "Nothing at all."

Keith swallowed hard. "Okay. Don't say I didn't try."

Kailah cleared her throat. "Just tired, that's all."

Keith pounded his fist, causing Kailah to jump in her seat. "You must take me for stupid or something."

"No, I don't," Kailah responded with a slight smile. "Keith, really, I'm okay." She gestured with her hands. "I just need a little time to get used to this."

She studied his face to see if he believed her.

"Somehow, I don't think you're telling me the truth," Keith uttered slowly. He turned to face her. "Is this about your friend?"

Kailah looked to see if her in-laws were still out of earshot. "This has nothing to do with him. And I would appreciate it if you didn't bring it up." She cleared her throat, then continued. "It's our first morning together, so let's just enjoy it, okay?"

"Anything you say, wife."

......

MIXED MESSAGES

Kailah found Keith sitting on the floor in the family room wrestling with the kids. Kailah's eyes swept the empty room with bare walls where her paintings and family pictures once hung.

Keith paused when he saw his wife. "How did your last day go?" Hunter jumped on him, and Keith playfully body slammed his son.

"It went fine." Kailah folded her arms and kicked her foot forward. "They threw a party for me. I saved you some cake." She tried to force a smile.

"Thanks." He had a pleasant smile on his face.

"Mommy, do you want to play with us?" Kamryn asked.

Kailah hesitated for a moment. For years, she prayed for this day to come. And for some reason, she wasn't as thrilled as she imagined she would be. Anger and bitterness resided in her heart, replacing the love she once felt very deeply for her husband. Although her feelings were misplaced, Kailah didn't know if she could make it right. She looked at the happy smiles on her children's faces. Somehow, she would have to find a way.

"Yeah." Kailah slipped out of her heels and felt the coldness of the bare floor. She joined her husband in tickling Kamryn while Hunter hopped on her back with his tiny hands wrapped around her neck.

That night, Kailah and Keith said goodnight to Kamryn on the pallet they made on the living room floor. Hunter was already fast asleep on his pallet. Keith snuggled next to his wife on the air mattress in the dining room. She grabbed his hand close to her and kissed it.

"You think we should find a marriage counselor once we get settled in?" Kailah asked.

Keith kissed her neck. "Yes." He sighed heavily. "I'm relieved."

Kailah turned around to face him. "Relieved?" She held her hand up to hold her head.

Keith ran his fingers through her hair. "For a minute there, I thought you were going to ask for an attorney."

"You're kidding, right?" Kailah raised her thin eyebrows.

Keith shook his head. "No, I'm not." He shifted a dangling curl from her face. "You've been acting funny around here lately." He rubbed her chin.

Kailah twisted her lips. Keith knew she had her ways, but it was obvious things were not right between the two of them.

He tried to adjust another strand, but Kailah grabbed his hand. "Would you stop? I'm trying to talk to you."

Keith snorted. "Sorry. I don't want one hair blocking my view." He kissed her on the forehead. "You're the most beautiful woman in the world."

"No, I'm not. But, I'll settle for being the most beautiful woman in America." She laughed at her own humor.

Keith licked his sexy lips. "Okay, it's a deal."

He gazed into her eyes and Kailah locked eyes with him. He ran his hand across her mocha-colored face very softly. Kailah's head followed his hand.

Keith moved in closer and kissed her on the neck. Kailah ran her hands on his back in a circular fashion as he climbed on top of her. He slid her pink nightgown past her shoulder and kissed her shoulder blade.

"Oh, Keith."

His manhood swelled in between her legs. Pulling the nightgown up over her head, Keith sucked on her small breasts and slowly swirled his tongue around her navel. Kailah lifted her leg and shifted on top of her husband.

"Yes," Keith groaned as Kailah licked his chest. She slowly worked her way down and pulled down his black briefs.

MIXED MESSAGES

"Uuhhmm." Keith rested his arms behind his head as his wife performed oral sex on him.

Then she saddled herself on top and slowly lowered herself down on his penis. Keith pinched her hips every time she squeezed her vaginal muscles tightly as she landed fully on his member.

"Damn!" Keith squealed. "This is some good pussy."

Kailah smiled. "I know it's good." She licked her lips, tasting his manly juices in her mouth.

Just when Kailah was sure Keith was about to release, he lifted her up and turned her over. Kailah rose up on her knees as he entered her from behind.

"That's the way you like it, right?" Keith thrust deeper.

"Uh-huh!" Kailah shrieked. "That's it."

Keith grabbed her ass and rubbed it. Then he pumped harder. Kailah steadied herself on the mattress and lifted her head. Her hair dangled in her face. Keith pulled her hair back and kissed her on the cheek. Then he started biting her on the back as he continued to send shock waves through her body. In and out he moved inside of her, and she loved every second.

"Oh, Keith, I'm 'bout to—"

"Do it, baby." Keith suppressed a smug grin. He pushed with more force as he increased his momentum.

This time, Kailah let out a terrifying wail as she released the most powerful orgasm. Keith groaned with complete satisfaction, then reached his own climax.

"Oh fuck!" He exhaled and fell on his face onto the pillow beside Kailah. They were both panting like wild animals. She wiped the sweat from her forehead.

"Oh my God." Kailah took a deep breath. "Baby, I don't know what got into you." She grabbed her legs to stop them from trembling.

Keith leaned forward and pulled Kailah into his arms, nestling her head on his chest. Kailah was relieved her curious daughter hadn't woken up to discover her father working her mother doggy-style in the opposite room.

"I love you, Mrs. Kailah Terrence."

Kailah smiled as she snuggled up closer. "I love you, too." And for the first time in a really long time, she actually meant it.

MIXED MESSAGES

Epilogue
(1 ½ years later)

"Do you want some more iced tea?" Kailah stood over Mona with the pitcher in her hand.

Mona held her glass out. "Yes, please," she said as she gently cradled her sleeping newborn baby in her arms. Natalie was only five weeks old.

Kailah filled her cup. "You know, when the baby is sleeping, you put them down in a crib."

"Aawww, shut up." Mona rocked her baby in her arms as she wrinkled her lips.

"Girl, you're a mess." Kailah sat in the cushioned patio chair beside her. "That little girl is going to be spoiled just like her mama."

Mona kissed her baby once more. "There's no such thing."

"Oh, yes, there is." Kailah slid back in her chair as she put on her sunglasses. She rubbed her stomach hungrily while she waited on Keith and Davis to finish grilling the ribs, hamburgers, and hot dogs. Tori helped place the macaroni salad and baked bean dishes on the table. Kailah relaxed while Tori and her new boyfriend, Lem, continued to put out plates, cups, utensils and other items. Keisha and Tori were now attending college together at the University of Florida and sharing an apartment.

Davis and Mona's new home in Brandon was absolutely stunning. Of course, Bea used her interior decorating skills to add the finishing touches. Charles and Bea sold their home in LA and moved to Naples, Florida. Bea thought it was important to live near her granddaughter. Many times, babies had a way of bringing families closer. As a direct result, Mona and Bea spent more time together and developed a stronger relationship.

Admiring the view from the screen enclosure cascading over the pool with a fountain, Kailah gazed up at the beautiful blue skies. Most Florida homes had screened patios to escape the bugs. It was a wonderful Labor Day weekend.

Keisha waded in the shallow end of the pool with Brianne and Hunter while Kamryn showed off her swimming skills in the deeper end.

Kamryn pulled off her goggles and rested at the edge of the pool. "Hey, Mommy!" she yelled and waved wildly.

Kailah waved back.

Mona laughed. "That girl has a big mouth."

Kailah nodded. "I know." She scratched her head. "I wonder where she gets it from."

"Please." Mona cocked her head back. "From her loud cackling mother."

Kailah twisted her lips and shot her a nasty look. "You know you wrong for that."

"Mommy! Mommy! When are you going to get in the pool?" Kamryn yelled.

"Right now." Kailah stood up and peeled out of her daisy dukes, revealing her red bikini. She placed them on the chair.

"Go ahead with yo' sexy self," Mona said. "Everybody ain't able."

Kailah snapped her fingers. "Don't hate, appreciate."

They both burst out laughing.

As Kailah confidently strutted towards the pool, she heard Keith whistling at her. She smiled as she jumped in, splashing water three feet in the air. Kamryn screamed loudly as she held up her hands to protect herself. Kailah chased Kamryn around in circles.

After dinner, Kailah and Mona sat out on the patio while Davis and Keith watched the Tampa Bay Bucs' game inside the family room on a big-screened plasma television. Occasionally, Kailah heard hollering as the two men gave each other a high-five after a player scored a touchdown.

"It's such nice weather," Kailah said. "The temperature is already starting to drop in Virginia."

Mona sat up and looked at her. "Already?"

Kailah nodded. "Yep."

"How do you like it now that you've had time to settle in?" Mona asked, taking a sip of Coke.

"Virginia is so beautiful. Lots of green grass to make the landscaping resemble Florida." Kailah squeezed her shoulders. "I must say that I do enjoy it much better than Chicago. Living so close to my in-laws isn't as bad as I imagined it would be."

Mona's eyes widened. "I'm surprised to hear you say that."

"Why?" Kailah asked. "The only reason why I moved there was to work at AND. No one else offered me a job, so I jumped at the chance." She drummed her fingers along the glass table between the two of them.

"Yeah, I remember how worried you were right before graduation." Mona unzipped her denim shorts to allow more room. Seriously overweight and now fitting in a size 18, she vowed to go on a diet as soon as she stopped breast-feeding Natalie.

Kailah smiled. "Man, I was so jealous of you with all your huge six-figure job offers." Her smile soon disappeared. "It wasn't easy being friends with someone who had everything."

"No, I didn't," Mona defended as she placed her hands on her wide hips. Her plump face turned red. "It's funny how the tables turned. Suddenly, you were the one with everything, and I had nothing."

"Yeah, right." Kailah sucked her teeth. "My life has taken more rough turns than a roller coaster."

Mona took a deep breath. "That's just life period. No matter what, I wouldn't change a thing. Not even the rape. I wouldn't be who I am today if I hadn't gone through it."

"Wow!" Kailah said emphatically. "I don't know about that. I sure would change some parts of my life if I could. I'm not going to even front." She folded her arms.

She never shared the details of her affair with Mona. Attending marriage counseling for a year had certainly helped mend her relationship with Keith. She figured it was nobody's business, so she and Keith agreed to keep their problems secret. The prison sentence had created a wedge between them, and it took time for them to get to know each other again. They started with long honest talks when the kids weren't around.

Keith had forgiven her for sleeping with another man, and he was more than ready to move on. Kailah had to let her feelings for Corey run its course. It wasn't easy getting over a man she'd fallen madly in love with.

"I've had to get through some rough spots." Kailah rubbed her arms.

Mona nodded. "Yeah, we both have. Life has never been more pleasant until I gave birth to my daughter. At that very moment, I felt like I was alive."

"I know. When Kamryn came out screaming, I cried like a baby."

"I finally understand why you stayed with Keith," Mona explained. "There is nothing I wouldn't do for my daughter. Some lessons in life aren't learned until you first love someone, and second when you have a child."

Kailah nodded. "True."

Keith hollered at the top of his lungs. Kailah and Mona laughed.

"That's my man in there acting a fool over the Bucs. But seriously, at one time, I considered divorcing him."

Mona sat straight up and leaned forward. "What? You didn't tell me about that."

"I was too embarrassed to tell you," Kailah said in a voice barely above a whisper. "After you forgave me for sleeping with Derrick, I didn't want to lose your respect again."

"Oh, Kailah," Mona grabbed her chest, "I'm sorry to hear that. I admit it wasn't easy for me to trust you at first."

"I could understand," Kailah said awkwardly, massaging the back of her neck.

Mona stood up and stretched. "Eventually, I learned to trust you and our friendship again. And now, I love you to death."

Kailah got out of her chair. "Yeah, sometimes you have to go through the hard times to truly appreciate the other person. I certainly learned my lesson."

"You needed to," Mona said. "Girl, you were sleeping with almost every guy you met. How many guys was it?"

Kailah shamefully dropped her eyes to the ground. "Thirty something. I stopped counting," she lied. "I know women who have slept with way more than that. Anyway, I couldn't be perfect like you, Ms. Virgin USA."

Mona playfully threw a punch at Kailah. "Uh-huh. And I guess you expect me to believe you *worked* your way to that VP position at AND."

"Oh, so now you're trying to be funny." Kailah threw her hands up in the air. "Just like you don't expect me to believe that you didn't steal Davis away from his wife. What's her name? Doris."

Mona held her fingers to her lips. "You wrong for that. You know her daughters are right there in the house."

"And? So what." Kailah puffed out her chest like she was big and bad. "Doris can't beat me. And you can't beat me either, short stuff."

"I ain't scared of you. What do you weigh, a buck o' five? Please." Mona danced around like she was Ali. "Don't make me body slam you out here and embarrass you in front of everybody."

"Oh yeah?" Kailah wiped her nose. "Well, there ain't nothing between us but air and opportunity."

Mona laughed so hard that she collapsed onto Kailah. The two of them held onto one another like two drunks.

"You're so crazy," Mona said.

Kailah pointed her finger. "No, you're the crazy one." She pulled open the sliding glass door to the house and followed Mona inside.